CW00395005

J. A. BOULET

The
STRONG
WITHIN
US

Copyright © 2020 J. A. Boulet

Published by J. A. Boulet

Book cover design: Emily's World of Design

ISBN: 978-1-7772112-4-0

The front cover Ross MKII is an original photograph of the Norwest rifle on display in the gallery of The King's Own Calgary Regiment Museum, located within The Military Museums, at Calgary, Alberta. This Ross Rifle is the second of three that was actually used in battle during WWI by Lance Corporal Henry Norwest (MM and Bar), a Metis Cree from Fort Saskatchewan, Alberta. Lance Corporal Norwest served as a sniper with the 50th Canadian Infantry Battalion from Calgary enlisting in 1915 and recorded a total of 115 observed hits until he was killed in action on August 18, 1918. Much thanks to Colonel Roy Boehli (Ret'd) and The King's Own Calgary Regiment Museum for allowing the photograph to be taken and displayed on this front cover.

This book is dedicated to my late father, Mike. He bravely fought during the Hungarian Revolution, fighting for his values and beliefs, a strong pledge that I stand by to this day. Always be one of the last soldiers standing and never sacrifice your values or passions.

Note to Reader

This book is a work of historical fiction. I have attempted to be accurate with most historical events although some details have been intentionally skewed to propel the story. This is a fictional saga of courage, grief and hope. It should be read as such.

J. A. Boulet October 6, 2020

PART ONE

1893-1894

Chapter 1

She was a stunning woman with beautiful long black hair, shockingly rare blue eyes and tanned skin. She was captivating and absolutely gorgeous. Ivan thought that he didn't have a chance until he found out that she lived down by the pier with her father. He bought fish from her father regularly, trading vegetables and grains some days. Every time Ivan visited the large fishery at the pier, he was always scanning the crowd for the beautiful blue-eyed fisherman girl. He found out that she was almost the same age as himself; she was 18, and he was 19. How she had managed to remain single was something beyond his stretch of knowledge. Maybe she was too beautiful, he thought. No man was courageous enough to approach her. Until this day, he thought.

Ivan straightened his tie and proceeded to the fishery. He ran his fingers through his hair, adjusting his cowlick. The pesky tuft of hair at his crown annoyed him greatly. It seemed to have a mind of its own, especially in tense situations; it would stick up like a fork in a haystack. Otherwise, he thought that he was quite a handsome fellow, standing at six feet tall, slim but fit, with dark blonde hair, a young uneven beard and captivating green eyes. Women looked at him often, so he knew that he was attractive, but he still felt unsure of himself some days, especially around stunning women like her. Ivan pulled the door to the fishery open, unconsciously licking his hand and smoothing down the cowlick again as he stepped inside.

"Good morning, Ivan," a giant voice boomed.

"Good morning, Garth," Ivan responded. "How is business today?"

"All is well, all is well," Garth replied, happily. They had prospered over the years, there were good years and bad, but the Icelanders finally found ways to increase the number of fish caught. They had scoped the areas that had the best fishing at certain times of the year and pulled in so much fish sometimes that selling them all blossomed into big business, a profitable industry. Nath and Garth had become business partners in late 1877, building the most significant fishery in Gimli. The whole family helped, as well as many employees and local fishermen. It was something to be proud of and continued to be a successful venture. Both families lived in two of the most affluent homes in Gimli, built right along the shoreline street, with the beautiful beach in their backyards. Bea and Garth lived in the brown house; Nathan and Annabella lived in the tall white house. It was something to be thankful for every day. "What can I do for you today, Ivan?" Garth asked. "I thought you were just here yesterday. Did you forget something on your list?"

"No, no, actually, I came to speak to Nathanael," Ivan said, his voice cracking. He talked to Nathan several times before, but the large muscular older man was still intimidating. Especially now, he thought. "Is he around for a quick chat?" Ivan asked.

"He's just in the boat with Annabella at the moment, pulling the days catch in," Garth replied. "You are welcome to go talk to him; they are almost done for the day."

Ivan looked nervously behind Garth, staring out the window towards the massive boat, where Nathan and his daughter were. He stuttered briefly and then coughed. "Ok, I will go talk to him at the boat then."

"Are you okay?" Garth asked. "You just looked a bit pale there for a second. You should drink water! Dehydration can be a beast during the summers here! You need to be careful when you are working hard, sweating in the fields. Go, I need to attend to the other customers now. Drink, boy!"

Ivan laughed nervously. "Ok, thanks," he replied as he walked out towards the boat. His nerves were starting to make him think twice. Maybe he shouldn't do it this way; perhaps he should approach Annabella more, talk to her more. She just seemed so withdrawn. He sometimes tried just chatting with her about the weather, when he caught her in the store, but it was rare, and she just seemed to shy away, retreating into her fishing boat. But one day, he had caught her looking at him. Several times actually, she had glanced demurely away every time he had looked her in the eye. It made him think. What does a man need to do to talk to a woman so she would marry him? It sounded so foolish when he thought of it that way, but she was the only woman he wanted. Ever since they arrived in Gimli, she was the one he dreamt of, only her face and her smile filled his dreams. Annabella was his favourite person in the entire world. He couldn't think of anyone else he would love to spend his days with, today and into the future.

His shoes clicked on the wooden dock until he arrived at the boat. There weren't as many people around this late in the morning. It was relatively quiet until, of course, he heard Nathan's voice booming.

"Annabella! Grab that net before it falls in the lake!" Nathan shouted.

Annabella ran across the boat, right past Ivan to the net. She noticed him briefly, grinning curiously and grabbed the net as her father snatched the other end, just in time. They rolled the net and hauled it aboard. "Pabbi," she said. "Someone's here, looks like he wants to talk to you."

"Oh?" Nathan said inquiringly.

"Yes, Nathan," Ivan interrupted. "It's me, Ivan. I wanted to ask your approval of something." He stood a bit taller, pushed his chest out a bit and smiled his most handsome smile.

Nathan lifted his head over the boat and whipped his hair over to the side. He had aged well. His brown tanned skin was still tight, his hair still full, and his body muscular and quite fit. A life of working hard in the commercial fishing industry kept him younger than most his age. Nathan was in his mid-thirties, but he felt as young as when he had first met Anwa. "Is that so?" Nathan replied. "Then come aboard!"

Ivan nervously stepped onto the boat as Nathan grabbed his hand. Annabella ran around the vessel, standing beside her father. "Hi, Ivan," she said, simply, her hypnotic blue eyes piercing right through him.

His heart melted into a puddle at her feet. She has such an immediate effect on me, Ivan thought. He smiled and reached over, grasping her hand and kissing her knuckles in the gentlemanly style that was common these days. "Hello, Annabella, you are as beautiful as ever today."

She giggled briefly, then scowled, not sure where this was all going.

"What brings you here, lad?' Nathan asked inquiringly.

Ivan took a deep breath. "Well," Ivan started, letting out his breath as he talked. "I came to make it known of my love for your daughter." He paused momentarily then continued in a rush of nervous words. "I have been hoping for the past year that she would talk to me more or acknowledge me more, but I believe we are both the shy type, and we seem to be having difficulty connecting in the normal ways. So I thought I would ask you, her father, if it would be alright if I could begin dating your daughter." He let out another gulp of air as he braced himself for the rejection.

Nathanael stood in shock then started chuckling. Annabella looked at her father and then at Ivan, grinning but still confused. Nathan grabbed Ivan by the shoulders, half hugging him with one arm. "You have guts, my boy!" Nath replied heartily. "I don't believe any man has ever tried even to approach my stoic daughter."

"Pabbi!" she scolded, immediately, stepping a bit closer to the two men.

"Annabella," Nathan said. "You know I am right!"

Ivan was relieved; Nathan had not said no, and Annabella was stepping increasingly closer. His heart lifted higher as Nath squeezed his shoulders in a friendly gesture. Ivan winced, as Nath's grip sent pain through his limbs. The older man was strong!

"Let's go for a walk, Ivan," Nathan said, laughing.

"Pabbi!" Annabella shouted at him angrily.

"Sweetie," Nath said, looking back at her. "I will be back. Don't worry; I love you more than anything in the world. Give us a moment."

Annabella stood there stubbornly, then whipped her hair to the side, just like her father did, but she was female, and her hair was incredibly long and thick, reaching to the top of her buttocks, so it had a very alluring effect on Ivan. He gazed up at her, his eyes turning glossy and silly looking. She smiled and shook her head. She was trying to act stubborn, not gorgeous! Men are weird, she thought.

"We will be back, Annabella," Ivan said, waving.

Nathan let go of the young man's shoulders and walked with him along the sand. Once they got out of earshot, Nath started talking. "Do you know why my daughter is so withdrawn?" he asked.

"I heard her mother died when she was young," Ivan replied.

"Yes, her mother, Anwa, died in my arms," Nath said, gulping in his emotions. The memory tugged at his chest, piercing his heart silently. Nath looked down and ran his fingertips over a beautiful beaded bracelet on his wrist, momentarily lost, then inhaled sharply, swallowing his emotions. "It was a very difficult time for me. I poured my entire heart into raising Annabella. But I think as Annabella grew older, she started assuming the role of her mother, the missing parent. It was not something I even realized she was doing; my daughter is a lovely soul. It just became natural for her to help me through the rough times." Nathan shuffled his feet in the sand. "As time went on, I healed. We all healed, but for me, there will always be a missing piece that I don't think can ever be replaced. I don't believe many people can truly understand this." He smiled weakly. "Annabella, I think she tried to be that piece for me. Her whole life. I also raised her on a fishing boat. She learned about fishing, nets, boats and spent most of her childhood on the water. She still went to school but always looked forward to fishing in the mornings and evenings. She became somewhat socially awkward as a result. Even though she loves fishing as much as I do, I think she began sacrificing her own happiness by spending all her time with me. And I feel that it is my fault. My sorrow was not something I managed well."

"I'm so sorry to hear of your anguish," Ivan said softly, watching Nathan's wrist rest on his shoulder. He noticed a blue beaded bracelet woven together with string on the older man's wrist. "Do you mind if I ask where you got that man bracelet? I've never seen anything like that."

"It's not a man bracelet," Nathan said, fingering the beaded jewellery on his wrist. "It was Anwa's. I found it in her belongings years after her death. I liked the colours, so I started wearing it a few years after."

"I'm sorry for your loss," Ivan said.

"Thank you," Nath replied. "It was a long time ago. I think when you find that right person, Ivan, when it feels like your heart is going to jump right out of your chest and you think about that person almost every single day, then I think that kind of love never fades, no matter what. It just stays." Nathan patted his chest. "Right here."

Ivan stopped, momentarily stunned by Nath's words. "That's how I feel about Annabella, Mr. Olason," he said. "I think about her every day. It's making me crazy trying to figure out how I can possibly be with her. My parents know this because I talk about her, and no one else. Even when Annabella and I just talk randomly about the weather, my heart sings! My parents pushed me out the door today to do something about it because they are sick of seeing me in such turmoil over a girl."

Nathanael's face broke into a wide smile. "I'm so happy you feel that way about my daughter," Nathan said, his eyebrows lifting. A question formed in his mind. He was curious about this young man that was interested in his daughter. "What country did you emigrate from, Ivan?"

"Ukraine, sir," Ivan responded.

"Ah, yes," Nathan nodded. "Lots of tensions in Ukraine right now. What kind of work did you do while you were in Ukraine?"

"I was in the military, sir," Ivan replied, uneasily.

Silence filled the air as Nathan absorbed this information. "Military?" Nathan said, cocking his head to the side. "What was your position?"

"Private," Ivan answered. "It was a compulsory service. I had no choice."

"Oh," Nathan said thoughtfully.

"I was beaten," Ivan blurted out.

Nathan glanced at the young man. He was tall and strong, holding his head high.

"The Germans were brutal," Ivan continued. "They were abusive and belligerent. And I had some trouble with them."

"What happened?" Nathan asked.

"Well," Ivan said, his voice cracking. "You have to know that we could not understand the orders. They were speaking German, not Ukrainian. There was a considerable amount of miscommunication." He swallowed bravely and continued. "I was ordered to bring in some ammunition, and I brought in the horses instead. One soldier yelled at me and then struck me. I blocked his arm and accidentally elbowed him sharply in the face. A scuffle ensued." Ivan exhaled slowly, trying to forget the horrific details burned into his mind. "A group of German soldiers swarmed me. I was beaten unconscious. I am lucky to be alive, Mr. Olason."

A gust of wind blew along the beach, whipping up sand, swirling it in front of them. Nathan shielded his eyes. "I'm sorry," Nath said. "You are alright now?"

"Now, yes. It took me months to recuperate," Ivan said quietly. "They dropped my battered body off at my parent's door, using me as an example of what would happen to the other soldiers if they misunderstood instructions." Ivan paused, breathing in. "My parents made plans the next week to leave Ukraine. It took three months before I recovered enough to travel. We packed our meagre belongings and boarded a ship to Canada soon after. It was one of the best decisions my parents made."

"You've been through a lot," Nathan said, his face in the wind. "You are a strong man."

"Thank you," Ivan responded. "I plan on making a good life here in Gimli."

"That's exactly what I thought when I first came here from Iceland," Nath said.

"You are from Iceland?" Ivan asked.

"Yes," Nathan replied. "I am one of the original explorers that settled here. It was extremely difficult. There were many hard years here before it became easier."

"I'm prepared for that," Ivan said, smoothing his cowlick down again. "I can never go back to Ukraine. I have nothing to lose and everything to gain."

"You have a good positive attitude," Nathan pointed out.

"Thank you, sir," Ivan replied.

"Stop calling me sir," Nathan said, hugging the younger man with both arms and patting his back. "You can call me Nathan. Okay, let's head back now," Nath pulled his arm away and thoughtfully gestured his hand at the dock in the distance. "If Annabella agrees, I would love to accept you into the family, Ivan."

Ivan's face broke into a huge smile; he wasn't expecting this. He reached over and hugged Nath spontaneously. Nathan laughed, and so did Ivan. "Thank you, Mr. Olason," Ivan replied happily.

They both walked briskly back to the boat, speaking in hushed tones, Ivan almost skipping and Nathanael with his head slightly down, grinning.

Annabella stood defiantly on the boat, watching them both return to the dock. She laid her hands firmly on her shapely hips, trying to maintain a stubborn disposition. Annabella flipped her hair as it fluttered in the wind, slowly allowing a smile to creep onto her lips. She couldn't help it; a giddy feeling was inching through her body.

Ivan looked up, gazing at her silhouette, the glossy look coming back into his eyes. "She is a stunningly beautiful woman," Ivan said, as he admired her curvy figure and the odd smile she wore on her face.

"That's exactly how I felt about Anwa," Nath said softly, nodding.

The forest was dark, and he could hardly see anything. The wind blew through the shrubs, swaying the branches. The forest floor was full of deadwood, so much that it was impossible to clear it all. The trees hid everything in the dark; you could never see where you were going in the blackness.

But it didn't matter; he knew the way in these woods.

He looked up and noticed the stars glowing down upon him. The crescent moon rose higher in the sky.

No full moon tonight to guide him.

He walked through the bushes with a purpose, fuelled with a mix of anguish and recklessness. He swatted the branches away, blazing a path into the darkness. The trees swayed back as if in answer. Don't come here, they said. It's not safe. You may lose your way and never return.

He didn't listen.

His footsteps crunched the ground until he arrived at his destination.

He knew it well. He could find it with his eyes closed.

"How did your talk go with Annabella?" Ivan's mom asked, her voice lilting in the air pleasantly.

"It went well; I think," Ivan answered happily. "I talked to her father more than her, but he approved of me courting his daughter."

Ivan watched as his mother folded the cabbage rolls over the rice and meat mixture. Along the other table were numerous dough-wrapped potato mixtures called perogies. These were Ivan's favourites, amazingly delicious with cheese mixed into the mashed potato filling. When they first arrived in the summer of 1893, he noticed many of the Icelandic people in Gimli thought these foreign foods were a welcomed addition to meal preparation. The bland flatkaka, an unleavened rye bread, and salted fish were the Icelander's main dishes; Ukrainian cooking was an appreciated bonus.

The Kozak's arrived together as a family moving to the outskirts of Gimli, registering their free farmland for ten dollars. They invested in the land, cultivated it, grew grains and vegetables, then sold the goods in locals stands at the market. It was hard work. They had slaved together as a family unit, growing as much wheat, oats and root vegetables as they could. They were low on funds but desperate for a chance to make it in this new country, Canada.

Gimli had welcomed many settlers from Ukraine, Hungary, Germany and Poland; people that were being forced out of their countries from the Austria-Hungary tensions.

Ukraine was being splintered into several parts, with Western Ukraine falling into the Austria-Hungary rule. The average peasant's main occupation was farming; although forced to farm the lands of their lords in Ukraine, paid nothing more than just room and board, they became landless peasants, never able to grow and prosper.

Even the languages were changing; Western Ukraine was now a mixture of German, Polish and Yiddish speaking inhabitants. The Ukrainian farming labourers began to feel like foreigners in their own country. Many young Ukrainian males, like Ivan, were enlisted in the compulsory service in the Austrian army, with disastrous results. Ivan's experience with the military was not something he would ever forget. Left with a deep scar on his scalp, Ivan had deep-rooted resentment for his occupied country. Emigration was the only option left for Ivan and his family. He felt so lucky that his parents had managed to save enough money to leave.

When they learnt of what Canada was offering, they were hopeful. The Canadian government embarked on an aggressive immigration strategy to attract farming labourers from many countries, including Europe. Coinciding with the Austria-Hungarian crisis, Canada was experiencing an intense period of economic growth. With the completion of the transcontinental railroad opening up the west, demand for wheat and grains increased substantially. Massive areas of the country that were inaccessible before were now demanding train shipments. Settlements were growing everywhere, and labourers were in high demand, especially wheat farmers.

Ivan and his parents were desperate for a country to call home, and Canada was calling them. So, a deal was born. One hundred sixty acres of land was offered free as a homestead for just a registration fee of ten dollars. His parents thought this was a sweet deal. They scraped together the hefty boat fee to cross the Atlantic, gambling on a better life. Thousands of Ukrainians flocked to Canada with them, stretching from Manitoba to Saskatchewan to Alberta. Canada was everything they had dreamed of; their promised land.

Once they started farming the land, his parents began building a second home on the property for their son and his future bride. The only problem was that the bride didn't know it yet.

"So how did she react?" his mom asked.

"I don't know," Ivan said, trying to smooth the pesky cowlick on his head. "I don't understand women much, Mom. At times she would smile at me, then at other times she would appear aloof and perturbed."

His mom laughed, "That's wonderful news."

"How do you think that's wonderful news?" he asked incredulously.

His mom smiled sweetly, "She likes you, Ivan."

"I sure hope so," he smiled, nervously running his fingers through his hair. "Because I'm going to ask Annabella on a date tomorrow."

Chapter 2

Annabella's eyes narrowed as Ivan approached. He sensed something. He wasn't sure what, but it felt like he had done something wrong.

"Good morning, Annabella," Ivan said softly, as he watched her clean out the boat, her hair tucked sloppily into her fishing hat.

"Good morning, Ivan," she replied, stiffly, glancing away.

Ivan swallowed hard; nervous tingles crept up into his stomach. He wasn't sure why she responded in this cold manner, but then Ivan did not have much experience with women; they often left him bewildered and confused. He scratched his head. "Is there something wrong?" Ivan asked.

Annabella looked up, spearing him with her stunning blue eyes. She scoffed and turned away into the boat, grabbing the fishing boxes, stuffing them with bait.

Ivan was worried. He had thought everything was going well. He had obtained her father's approval, and she had seemed somewhat receptive. Now Ivan was here to ask her on their first date. He was not sure what they would be doing for their first time together, but he was slowly forming an idea in his mind to make it special.

"What makes you think that all you need to do is ask my Pabbi and not me?" Annabella said suddenly, blurting it all out. She stood before him, with her hands on her hips, so beautifully stubborn. In that instant, Ivan felt so immensely attracted to her that he had to keep himself from smiling, fearing that he may anger her more.

He smiled gently. "I am truly sorry if you have misinterpreted my actions," Ivan said.

"Misinterpreted!" Annabella responded, scoffing back.

Ivan was confused. His lovely date was being tenacious. Was it because she didn't like him, didn't want to date him or was it just that she wanted the choice to be hers? Or maybe, she wanted to be pursued in a different method than he had chosen. He looked up at her, following her movements with his eyes as she rummaged in the boat. "Can we go for a walk along the dock and talk?" he asked softly.

Annabella glanced at him, flipping her hair to the side briefly. She didn't respond; her thoughts were swirling in her mind, frantically. Her heart beat loudly. She liked Ivan, but she felt like she didn't have a voice. At the same time, she found it difficult to articulate what she was feeling. Her mind screamed at her. She had to say something!

Ivan watched her silent body language. Dejectedly, he took her silence as a rejection and began to walk away, confused and deflated.

"Yes," she said firmly, at the last moment. "I will go for a walk and talk."

Ivan smiled, relief flooding his body. He reached out his hand to help her out of the boat. She looked down at his offered hand and refused his assistance. "I am able and strong," she said. "I was raised in this boat. I can get out on my own just fine, thank you." She stepped out with her dirty fishing boots, placing her feet squarely on the dock.

Ivan let her lead the way. The town of Gimli had built the wooden dock with some reinforcement from rocks and boulders. It was an unstable structure, often washed away with the autumn storms, needing to be repaired or completely replaced every year. "When will they build a more sustainable dock?" Ivan asked. "Something that won't get washed away every year?"

Annabella's eyes flashed angrily. "And I suppose you have a better idea?" she asked. "We have been struggling with this dock for many years. Water is not that easy of an opponent. What would you suggest?"

Ivan looked at her blazing eyes and immediately felt a strong attraction again. His reaction was confusing and alluring at the same time. She was amazingly beautiful with that intelligent look on her face. She was a strong, willful woman, and he was falling for her even harder now. "Well," Ivan said softly. "Maybe, we could build up more of the dock with dirt and rocks. See here." Ivan pointed to the portion of the dock reinforced with mud and rocks. "This seems to be more stable than the wooden parts. And maybe build a lighthouse as well."

Annabella grinned. "Hmm," she said thoughtfully. "You may be right." She pointed out towards the lake. "But the lighthouse would need to be farther out. How would we accomplish that?"

"I would think," Ivan said, brushing his arm lightly against hers, appearing almost accidentally. "We would need to build portions of the dock with reinforced cement and build the entire dock farther out."

Annabella felt the electricity shoot up her arm at his slight touch. She felt attracted and drawn to him. He was an intelligent man and just as stubborn as she. His thoughts on fixing the dock were impressive. "Where do you get these kinds of ideas?" she asked, smiling.

"I was always good at planning," he replied, smoothing his cowlick. "When I was in the Austrian army, they often gave me orders to build structures quickly; guard posts, fences and reinforced structures. I didn't understand much German but was quick to determine what they needed from their actions."

"You served in the army?" Annabella asked, impressed.

"Yes," Ivan said. "Every young man was conscripted to the Austrian army. Many of us were beaten."

"Were you beaten?" Annabella asked.

"Yes," Ivan said softly. "It was one of the reasons that we left as a family."

"That sounds dreadful," Annabella said.

"It was," he said.

They walked along the dock approaching the end and turned around to go back. Ivan brushed his hand against hers, then lightly laced his fingers within hers. She cocked her head to the side but left her hand in his. They walked in silence back to the boat, hand in hand, not speaking another word. Arriving at the vessel, Annabella took her hand away and busied herself with tying the anchor rope tighter.

"I am eighteen years old," she said, looking down at the rope. "I would like to choose for myself. My Pabbi doesn't choose for me."

"I understand now why you were angered," Ivan said. "My apologies." He looked down at his hands, wishing he could hold her hand again. It felt lovely and warmed his heart. "I was shy, and you are so beautiful that I became tongue-tied every time we talked. I racked my brain on how to approach you. So, I decided I would ask your father instead." Ivan looked up. She was intensely staring at him, her blue eyes burning through him. "I will talk directly to you from now on and give you a chance to express your wishes."

Annabella's face lit up into a huge smile. "Thank you for that," she said. "You are a nice man."

Ivan smiled. "Does that mean you will go on a date with me?" he asked, beaming.

Annabella laughed. "Yes," she replied, smiling broadly.

Ivan had spent days mulling over what they would do on their first date. He walked into Yuri's farm, intent on buying a promising strong colt for the farm. He was surprised and delighted to bump into Annabella there. She was visiting her cousins, Julia, Aron and their daughters. They were all sitting around the kitchen, sharing stories, when Ivan walked in with the ageing Yuri.

"Hi, Ivan," Annabella said immediately.

Ivan smiled broadly, a boyish grin gracing his handsome face. "Hi, Annabella," he said. "How have you been?"

"Great, actually," she said. "I proposed your idea to fix the dock to my father, and he is trying to put it through the town council. Pabbi is a retired assistant reeve."

"Oh," Ivan said. "I didn't know that." Ivan looked at Annabella wondrously. She looked as gorgeous as ever again. He felt his mind turning to mush. "You look very beautiful today, Annabella."

"Thank you," Annabella said, blushing.

Julia looked at Ivan and grinned. Her daughter's giggled.

"Would you like to take a walk with me, Annabella?" Ivan asked. "It's a beautiful day today. I can resume my negotiations with Yuri afterwards."

Annabella smiled. "Alright, let's go," she said, standing up.

Ivan gestured with his hand towards the door. "After you, my beautiful lady," he said.

Julia giggled, and her daughters glanced shyly at the handsome Ivan. "Ladies," Ivan said, tipping his small hat. "We will be back. Have a wonderful day!"

He closed the door and stepped outside. Ivan saw Annabella already walking towards the old horse road; he ran to catch up. "Hey," Ivan said, laughing. "You are a fast walker."

"I am," Annabella replied, grinning. "You look handsome today. You had my cousins blushing."

Ivan laughed. "Thank you, my dear," he said, gazing around, scanning the distant fields. "Where did you want to walk?"

"Hmm," Annabella said thoughtfully. She scanned the farmlands, her eyes lighting up. "I know! Why don't we get two horses and take a quick ride over to Willow Point? It's beautiful there. Have you seen it?"

Ivan laughed wholeheartedly. "You're serious?" he asked.

"Yes," Annabella said. "As you said, it's a beautiful day."

"Okay," he said, his boyish grin lighting up his face. "My father has some horses that are rideable. Do you know how to ride horses?"

Annabella laughed. "Of course, silly," she said. "Who doesn't know how to ride?"

"Ok, come this way," he said. "My farm is not far." He pointed in the distance to the west. "See that brown house? That's where it is."

They walked across the field. After several minutes, Ivan's hand brushed against hers again. She felt sensual currents run up her spine. Then his hand slipped into hers. She loved that feeling. Her heart melted. They continued walking hand in hand in silence until they reached the brown house. Across the field, there was a house half-built. The roof was constructed and the walls standing, but there were no windows or doors yet. The front steps were just a rough bare wood structure, enough to allow access in and out while working.

Annabella pointed. "Whose house is that?" she asked.

"That's my house," Ivan said nervously. "My parents are building it for me. Well, I am building it too. But, yes, it's my house."

"It looks like a big house," she said. "Just for you? Aren't you too young to be living alone?"

"Well, I hope that I don't live alone for long," Ivan said, glancing at Annabella sideways.

"What does that mean?" she asked.

Ivan coughed. "Let's discuss it after our day at Willow Point," he said, pointing. "There's our horses now. See them by the barn?"

"Oh, my," Annabella said. "They are beautiful!"

"You can have the light brown one," Ivan said. "She's a mare. I will take the dark brown one."

Annabella quickened her step until they reached the horses. She smoothed the mare's neck and spoke gently to her. "What's her name?" Annabella asked.

"Lily," Ivan said, giggling. "And this is Dash; we just bought him in March. He is a good strong horse. He took quite a liking to Lily as soon as he got here. They adore each other quite a lot; they have been inseparable since his arrival."

"That's so cute," Annabella said, laughing, patting Lily's neck. Ivan handed her a saddle, and she laid it gently onto the mare's back.

"She likes you," Ivan said. "She normally would flinch if a stranger put a saddle on her." Ivan fastened his horse's saddle on, adjusting it until it was perfect. He turned to help Annabella onto her horse and was astonished to see she had already mounted the mare.

"Ready to go?" she said inquiringly, sitting high up on her horse. Lily was stepping her front legs out anxiously, ready to trot.

Ivan laughed and mounted his horse, grabbing the reins. "You are amazing, Annabella," he said. "Okay, let's go." He snapped the reins, and they both galloped out into the field. Annabella was quite good at riding, he noticed. This woman was showing him all sides of her personality, and the more he learned about her, the more he liked her. She was beautiful, adept, wilful and spontaneous.

As they both neared the road, they slowed down and rode side by side. Annabella's hair flowed beautifully in the wind behind her. "It's not much farther," she said. "There will be a small clearing and another smaller horse road going towards the east."

"Do you go here often?" Ivan asked.

"Sometimes," Annabella answered. "I will just walk to be alone with my thoughts. It only takes an hour." The horses slowed to a trot. Annabella glanced sideways at Ivan; the movement caused a large strand of hair to fall forward onto her breasts. He tried not to look down, but his eyes didn't listen. Annabella caught him looking and smiled. "And sometimes, late at night, I will go swimming naked there. It's so peaceful and serene."

Ivan felt his groin harden. He tried to ignore it, but it grew valiantly without his consent. He shuffled on the horse uncomfortably. "Maybe we could do that together one day," Ivan said.

Annabella laughed, "Yes, maybe one day." She pointed to a clearing a mile away. "We turn east there."

"Alright, my beautiful," he said. "You lead the way."

Annabella smiled delightfully, happy to be offered the chance to showcase her home-grown knowledge. They trotted side by side until they reached the clearing, then the road narrowed quite a bit. The horses led them into Willow Point, with Lily in front of Dash. Ivan watched from behind as Annabella's buttocks bounced on the horse rhythmically with every trot. She had a lovely round shape to her buttocks, and he began getting quite aroused from seeing this. Finally, he had to avert his eyes away from her backside, lest he gets off his horse with a raging hard penis.

The branches and bushes started crowding the road; they pushed the stray branches away as they made their way to the point. They crossed a muddy ditch then arrived at a beautiful small beach. The sand was fine and more whitish in colour than the brownish sand on Gimli beach. Annabella jumped off her horse and led Lily to the water's edge. "Drink, my sweet," she said. Lily dipped her large head into the lake water and lapped up the cold liquid.

Ivan also disembarked, following her example. Dash gulped at the water, splashing his big head with the wetness. He glanced at Bella. "You are a very good rider," Ivan said.

"Thank you," Annabella replied. "My father taught me when I was just very little. He said my momma was a good rider too."

"I heard you look like her," Ivan said, leading the horses to the trees and tying them loosely to a thick tree trunk.

"Yes," Annabella said. "My Pabbi said I look so similar to her that sometimes he stopped in astonishment. Although I have my daddy's eyes."

Ivan gestured for her to sit on the sand beside him. "You have beautiful eyes," he said.

Annabella stood boldly by the water's edge instead. "Thank you," she said, looking away.

"Please sit," Ivan said, gesturing to a patch of grass.

She turned, looking down at the grass and walked over to him, choosing not to sit. She stood, narrowing her eyes. "Why do you want me, Ivan?" she blurted out suddenly. "Why do you not choose the other girls that are blushing over you? You have so many to decide from."

Ivan sifted the sand through his hands. "Because you are special," he said simply. "I find you fascinating; I've been enthralled with you since we first met. I think it was the week after we moved to our new parcel of land. I saw you walking with your dad down Main Street, and your hair looked so unkempt and tangled. You must have just come back from fishing. But there was something about you; all I could see was the beautiful woman that you are. And I still see that."

Annabella smiled. "That's sweet," she said, finally sitting down. Ivan shuffled his hips closer to her. One of his hands drifted to her knee, and he left it there; she didn't object. He hugged her loosely with his right arm. She grinned and snuggled into him.

His heart rejoiced with this wonderful woman in his arms. "Want to know something strange?" Ivan asked.

"Sure," she said. "What?"

"The more defiant you are," Ivan said, smiling sheepishly. "The more I like you. I don't quite understand it myself."

Annabella laughed, stretching out her luscious neck as her head tipped back.

Ivan watched her laugh, grinning. He felt so drawn to her right now. The heat built between them instantly. He felt a strong urge to kiss her. He shuffled his legs closer until their knees were touching.

Ivan grasped her hand and kissed her knuckles, slowly, very slowly. He looked up at her; there was a smouldering dark blue glint in her eyes, saying yes. Ivan leaned forward, grasping her chin and gazed into her eyes. Her sapphire eyes burned through his. He felt his heartbeat in his head, his body urging him to kiss her now. Yielding to the chemistry, he moved his lips gently to hers. The touch of their lips was electric; it spread through his veins like a current of desire.

Her lips were so beautifully soft and feminine. His penis hardened fully, instantly awake. He leaned into her, grasping the back of her head lightly as he kissed her fully. Her mouth opened effortlessly, letting him in. He could feel her body begin to melt in his grasp. Her response was so quick and sensual that it carried him away, making him forget exactly what was happening. He kissed her deeply, his tongue now exploring her sweet mouth. They moved together, stretching back onto the sand, still kissing, their hands moving naturally into each other's hair.

She moaned, and her hips moved involuntarily, slightly rocking into him. He laid on top of her, naturally moving to a more comfortable position, his leg between hers. She grasped his shoulders and began kissing him back with a fury like none other. Testosterone jumped crazily through his veins. Her body pressed against him urgently, and his body responded just as quickly, his penis straining against his pants. He felt the urge to undo his belt, then stopped.

His brain was not working, he thought, strangely.

He could not undo his belt here on the sand in a secluded beach! This was their first kiss! They hadn't even gone on their first date! Be a gentleman!

Ivan pulled back, breaking the kiss. He caressed her cheeks and looked into her smouldering sexy eyes. "One day," he said. "We will do this here in the sand. Swim nude in the lake and make love right here. But not today."

Her blue eyes closed, accepting this statement. "Yes," she said. "You are right. It is too early."

"Yes, my dear," he said. "It is."

"My body feels on fire when I am with you," Annabella said. "I want to challenge you, touch you, feel you and kiss you all at the same time. I want you to feel you deep inside me."

Ivan breathed in sharply. "I want that too," he said numbly, no other words coming to his brain.

They both looked into each other's eyes so closely and so deeply, as if they were reading each other's thoughts, each other's intentions and feelings. Ivan leaned forward and kissed her again; his tongue penetrating her sweet mouth. His penis hardened almost painfully in his pants, straining to get out. He tried to ignore his body's response and kissed her deeply. Annabella kissed him back urgently, her hand fluttering down to his groin, ever so slightly touching him there.

Ivan broke the kiss, breathing heavily. "We must go, my sweet," he said, inhaling her scent. "Or else I won't be able to control myself any longer."

Annabella stared into his green eyes and blinked slowly, allowing the sexual energy to dissipate slowly. She inhaled deeply, calming her desire and exhaled forcefully. "Okay," she said. "Hug me first."

"That I can do," he said, gripping her in a ferocious hug, squashing her magnificent breasts against his chest. "You feel so good," he murmured in her ear, little pulses of electricity running down his spine.

"Mmm," she murmured, lying there underneath him, so soft and willing.

"Alright," he said, moving off of her, grasping her hand and pulling her up. "We must go before this kissing progresses into something more."

She stood, feeling light-headed. "Okay," she said. Annabella hugged him briefly and walked towards her horse, untying the rope from the tree. She turned and faced him suddenly. "I have a question that you didn't answer earlier," she said.

"What is it?" he said inquiringly.

"Are you really planning on living in that big new house all alone?" she asked, shading her eyes from the sun.

Ivan smiled nervously, looking directly at her face. "Honestly," he said. "I was hoping to live in it with you."

Annabella's heart flipped happily, and her lips spread into the biggest smile Ivan has ever seen. He laughed and hugged her warmly. "I just need to convince you to say yes first," he said, kissing her on the top of her head.

She laughed. "You are persistent," she said, smiling.

"Well," Ivan said. "I have an extraordinary woman in my arms. And I don't wish to let her go. Ever."

Her heart burst into a cascade of warmth that spread throughout her entire body, her limbs, her feet, everything. They walked together to the horses and kissed briefly before mounting them.

Ivan grinned thoughtfully, fitting his feet into the stirrups. "Do you ever think of having a family of your own?"

"Yes," she responded immediately. "Quite a large family, actually. Many children."

"Oh?" Ivan said, surprised.

Annabella blushed and looked down shyly. "I always thought a big family would be lovely," she mumbled quietly.

Ivan smiled. "That's wholesome," he said reflectively, his heart warming at the thought. He pulled the reins and led the way, his horse leaping to the front.

As they trotted through the bushes back to Gimli, Annabella looked behind her. Something she had forgotten tugged at her mind. "What are we doing for our first date?" she asked.

"I am planning a surprise," he said, grinning boyishly. "I will let you know more when I get some details finalized."

The horses continued trotting all the way back to Gimli, leaving Annabella smiling and mulling over all sorts of possible scenarios in her mind. She liked Ivan. She was growing quite fond of him.

Nathan watched from the boat as Annabella returned home late. He saw her rush guiltily into the house. Nath knew she was concerned that her dad might be waiting for her. And he was; until about an hour ago.

He had left the house and decided to go fishing. He had several old fishing rods that he had put together and enjoyed his solitude on the lake. It made him think and work things out in his head, what seems right and what seems wrong. Right now, he felt that it was healthy to start letting his daughter Annabella go. But in his heart, he was fearful that he could possibly lose his daughter. She would leave, marry and never come back, he thought.

Nathan mused over this as he led the boat out onto the lake, glancing back towards his home on the beach. He loved his home, his family and his hometown Gimli. They had called it New Iceland back in the beginning. The Canadian govern-ment had declared it part of Manitoba later on, but it was still

New Iceland in his mind. They had formed an Icelandic government from 1878 to 1886, but it didn't last.

Following the smallpox epidemic, a sombre mood fell upon Gimli, leaving people feeling defeated. By forming the united government of New Iceland, they were hoping to keep everyone together. Despite their efforts, there was widespread emigration. Hundreds of Icelanders moved south to Winnipeg, Dakota and farther south. Many people also moved farther north along the Icelandic River, into Arnes and Riverton. Gimli was being abandoned. In 1881, after the exodus, the population of New Iceland struggled to stay at 100 people.

Several years later, a New Iceland revival had begun to form. The fishing industry that Nathan had worked so hard for began developing many opportunities for employment. The farmers began cultivating crops more successfully; people started moving back, and New Iceland was recovering.

Nathan served as assistant reeve in the district Vidinesbygd, which included Willow Point and Gimli. Several other reeves were serving in the other three districts; Arnesbygd, Fljotsbygd, and Mikleyjarbygd, which encompassed Arnes, Icelandic River and Hecla Island. A five-person council, including a reeve, an assistant reeve, and three other members, governed each of the districts. The members met regularly and deliberated over issues within their regions and also dealt with matters concerning the colony as a whole.

In 1887, New Iceland was incorporated into Manitoba as the Gimli Rural Municipality. As an official part of Canada, Gimli prospered. In 1897, Nathan helped build the grand steamboat named the Lady of the Lake. It was a celebration like none other. It was the largest boat ever. He was always good at building things. He had built his large family home too, along with the help of dozens of relatives, all the while raising his baby daughter as best as he could. He was proud; they were able to make Gimli a home, prosper and build a solid foundation for the future. He had accomplished all of this even while continuously struggling with his grief from Anwa's death. Nath smiled wistfully at the memories, as he glimpsed his daughter rushing to the house.

He watched her small agile figure fumble with the keys and enter their home.

He set sail, and the boat slipped effortlessly farther into the lake. He turned his eyes away from their home. He was a good father; he had poured his heart and soul into raising his sweet daughter.

Annabella was what made his life worth living.

For the first few tender years, he would hug his little baby girl, and they would rock each other to sleep. He put everything, his heart, his soul, his emotions, his entire being was channelled into raising his only baby girl.

But she was 18 now. She was an adult.

She was falling in love with a man.

Nathan grabbed the rudder and watched the wind, adjusting it accordingly. He aimed the boat for the northern part of the lake. He wouldn't go too far because it always became dangerous if you travelled too close to the remote northern areas. He knew of a small spot near a deserted shore that the fish were plentiful. The boat moved swiftly, the wind carrying it along. The water splashed behind the vessel, creating a beautiful wake that grew larger and larger in the distance, setting off rippling waves.

He couldn't see the house anymore now, but he knew that Annabella was panicking, running through the house looking for him. She would now be slumping on the sofa, worrying about him. After a half-hour, though, Bella would realize that he had gone off on his own, fishing, and hopefully relax. She would still worry that she had somehow abandoned him.

He was going to stop this dependency tonight.

She needed to start living her own life. It pained him; unnerved him. It formed a lump in his heart, knowing that he might lose her. But he knew in his gut that this is what a loving parent must do.

He had to push her to go out and start living her life.

He had enjoyed an incredible 18 years with her, living on the boat during the busy fishing seasons. He had sent her off to school, helped her with homework, taught her to fish, taught her to cook, everything a good parent would do.

But he also realized, at some point, the parenting would end. She would grow into a beautiful young woman and fall in love with a man.

He steered the boat towards the little deserted shoreline, adjusting the rudder until he finally reached the destination. He let the sails go and floated, bobbing on the lake. Nathan threw an anchor over and fumbled through his fishing supplies; he pulled the crude fishing rod out and launched the line out into the lake. He relaxed back and gazed at the setting sun.

It was so quiet and thought-provoking out here, like the spirits and the heavens were looking down on you. He took a deep breath and inhaled the fresh sea air. He loved it out here. If he could, he would stay out on the lake all the time, never going back home. Time didn't exist out here, nor did personal struggles, stress or hard decisions. Everything slowed to a wonderful state of gratitude.

This was his comfortable place, where he gathered his thoughts. He would muse over difficulties with his work or his family. He would always come back with the right answers. But this time, he already knew the answer.

He would come here more often. Maybe every evening.

Then Annabella will stop coming home so often. She will stop feeling guilty and find her own path. Tears welled in his eyes; he knew it was the right thing to do. And he also knew that she was part Nath and part Anwa; she was raised to have strong family bonds. The chances are that she would have children soon, and those grandchildren would be in his life too, maybe even more than he wished for, he thought, chuckling.

She was a wonderful young woman. He trusted that she would make the right decisions. And he knew in the depths of his soul that she was not leaving, she was beautifully spreading her wings and that whatever happened, she would do it with integrity, love and family in mind.

Nath was proud, sad and happy all at the same time.

CHAPTER 3

Annabella burst onto the deck at Ivan's house, knocking on the door urgently. He raced to the door.

"What is it?" Ivan said.

"Pabbi has been absent a lot," she said. "I'm worried. It's not like him. Lately, it's been every evening. He leaves a cold dinner for me in the kitchen, and by the time I'm back at home, he's gone."

"Maybe he just wants time alone," Ivan said, reasoning.

"Yes," she said. "He does that. But normally it's only sporadic, maybe once a week. Now, the only time I get to spend time with him is during work. But sometimes the fish store is so busy that we have little time to talk."

Ivan smiled. "Hmm," he said. "I'm not sure then."

"What are you smiling about?" Annabella laughed.

"Just noticing how beautiful you are," he replied, a grin spreading on his face.

She laughed. "You're so silly," she said, immediately hugging him.

He kissed the top of her head and delighted in the warmth of her body against his.

"Hey," Annabella said, abruptly. "Did you figure out what we will be doing for our first date?"

"Yes," Ivan responded excitedly. "We will be going to Winnipeg!"

Annabella snapped her head around in surprise. "What?"

Ivan laughed, "Yes. I have it all planned. We will leave early tomorrow."

"When will we be back?" she asked.

"We are staying overnight," he said. "So, pack a bag and be prepared, my beautiful!"

"You are serious!" she said, laughing in surprise.

"I am, my sweetheart," Ivan said, squeezing her close. "We will have a wonderful first date. I promise."

He sat in the dark. The forest surrounded him, engulfing him and accepting him at the same time. The wind swayed the leaves, the breeze filling his nostrils with the clean lake air. It wasn't a good place to sleep, but he had nodded off briefly, napping on the forest floor. He would hunt some deer tomorrow. They were jumping out of the bushes again, teasing him with their agility.

He heard a rustle in the bushes, and his mind flashed back into time briefly. He peered into the bushes, trying to see through the night. It was an animal; he knew this. It moved like a deer. He would have deer meat tomorrow.

He stood and brushed the dirt off his torn pants.

The blackness closed in on his mind. The forest was a serene place in the darkness, but the night also held clues to answers that he didn't want to hear.

He stomped away wearily, knowing that it wasn't going to be easy. Nothing was.

Annabella had packed. Ivan loaded the carriage, and they had spent the entire morning and afternoon in transit. Ivan was feeling slightly tired but mostly insecure. He tried smoothing his cowlick several times without success. Ivan wasn't sure why he felt nervous; he had spent several weeks courting Annabella, his nerves should be calmer. He glanced at her and understood now that it was most likely because she looked absolutely stunning tonight.

She was wearing a wide, blue dress, and her hair was pinned up in the current style of single ladies. But he could tell that she wasn't herself in the beautiful dress. She itched, scratched, pulled at the pins in her hair, shuffled her feet, didn't sit down properly, just generally looked like she was imprisoned in the beautiful dress. He found this funny, and it helped him to relax.

"You don't like the dress," Ivan stated, smiling.

"Can you tell?" Annabella replied, pulling a pin out of her hair. "Now, I'm embarrassed. Both my grandmas made me wear it. They insisted that its customary to dress up beautifully on your first courtship date."

"You look stunning, Annabella," Ivan said, smiling.

"Thank you," she replied softly, cocking her head to the side, pulling at another pin in her hair. A thick lock fell loose and cascaded down her shoulder, curling up at the end. "But I really don't feel comfortable dressed like this. I usually wear fishing pants and a deerskin coat, not this wool coat grandma Bea gave me."

"I know," Ivan said, nodding. "You look beautiful in anything, Annabella. Fishing pants or frilly dresses. Honestly, it doesn't matter to me. I like you just the way you are."

Annabella's face lit up in the biggest smile he had ever seen. "Thank you," she said, beaming. "That's one of the nicest things anyone has ever said to me."

Ivan reached over and touched her shoulder. "May I?" he asked. "A lock of hair has come loose. I will pin it back."

"Yes," she said softly.

He stood, pulling his chair out, walked behind her and gently lifted the silky strand back onto her head. As he searched for the pin, his left palm fluttered down absentmindedly onto her neckline, ever so lightly brushing against the sensitive skin there.

Annabella shivered slightly from the erotic sensation of his touch. She wondered if he knew the sensual response of his light fingers on her body. Electric vibrations tingled throughout her entire spine, spreading warmth to her lady parts. "Did you find the pin?" she asked, trying to calm the erotic shivers from melting her entire being.

"Hmm," he said sensually, concentrating. "I believe so." He plucked a pin out, put the hair through it and tried fastening it to her bundled hair. "But I believe that I just made it worse. I am not good at pinning hair."

Annabella laughed. "Either am I," she said. "Don't bother with it. I will be taking all these pins out the minute we leave this restaurant."

Ivan laughed. "Sounds good to me," he said, seating himself back at the table.

"Where did you come up with the idea of coming to Winnipeg for dinner?" she asked, grinning.

"I don't know," Ivan said, smiling. "I just thought it would be fitting that our first date would be special. My parents have a carriage and the horses, of course, so it was the beginning of the idea, I guess."

Ivan had deliberated about the date much more than he wished to tell her. He nervously planned it, searched for suitable first-class restaurants, which there were very few, so he settled on the Winnipeg Hotel. It was a three-story building built in 1881; it featured a restaurant and bar on the main floor and 60 beds on the upper two floors. They had travelled all the way from Gimli to the west side of Winnipeg Main Street to reach it. The owners, Oswald and Thomas Montgomery, were often seen in the restaurant and hotel lobby, even though they had several hotel employees. Ivan's father had a brother who knew the Montgomery's well, and they had put a good word in for Ivan, securing him two rooms and a table in the hotel restaurant. In exchange, he had brought an entire wagon full of vegetables and flour. Thomas had shaken his hand in the front entrance, a gentleman's handshake, showing him the way to the back to unload. It made Ivan feel very influential, mostly since Annabella was smiling beside him. They both had to ride in the front of the carriage, though, because the actual carriage was full of vegetables. But Annabella didn't seem to mind; it looked like she preferred to sit in the riding seats, with the reins in both their hands.

Ivan reached forward and grasped her hand, kissing it softly. Bella watched his lips caressing each knuckle. "Why do you put so much effort into making special moments with me?" Annabella asked thoughtfully.

Ivan smiled. "That's simple," he said bluntly. "Because I want you to be my wife."

Annabella inhaled sharply, but could not keep the grin from spreading across her face. "You are such a romantic gentleman," she said. "But how can you just blurt out such a serious thing?" she asked mischievously, trying to hide her elation.

He was smiling again. He seemed to smile quite a lot, she mused.

"Because it's true," Ivan said. "I have felt like this ever since I first met you. I cannot describe it. I just knew. I think of you every day. You captivate my thoughts and my heart."

Annabella grinned sheepishly, her cheeks blushing. She looked down at her hands, trying to will her face to return back to her normal colour.

"You are cute," Ivan said, chuckling.

Ivan lifted her hand from across the table and gently kissed the top of her knuckles again. His full lips kissed her skin, softly and ever so slowly. The sensations sent erotic tingles throughout her body again. "I like it when you touch me," she said. "It makes me feel warm and tingly inside."

Ivan's smile transformed into a sexy grin. His green eyes looked up at her as he kissed her hand once again. "I could kiss you all night," he said. "I enjoy the feeling too."

Annabella looked into his alluring green eyes, and for the first time in her life, she felt so extremely giddy, excited and elated, all at the same time. Every moment that they spent together moved them closer and closer to each other's hearts. She treasured this feeling. It made her feel so comfortable and relaxed like she didn't have to try to be anybody other than herself. It warmed her heart.

Ivan was still smiling, and he still had her hand in his. A silly boyish grin spread on his face. Annabella laughed.

Ivan laughed too. He was delighted that she was warming to him so much. She was the most beautiful kind woman he had ever met, and she was allowing him into her life. A part of him felt incredulous that this was happening, and the other part was entirely grateful.

After dinner, they had retreated to their rooms, as was customary during courtship. Annabella was astonished at the lavishness of the hotel room. She had never before experienced such luxury. It must have cost Ivan a fortune to do this, she thought. She immediately pulled the pins out of her hair, removed her Victorian-style dress and the many layers of undergarments. She now felt foolish wearing such an elaborate gown, since Ivan had said he liked her just the way she was. But grandma Margret had insisted she wears it. Maybe it was right because she would have felt foolish entering such a beautiful hotel wearing a simple grey dress.

She washed her face and hands, then slipped into her peasant dress. It was a plain dark grey dress with a nice collar; it was her favourite. It was worn but comfortable.

She looked at the time; it was only 8 o'clock in the evening. It was so early! She was accustomed to not sleeping until well past 11 pm. She paced the room and then drank some water. She rummaged through her luggage, then fidgeted, shuffling through the newspapers and pamphlets on the stand.

Finally, she leapt up, slipped on her peasant shoes and reached for the door. This was ridiculous, she thought. He was in the room right next door! And they weren't supposed to see each other at night? Now, what was the reason for that? Her mind couldn't rationalize the logic behind such silliness.

Annabella walked wilfully out into the hall and knocked on Ivan's door.

She waited and waited. She knocked on the door again, confused. She heard rummaging, then finally footsteps to the door; she smiled with relief. Finally, he was going to open the door.

Ivan unlocked the door and flung it open, all the while muttering. "I did not order anything from the bar. Who is it?" he said.

When he looked up, he was in shock.

Annabella smiled happily.

"What are you doing here, my dear?" Ivan said, peering down the hall nervously. "Hurry, come in." He grabbed her arm and pulled her into the room, closing the door swiftly.

Annabella was anxious and flustered. "What's wrong?" she asked, clearly confused. "Did I do something wrong?"

Ivan locked the door nervously. "I could be in a lot of trouble with you here in my room."

"But whatever for?" she asked, innocently. She smoothed her dress and hugged him warmly.

"Annabella," Ivan said, bewilderedly, her warm arms around his waist. His physical response was immediate. His palms started sweating, and his groin tingled. He pulled her slightly away and looked into her eyes. "An unmarried woman should never be in a man's room at night." He watched her eyes fall in embarrassment. "It's alright, my dear. You didn't know."

"I was bored in my room," she said. "And I just thought that it's ridiculous that I have to spend the entire evening alone in my room, with you just next door, doing exactly the same thing! It's ridiculous."

He hugged her. "I'm glad you did it," he said, chuckling. "I was missing you too. Come have some tea with me, sweetheart."

His hand fluttered to her waist, leading her to the side table with two chairs. He pulled out a chair for her and poured the dark liquid from the teapot. He seated himself across from her.

"I love your hair down," he said immediately. "You look so beautiful."

Annabella smiled. "Thank you," she said. "You look very handsome in that suit as well."

Ivan smiled foolishly with a wide, boyish grin.

Annabella laughed. "I love that boyish grin of yours," she said. "It's so cute how your dimples show."

Ivan laughed. "And I love your innocent stubbornness," he said.

"About that," Annabella asked. "Why am I not supposed to be in here at night? I like you quite a lot. We enjoy talking together. Why can't we be together at night?"

It was Ivan's turn to blush. "Annabella," he said softly, explaining. "Because people would think we are having sex before marriage."

"Oh!" Annabella shrieked, her eyes opening wide in shock. Then she demurely looked down at her hands embarrassingly. Bella had no idea people thought such things and nervously fiddled with her hands. To be honest, she had imagined having sex with Ivan several times over the past few weeks, dreaming of his hands all over her body, most times awakening to her own hands touching herself. They had gone for several more walks and kissed in the bushes often; every time, the heat had escalated between them, and they had to stop themselves. When she went home afterwards, she was always intensely aroused, often touching herself. She was 18 years old; she knew how to please her own body, but this was the first time she thought of a specific man every time. She really liked him.

Ivan slipped his hand inside of hers. "You have nothing to worry about, Annabella," Ivan said. "You are safe with me. I will always be a gentleman. I care about you quite a lot. I hope you know that."

Annabella looked up. His green eyes were a shade darker, more handsome somehow than they were earlier today. His hair flopped over his brow sensually, and his hand was calloused but warm in her hand. She could sense that his breathing had quickened. She was intensely aware of something, she wasn't sure what it was, but a strong force was pulling her body into him. It was some sort of chemical energy. Her breasts felt warm, and the spot between her legs felt very moist, almost uncomfortably so.

"Can we kiss again?" she asked, her voice so incredibly soft and innocent.

Ivan breathed in sharply. "Yes," he said, his control quickly being whisked away.

Annabella leapt up and immediately sat in his lap. Ivan sat stiffly in the chair with her soft buttocks on his groin, trying to will his instant erection down.

"Are you okay?" Annabella asked.

"Yes," Ivan replied simply, his mind not being able to form many words.

"You are breathing fast," she said.

"I have a gorgeous woman that I have many feelings for, on my lap," Ivan said, his voice catching.

Annabella gazed into his handsome green eyes and took the initiative. She leaned forward and kissed his lips. Ivan made her feel so safe and comfortable that she felt free to show her feelings and desires. It was a lovely feeling.

Ivan's lips were so soft and plump, her mouth melted into his and sent incredible sensations throughout her body. She kissed and pecked his lips until he opened his mouth slightly. Then she used her tongue, licking his open lips, lightly at first, following the curve of his mouth, licking around the creases to the top and back down to the bottom. Ivan groaned.

"You like that?" she murmured.

"Yes, my dear," he replied dumbly. "I certainly do."

"Then I will do that more," Annabella said, licking his lips more, feeling his breath coming out in gasps. She felt spurred on by his sensual breathing. Bella just followed what her instincts told her, no longer thinking, just doing. Her hands moved all along his face, caressing his light facial hair, his cheekbones and his jawline. Her fingers slid through his hair as another groan escaped his lips. She felt so empowered. This handsome man was in her grasp, groaning from her touch. She leaned into him and kissed his lips fully, peeking her tongue into his mouth. She grasped the back of the chair and pushed her breasts onto him.

Unexpectedly, the chair wobbled from their combined weight; then, it teetered and faltered. Before she realized what was happening, the chair was crashing onto the floor with both their bodies together. She landed fully onto him. They both squealed in laughter.

Ivan's smile lit up the room. His eyes turned a dark green emerald colour, his gaze piercing joyfully through her soul.

Annabella couldn't help but wonder how naughty it must be that she was in his room when she was not allowed by society standards. Something inside her, a rebellious streak, took control of her senses. She wanted him so badly. She was tired of arousing each other over and over again and never completing it. Her vagina contracted almost painfully, sending sharp currents to her lower abdomen. She knew it was naughty but somehow knowing it was forbidden made him impossible to resist.

Ivan looked into her eyes. "I love you, Annabella," he said.

That was all she needed to hear. She tore at his shirt, unbuttoning the crazy small buttons, her fingers fumbling wildly over his shirt, finally opening it to reveal his well-muscled chest. She inhaled sharply, admiring his masculinity. She felt an urgency pushing her beyond her rational constraints. She began sliding her hands all over his chest, instinctively lowering her lips to his chest, kissing his pecs, his nipples, licking his neck and inhaling his scent.

Ivan moaned heavily. He was at the mercy of her touch. She was all over him, kissing and licking his chest until his resolve had dissipated entirely. He could no longer resist this woman; she was unleashing her sexuality on top of him on the floor of his hotel room, with the chair still wedged under his buttocks. His penis strained urgently against his pants, screaming at him to break free. He tried adjusting himself by moving his hips slightly. It did nothing but made her notice his erection.

Annabella looked down at the lump in his pants, and her mouth watered. She felt an animalistic urge bubble up to her throat, and a groan escaped as her fingers fluttered down to his groin. Her hand brushed over the tip of his penis and slid down lower, feeling as much of his groin as she could through his pants. She was fascinated by this part of his body. It hardened and grew substantially bigger whenever she was around. She had noticed on many occasions. Every time they kissed, it grew larger and became very hard.

Ivan groaned, and his breathing came out in heavy exhales. "Annabella," he said. "I love what you're doing, but I am afraid that I will lose control."

"Oh?" Annabella responded. "What happens when you lose control?"

Ivan laughed at her innocence. "I will ejaculate prematurely," he replied. "And I definitely do not want to do any such thing on my first date with you."

Annabella smiled mischievously. It somehow felt wonderous that he would lose control because of her touch. She kissed him again. Just brushing her lips against his lips, savouring his moist mouth.

Her large breasts squashed onto his chest, and her scent covered him, blanketing Ivan in a whirlwind of sensual desire. His heartbeat quickened, and he felt his resolve fading again. His mind told him to wait, but his hormones were inhibiting his brain from thinking any further such rational thoughts.

Annabella began kissing his neck, his shoulder, his pecs, then she opened his shirt all the way, sliding her kisses down his abdomen.

Ivan's body splayed out on the floor, with his head bent forward, watching the woman that he loved ravage his body. His penis was so incredibly hard that he struggled to control his instinctual urges. "Annabella," he said, his voice cracking, the words in his brain not quite working. "I want you."

Annabella looked up at him, their eyes connecting. Her dark blue eyes glimmered, piercing through his soul, as she laid her hands gently on his belt.

Ivan breathed in sharply. "Babe," he said softly.

"I want us to do it tonight," Annabella said, pulling a length of belt out of the loop. "I know it's not perfect; I know it's not what everyone else expects us to do. And I know I'm not supposed to be here in your room, but I just can't wait any longer. We can keep it our secret. No one will ever know. I will slip back into my room in the early morning. I promise."

Ivan fought the urge to pre-ejaculate. He closed his eyes and took three deep breaths.

"Are you alright?" Annabella asked.

"I'm fine, sweetheart," Ivan replied. "I'm just getting a bit too excited." He clutched her hair, smoothing his hands down the long locks and then slid his hands along her curves. He effortlessly lifted her body level to his and shifted her, so they were both face to face. He stared into her deep blue sexy eyes. "You are the woman of my dreams, Annabella. If we are to do this, I need to know something from you first."

"Okay," she said. "What is it?"

"Will you marry me?" Ivan asked, his heart beating fast in his chest.

"Yes," she replied without hesitation.

Ivan's face broke into a huge smile, the boyish grin creasing his dimples.

Annabella laughed and started kissing his dimples, as Ivan chuckled. He felt elated and so very happy. His skin tingled, and his heart soared. He felt like he was floating as if he had just entered some kind of fantasy. The girl of his dreams had just said yes! He held her head and kissed her hard on the lips, pushing his tongue into her mouth. She groaned and accepted his tongue. His hands slid onto the back of her head, and he kept her there as he kissed her lips.

Annabella's hand slid down to his belt again, slipping the other loop through while they kissed. "You are my handsome husband, Ivan," she said.

"Sweetheart," he said. "I need to be inside you now."

Ivan pulled her up, pushed the chair back and sat them both onto the bed. "You are a little minx," he said. He fumbled with her dress and began undressing her as she wrestled with his pants. Ivan stripped his shirt off and threw it on the floor, while Annabella finally freed the belt and pulled his pants down around his ankles. She looked at the large bulge in his underwear. Her head was level with his groin as he stood at the end of the bed. Her mouth watered as she looked up at him. He stared down at her with a sensual longing. The potency of his desire hit her with the force of a tidal wave. Her entire body felt washed away in a surge of passion. She felt light-headed and giddy like she was floating on a tide, not really present in the moment. Her previous wilful nature dissolved into a puddle at his feet as he took control. She was his humble servant.

"Ivan," Annabella moaned as she slid his underwear down his legs, amazed at his penis.

Ivan breathed in sharply and moaned, watching his future wife remove his underwear so sensually and lovingly. He whisked a lock of hair from her eyes; lust was written all over her beautiful face like she had been waiting for this moment.

Annabella watched him step out of his underwear, and her eyes felt hypnotized by his penis. She was so intensely fascinated by this body part of his, feeling so strongly connected to him that she yearned to feel him inside her, the urge so strong, like a magnet pulling both of them together.

Ivan kissed her lips and pushed her shoulders gently back onto the bed. He finished undressing her, pulling her underwear off, exposing her naked curvy body for the first time. He marvelled at her beauty as she laid back; she was the most exquisite woman in the world. Her small waist highlighted her hips and her breasts, like an hourglass. Her large breasts were round and perky, the large nipples hard and pointing directly at him. He immediately grabbed one and licked at the nipple. She groaned and arched her back. He sucked at the nipple harder, and her groans increased.

"Shhh," he said softly. "We must be quiet, my sweet."

"Okay," she whispered back, nodding.

Ivan sucked on the other breast, massaging it with his hands, while she shuddered in his grasp. He loved the feel of her skin; it was so soft and supple. Her breasts felt warm and squishy in his hands. He continued his worship of her body, her breasts, her hips and her buttocks, squeezing her round backside while she lost all control, squirming all over the bed.

Finally, he could take no more. He grabbed his penis and mounted her. He momentarily stopped, looking into her eyes and kissed her mouth deeply. "My future wife," he said. "Mrs. Annabella Kozak." Then he slid his penis gently inside her, claiming her body as his wife.

Annabella gasped as he entered her tight vagina. Her thoughts left her head, and she succumbed to the desire coursing through her veins. His penis felt so exquisite inside her. A wave of passion gripped her as she moaned into his shoulder, his penis rhythmically sliding into her, then out. Her entire body felt like it was on fire; her vagina was so moist, she could feel the wetness spreading along her inner thighs and covering his penis. With every stroke, he brought her to a pinnacle; she wasn't sure where or what, but she felt like she was on a cliff of desire, and all she had to do was jump to experience it all.

Then his panting changed. Ivan began to breathe heavier and heavier. She instinctively knew he was close and that it was her turn to jump; she had to; there was no other way. Her vagina contracted so tight, almost painfully, clamping down on his penis.

"Ah," Bella groaned as a rush of moisture spilled out of her, coating him with her warmth.

Ivan squeezed his eyes shut and moaned, attempting to fight the urge to release. Her vagina gripped him so tightly that it was simply futile; he knew this. He was past the point of no return. He groaned heavily and thrust inside of her, releasing a torrent of semen. His legs shook as he instinctively pushed deeper inside her, feeling waves of desire flow out of him. He groaned again as all the pent-up sexual energy drained from his body.

Annabella felt his penis twitch inside her as he lay breathing heavily on top of her. Her legs shuddered as she accepted his semen into her body, so lovingly, so willingly. She felt so connected with him at this moment like everything was right; everything had finally fallen into place. His body, his soul, his entire being was hers, and she was his. It felt so encompassing and so complete.

After a few moments of rest, he raised himself on his elbows and kissed her mouth softly, then looked her into her eyes. "I love you, Annabella," he said. "I love you so much."

She began to cry, happy tears of joy.

They slept fitfully in each other's arms, waking several times to have sex. The attraction was simply too strong for both of them. They slept intermittently, only four hours the entire night. They would cuddle and drift off, then Ivan would awaken with Annabella on top of him. They would wrestle and giggle, kissing and touching until he entered her again, loving her inside and out. Then they would fall asleep again, exhausted, only to wake up an hour later repeating the whole sexual act over again. Ivan counted; they had made love four times before she finally kissed him and slipped out of the room, tiptoeing into her hotel room at 5 am.

They had breakfast three hours later, both of them looking quite dishevelled but bright-eyed and happy. They packed up the carriage with their luggage, stopping briefly to pick up some supplies in Winnipeg for his father, then they set off on the horse trail back to Gimli. The road was maintained, gravelled often, but still suffered from the weather; some large potholes and muddy areas appearing here and there. Ivan slowed the horses in these areas, keeping a good pace but also making sure that the horses were stable on the dirt road.

The sun shown down on them from the west as they rode north to Gimli. Annabella refused to sit in the carriage, as he thought she would. It was funny how he picked up on these little things about her already. Annabella smiled at him, jostling beside him in the riding seat. He had the reins in his hands; he smiled and handed them over to her. She grinned broadly and gladly took the leather straps. Ivan felt so complete with this capable, strong woman sharing the reins and driving the horses back home.

The countryside sprawled out before them; it was clear the terrain was being transformed by the Ukrainian settlers. The bush was still thick, but occasionally large patches of farmed land appeared, here and there, clearings as wide as a small lake, then just as suddenly, the bush would take over again, overgrowing into the dirt road in some places. It showed progress, he thought. One day, more and more of the land would be farmed, and more wheat could be transported to the west using the new railroad. Ivan felt empowered to be one of the families that were instrumental in achieving this ambitious goal.

Annabella tilted her hair to the side and smiled at Ivan; her face so radiantly happy. She handed the reins back to him.

He smiled back, taking control of the horses. She was everything he could hope for, he thought.

She looked thoughtfully ahead of them, staring down the dirt road as the carriage jolted side to side behind them. "I wonder what our future holds for us, Ivan," she said. "My parents had it so rough right from the beginning, landing in a foreign country, all the deaths, all the hardships. Your parents had it rough too; they left their home, their country, to take a chance here in Canada. Do you think we will have it rough as well?"

Ivan smiled as a wave of joy spread over him. "I don't think so, my sweet," he said, grinning happily. "Something tells me that we will be blessed with just a normal, long, happy life."

Annabella turned her head to the side, looking at him and then laughed heartily. "That would be lovely!" she exclaimed.

"Yes," Ivan agreed, as he curved his arm around her waist, gently squeezing her and kissing her shoulder. "It would be lovely, my sweet, yes it would."

PART TWO

1895-1912

CHAPTER 4

Nathan felt his heart swell with admiration and fatherly love. His daughter's swollen belly was huge. She waddled awkwardly all over town, picking up her things and moving them into her new home with Ivan. They had married quickly and were quite happy together, although the house took longer than expected to finish building.

Nath was sad that she was leaving, but he was also thrilled to be a grandfather soon. He helped her pack her things, giving her many baby items that he still had from when she was a baby. He loaded the items in the carriage.

"I can't believe you kept these little things," Annabella said, inspecting a long wooden rattle in her hand. "These are so cute. Why didn't you ever tell me that you kept my baby stuff?"

Nath looked down, shielding his eyes from her gaze. "I was nostalgic, I guess," he replied, feeling somewhat embarrassed. "It was just my private collection of baby memories. I never thought I would be giving them to my grandkids."

Annabella smiled, "That's so wonderful, Pabbi. Thank you for saving them."

Nath pulled the horses' reins towards the street, walking with the horses until they reached the right direction. He walked back to Annabella and helped her in the carriage. She was too large to fit in the riding set.

"I feel so fat," she said. "Look at me; I'm like this elephant that can't even get into the riding seat."

"Don't talk like that," Nath said. "Come on; we have to go."

Nath hopped inside the carriage, grabbed her arm and assisted her. Annabella put her weight forward, held firmly onto his other hand, hoisted herself into the small enclosed compartment and then slumped into the seat.

Nathan jumped out, landing on both feet and turned to close the door. "Oh," he said. "Just so you know, you look beautiful, my dear. You are so radiantly pregnant that your hair and skin shines with a new mommy glow. You have never looked so lovely before."

Annabella smiled, "Thanks, Pabbi."

He leaned over and kissed her cheek. "I'm taking you to your new home. You will love it. I can feel it."

"You won't be lonely?" Bella asked.

"Of course I will be," Nath replied. "But I will have a grandchild to take care of soon. Make sure you drop the baby off at my place often. I want to be involved a lot."

"Okay, Dad," Bella said, smiling warmly. "I will."

"It's a deal then," Nathan said, laughing. "Time to go now." He closed the door firmly, waved to his daughter and hopped in the riding seat as the carriage slowly lumbered along Main Street.

Several people glanced at the full carriage. Annabella barely had room to sit inside. Linens, luggage, pots and pans were stacked beside her. It felt strange leaving her family home. Part of her didn't want to go, but the other part knew that she must. It was time. She was nineteen years old, and the baby was due in a few weeks. She was married to a wonderful husband, and now they are finally moving into their newly finished home. Spring was just a few weeks away; her adult life was just beginning. She felt very sad about leaving her dad, though. She didn't want to go. Every little thing that she knew, her dad had taught her. Even the way she talked sometimes had inflections of his personality. She didn't want him to be lonely. She didn't want to leave him, but he was so persistent some days. It was like he was pushing her out of the house. She didn't entirely understand but accepted it as part of growing up and what parents must do. She giggled to herself as the carriage jostled down the road. She was going to become a parent soon, Bella realized. She smiled as she gazed out of the carriage window. Her father had said that he wanted to help with the baby a lot. Her heart gushed with love, and her eyes moistened with happiness. She felt so loved and cherished at this moment. It was as if all the stars were aligning, and everything was making sense. Bella rolled the wooden rattle in her hand and smiled. She was going to be a mother soon.

"Are you alright back there, Bella?" Nath shouted.

"Yes, dad!" she shouted back.

"Okay," he responded. "We are almost there."

Nath turned the horses to the left at the junction of highway 9 and main street. Several farming properties dotted the landscape. One of them had a gleaming white house, much farther back than the main house, but it was very quaint with its own parcel of land and fencing for the animals. Ivan was a good man. He was proud to have his daughter marry such a fine, hard-working gentleman. Ivan loved his daughter immensely; he couldn't be happier.

As the carriage slowed onto the property, Nath saw Ivan's form in the front yard beckoning them. His daughter was an adult now. She was going to be a mother and a good wife. Nath smiled to himself. It was her destiny, and he loved her for it.

Ivan pulled her chair closer to him as they ate their breakfast of eggs and porridge. He was deliriously happy to have her finally living with him. Her influence, her smell, her presence was everywhere in the house. Even her hair was in the sink, and he loved that too. He loved the good and the bad, all of it in a nice complete package.

They had only been living together for a few days, but it felt like heaven. Some days he felt like pinching himself to make sure that it was all real.

Ivan chewed and swallowed the hard-boiled eggs as he gazed at his wife. His hand was resting on her lap, keeping the physical connection constant. She looked extra sexy in the mornings. Something about having her hair strewn everywhere, and her eyes hooded and drowsy made him feel incredibly aroused.

He chuckled.

"What are you laughing about?" Bella asked.

Ivan grinned mischievously, "Oh, nothing."

Annabella eyed him suspiciously. "I don't believe you," she said doubtfully. "You must be laughing at my morning hair."

Ivan laughed, "Absolutely not! I was admiring your messy hair, actually."

"You are lying!" Annabella replied instantly.

Ivan kissed her cheek. "You are so silly. Do you have any idea how sexy you look in the mornings?"

Annabella grinned, "No."

"Well," Ivan said, pulling her closer to him. "I want you more when we just wake up with your messy morning hair and your sleepy eyes than any other time of the day."

"Really?" Bella replied innocently.

"Really," he said, sealing the confirmation with a kiss on her nose.

She giggled, "You're so sweet."

"So are you," he said, pushing his chair back. Ivan grabbed both plates, clearing the table as Annabella moved to get up. "No, you sit. I got this."

Annabella sat back down, watching her husband clear the dishes and fill the sink with soapy water. "I will clean those dishes, Ivan. Honestly, it's not that much work. You go feed the horses."

"The horses can wait," Ivan argued. "Have you not noticed how pregnant you are?"

"Yes," she replied. "My feet and back hurt all day. Walking around with all this extra weight is quite difficult."

"It's only a few more weeks, and then the baby will be here," Ivan said reassuringly.

"Grandma Bea says it could come any day," Annabella said.

"We are ready," Ivan said. "My mom and dad brought extra blankets and washbasins yesterday. The bassinet is all ready to go. I'm excited. Do you hope it will be a boy or a girl?"

"I don't care," Annabella replied. "As long as our baby is healthy."

"Well," Ivan said. "We have both names picked out for either gender, so it doesn't matter." Ivan finished rinsing the dishes and placed the towel to dry. He massaged her shoulders gently as she sat in the kitchen chair. "Everything will be fine. We will do this together. I'll go tend to the horses now."

Ivan grabbed his coat and laced his boots up, gripping the door. He paused as a thought crossed his mind. "Have you felt any contractions yet?"

"I think so, yes," Bella replied. "Just little ones, though. Nothing to worry about, I believe. Grandma Bea still knows how to deliver babies; I will be in good hands."

"Should we invite her to stay with us soon?" Ivan asked.

"Yes," Annabella said, smiling. "That's a good idea. I will ask her next week when I see her again."

CHAPTER 5

Nathan locked up the fishery and walked steadily down Main Street to Annabella's house. He fretted worriedly about his daughter. She was going to have a baby soon, and he remembered how sudden and urgent it was when Anwa had given birth. Grandma Bea was a lifesaver at the time. She had delivered many more babies since, becoming somewhat of a midwife in the town of Gimli. He was glad because that meant she would be there for Annabella too.

He was surprisingly comfortable without her in his home. He relished in the quietness and serenity. He did miss his daughter, but he also accepted it as the normal evolution of family life. The peace he felt at home alone was calming and centring. He liked it, although he wasn't sure that he wanted to live his life in complete silence for long. He was looking forward to holding his grandchild in his hands and caring for the small infant. He knew that he might not get to see the baby as much as he would like. Annabella and Ivan were the parents, after all. Ivan's parents would also be living right next door. One child shared by all these family members would be tough. He chuckled.

It wasn't a far distance for him. He could make it to Annabella's house in ten minutes, walking fast. He had long legs that could travel great distances. He would be there whenever she needed him.

Nathan looked over the horizon and felt the cool spring breeze blow his shoulder-length hair back. He relished in the feeling of the wind in his face. It signified that a new beginning was arriving. Something wonderful was happening, and change was in the air. The white house gleamed across the field now. He squinted his eyes from the glare of the sun and picked up his pace. Something told him to hurry. He hadn't seen his daughter in almost a week, but he assumed she was just enjoying her time with her husband in their new home. It was probably just his own desire to see her again.

He had some fish and deer meat in the large bag over his shoulder. He had gone hunting the day after she had moved out, catching a nice young buck. He was pleased that he could offer some food storage for the first few weeks of having a newborn. Routine things always seem to get lost in time when a new baby is present. It was a thoughtful welcoming gift.

He began to cross the field towards her house, his boots crunching on the snowy pathway. He felt elated and was looking forward to seeing his daughter in her new adult life. His steps quickened as he neared the front walkway. His long legs closed the distance. His right foot crunched onto the porch step, and he bounded up the stairs effortlessly, then knocked on the front door.

He hummed happily to himself and looked across the field. The horses weren't out. They were probably in the barn because the weather was too cold. He waited.

No one answered the door. He thought this was unusual. She could be at Ivan's parents' home, he mused, trying to contain the rising panic in his mind.

He knocked again.

And again.

Nothing.

His mind was telling him to go to the Kozak's home, but his gut was telling him to stay right where he was.

Nath knocked again. "Annabella," he shouted into the door.

He heard a muffled noise from inside.

His instincts went to high alarm. "Annabella!" he yelled, running to the window. He peered through, cupping his large hands against the glass, trying to see what was going on. The window had frosted over from the cold temperatures of the last few days. He removed his glove and scraped some of the ice away and peered through the tiny hole. He saw the kitchen area empty; a chair stood at an awkward angle. He looked towards the bedroom area. There was someone crouched on the floor!

"Annabella!" Nathan hollered through his hands on the glass window. "Is that you? Are you okay?"

A small groan answered. He strained to hear. Nath scraped at the ice to see more, but he couldn't see any further. The glass was frosted slightly on the inside as well.

Then he heard a feeble plea, "Pabbi!"

It was Annabella on the floor!

Nathan's hair stood up on the back of his neck. His entire body and mind reacted simultaneously; he ran to the front door and turned the doorknob. It was locked. He looked around. How was he going to get in?

"Dad," Bella cried weakly from inside.

Nathan felt the surge of adrenaline pump into his veins. His fists throbbed, and his heart pounded loudly. The urgency of the moment overtook his entire body. He slammed his shoulder against the door hard. The wood cracked but wouldn't budge.

"Hurry," Bella whimpered.

Nath backed up to the end of the porch and ran full speed at the door, crashing into it with his full weight. The door frame splintered from the jam and opened with a loud crack. The door slammed down onto the floor with a terrible bang. Nathan rushed into the house.

Annabella was on the floor, gripping her dress, exhaling in quick breaths. There was a strange watery substance on the floor, pooling around her feet.

"Sweet Jesus!" Nathan shouted. "Bella! What happened?"

Her face gleamed with sweat. The panic in her eyes was evident. "I don't know. I think my water broke," she huffed. "The contractions are so strong, daddy. Ivan left this morning to his parent's place to help with one of the sick horses." She paused, exhaling in short breaths again. "Pabbi, it hurts. I have to push!" She crouched over, grasping her round tummy and grunting loudly.

"Okay!" Nathan shouted, looking over to the washbasin. "Hold on, sweetie! I will grab some water and cloths. Where are they?"

Bella pointed weakly to the cupboard beside the sink.

Nathan rummaged hastily through the cupboard, pulling several towels out. He washed his hands in the basin, then poured fresh water into a pot and placed it hurriedly onto the wood stove. He poured more fresh water into a large bowl, grabbed the towels and ran over to Annabella with the materials.

He knelt on the floor, facing her. "Look at me, Annabella," he said.

She looked up at him, her face panicky and strained, her eyes wild.

"We are going to do this," Nath said, anxiously. "Everything will be alright. I am here, sweetie. You just push when you need to and breathe, always breathe."

Annabella smiled weakly. "Okay," she nodded, exhaling sharply and biting her lip as a new wave of contractions gripped her. "I need to push again!"

"Push, sweetie, push," Nath replied urgently, holding her legs.

She pushed hard and then exhaled in short bursts, sweat dripping from her brow. She relaxed briefly, then seized by the contractions again, repeated the cycle two more times until she was exhausted and perspiring.

The water began steaming on the stove. Nath draped a sheet over her knees and patted her legs; he rushed back, grabbed the pot and dipped one of the towels in the warmer water. He wrung the towel out and returned to Annabella, along with the basin of warmer water. Nath dipped the towel in the cooler water and wrung it out again. Hopefully, it wasn't too hot, he thought anxiously.

Nath laid down the dry towels and shuffled them under her buttocks. "Lift, Bella," he instructed.

She lifted her buttocks, and Nath scrunched the towel underneath.

"Dad!" she hollered. "The baby's coming! I can feel it!" Annabella propped her hands behind her and pushed with all her strength, groaning fiercely.

Nath positioned himself behind her legs, holding the wet towel, readying himself. He had never performed a childbirth but had witnessed Anwa giving birth. He just went with what he knew from that one time; wet towels, warm water and many dry towels.

"I'm ready, sweetie," Nath shouted. "Push!"

A visceral cry left her lips as she screamed for several minutes, all the while pushing.

"Good, you're doing great!" Nath said reassuringly. "Breathe!"

Annabella inhaled sharply, then focused on exhaling in short breaths again. Her chest rose and fell, rose and fell. Then the contractions gripped her again. She groaned like an animal, pushing with all her might. "Dad!" she yelled.

"Bella, oh my God," Nath said. "I see the head. Push, sweetie, push."

Another long guttural cry and Bella pushed even harder, sweat pouring down her face.

The baby's head slid out into Nath's offered hands. "Okay, sweetie, he's partially out, one last push, but gentle this time."

Annabella groaned, pushing again.

The baby's shoulders' slid out effortlessly, it seemed, and then the rest of the baby plopped into Nathan's hands and the wet towel. He quickly washed the baby as a barrage of people ran in through the broken front door. It was Ivan, his parents and Grandma Bea!

"It's about time!" Nath shouted. "Where have you guys been?"

"Oh my Lord, Nath," Bea shouted, rushing over. "We need to cut the umbilical cord. You keep cleaning the boy, especially his mouth and nose! I will cut the cord."

"It's a boy?" Annabella shouted incredulously.

"Yes!" Nathan shouted back. "Sweet Jesus! It's a boy!"

Annabella grinned, her face dripping with sweat. Her hair was wet and stuck to her cheeks. She fell back onto her elbows as Bea cut the cord.

The baby started crying, a guttural holler at the top of his lungs.

Annabella chuckled, "Exactly how I feel right now."

Everyone laughed, the tension easing dramatically from the room.

"Ivan," Bea instructed. "Help your wife onto the bed."

Ivan snapped out of the frozen state of shock he was in and rushed over. He wound his arm under her armpits and shoulders, lifting her to a crouched standing position, then eased her onto the bed. He put a towel underneath her buttocks and kissed her forehead. "I'm so sorry, babe," he said apologetically. "I had no idea the baby was coming so soon. We thought that he wasn't due for another three weeks. Please forgive me. I will never leave your side again."

"It all happened so fast," Annabella replied. "Next thing I knew, I had slipped on my water breaking on the floor. I must have blacked out. I don't remember what happened after that; then suddenly Dad was kicking down the door. Everything happened so fast."

Nathan handed the washed infant to Annabella. The tiny newborn cried with a fervour. For someone so small, the boy was surprisingly loud. His screech was surely heard for miles!

Bella nudged his small head and guided him onto her breast. The baby eagerly latched on, sucking urgently.

"You haven't told me what my grandson's name is yet!" Nath cried incredulously.

"Michael!" Annabella and Ivan shouted in unison. "Everyone, say hi to our new baby son, Mike Kozak!" Annabella finished the last sentence. "We decided to name him Mike, in remembrance of his great uncle Mikom."

"What a wonderful name," Nath laughed warmheartedly. "Quite the grand entrance, Mike. You could have given us some warning!"

The entire room erupted in stress-relieving laughter. Nath smiled warmly and looked down at his hands. His hands were the first thing that his grandson had ever touched coming into this world. Nath felt an instant bond with this tiny little human named Mike Kozak.

CHAPTER 6

I van kissed his baby's head while Annabella was busy bathing herself. The tiny boy was a handful. He had singlehandedly whisked away their former lives and created a tornado of change in the household. Everything was now about the baby. Does he need his diaper changed? Is he hungry? Is he sleepy? Why is he crying all the time? Rock the baby, that will make him quiet down.

Knowing his momma had left his side, the baby was starting to fuss. Ivan offered a thumb for Mikey to suck on. The baby searched with his lips and latched onto his dad's thumb happily. It worked! Ivan breathed out a sigh of relief. The boy was no more than three weeks old, but he was already a hellraiser.

He glanced up at Annabella's half-naked body as she slid the soap along her tummy and between her thighs. She washed her hair, the bubbles collecting along her beautiful neck as she leaned over the basin. She was so beautiful to him in whatever form, tired, bedraggled, half-naked, clothed, it never mattered to him. He always saw the beautiful person that she was. It just gleamed through her, like a glow lighting up the room with her presence.

"What are you looking at?" Annabella said, looking out from under her wet hair. "I look horrible. I have a sagging tummy; my hair is in knots, and I haven't brushed my teeth in two days."

Ivan laughed, "But you are my beautiful wife and such a great mother. I can't believe my luck sometimes. How did I manage to marry such a wonderful woman?"

"Aw, babe," Bella said, smiling, as she straightened and flipped her hair back. "You always know the best things to say. I've been feeling rather tired and clueless as to how to be a good mother. It seems like most things I do with Mikey are wrong, and only a few are right. I feel like I'm learning as I go along, and I truly do not have any clue how to be a parent."

"You are the best mother," Ivan said. "Don't worry, I feel the same, sometimes. When he cries, I'm not sure why, and I want to find the solution right away. I feel like I can do more than I have been to ease the burden from you, but he will only allow me to do so much. He wants his momma."

"That's normal," Bella said. "He's still a newborn. He needs to breastfeed a lot."

"I love your breasts," Ivan laughed. "Michael took them away from me!"

Annabella smiled, "My breasts are always yours, babe. They are just in practical use right now."

They both broke out in raucous laughter. Annabella felt tears well in her eyes as she laughed hard into her belly. It felt good to release the stress of the past few weeks. It had been difficult. She was only sleeping five hours a night, broken into intervals while the baby breastfed and slept. She had no idea having a baby was so hard. But she also suspected that it would get easier over time and with each subsequent baby.

Ivan smiled at her, reading her thoughts. "You said something when we first dated," Ivan said, grinning. "That you wanted to have a big family. Do you still want that?"

Annabella rinsed off with a wet towel then squeezed the water out of her hair. "Yes," she answered. "I still do want a large family."

Ivan smiled, "When do you think we can start again?"

Annabella's face lit up with a huge smile. She laughed, "I think we can start whenever it begins to feel better, and my tummy goes down back to normal size. Probably a few more months."

"Good," Ivan said. "I love you, Bella. We will wait until you are ready." He blew a kiss in her direction.

She towelled herself dry and pulled on a nightgown. Annabella combed her wet hair and breathed out a long sigh. "It felt so good to bathe," she said.

The baby began to fuss in Ivan's arms. He stood and began rocking Mike slowly, swaying him with each step. He tried sticking his thumb in between Mike's lips again, except it was futile. It was feeding time again.

Annabella scooped the baby into her arms and laid down with him on the bed, propping pillows behind her back. The baby latched on and began sucking her right breast. The hormones immediately hit her, making her drowsy. Her head flopped to the side as she fought sleep until the baby finished feeding.

Ivan cleaned up the bath basin and towels while his beautiful wife fell slowly asleep with the baby in her arms. He smiled. He couldn't think of a more pleasant sight than this.

It was 5 am, and the baby was awake again. Nathan had stayed over for a few days to help around the house. Annabella's home was a disaster, with clothes strewn everywhere. Ivan's parents had picked up the dirty diapers and left clean laundered ones. Since Nath wasn't that great at the laundry, he offered to help clean and cook.

His deer stew was the best in town. He had cooked a large cauldron of it last night and cleaned the kitchen. It seemed as soon as he cleaned anything, more dirty things piled up right behind him. It was an endless struggle to keep ahead of things. But he knew it was valuable to his daughter. And the bonus was he could hold his grandson more often.

Mike regularly cried, raising the roof on the otherwise quiet household. For such a small infant, the little boy had a loud presence. Annabella had awakened sleepily, fed him and rocked him, but it wasn't enough, and the baby boy was hollering at the top of his lungs. She walked back and forth, humming to the baby. She burped him and swayed with him; nothing seemed to work. Mikey screeched in her arms. Exasperated, she looked at her dad, handing him the inconsolable infant.

"You try," she said wearily.

Nathan chuckled, "Alright, let me try. You go back to sleep, sweetie."

Annabella shuffled sleepily back to bed, yawning.

Nath looked down at his baby grandson in the dark and smiled. The boy was clearly upset. His fists were curled into balls and his face turning red as his shrieks filled the air. "Shhh, You little bundle of fire. Hush now, baby, don't you cry."

Michael paused and opened his tiny eyes briefly.

Nath breathed a sigh of relief.

Michael started crying again, but with less intensity. Something had piqued his interest.

Nath pulled Mike onto his shoulder and patted his back, burping him. The gentle, rhythmic patting seemed to soothe the boy. His crying eased as Nath continued patting him in the early morning dawn.

Nathan paced through the home with a gentle rock in his step, patting and rocking. Then he remembered the song he used to sing Annabella. "Twinkle, twinkle little star. How I wonder what you are," he sang softly.

Nath looked out the window at the dark dawn. The sky was gradually lightening to a lighter purple, sending rays of mixed dark colours across the clouds. It mesmerized Nath. The stars were clouded over, although the beautiful glow of early dawn made up for the lack of stars.

"Up above the world so high," Nath sang, his deep voice filling the room.

Michael was trying to listen to the words; It worked! Mikey stopped crying.

"Like a diamond in the sky," Nath sang gently.

Michael squirmed, and then a large burp escaped from his mouth.

Nathan chuckled, "Oh my, is that what you were crying about all along? Had to let that one out, my boy!"

Michael visibly relaxed. Nath pulled the boy into his arms and rocked him in his arms. Mikey looked up at him in the dark room.

Nath continued rocking him back and forth, using his knees and his hips. The gentle sway started lulling the baby into dreamland. The baby tried to keep his eyes open, but it was futile; they were closing heavily.

"Twinkle, twinkle little star. How I wonder what you are," Nath sang, looking down at his grandson, adding his own ending to the song. "And how I love you just the way you are."

Mikey curled against Nath's chest and closed his eyes.

An adorable hand reached up and landed gently on Nath's arm, tiny baby fingers grasping his shirt sleeve. Nathan continued rocking and walking, singing the lullaby over and over again, watching Mikey's tiny hand grip his shirt. Tears formed in his eyes. It was like having baby Annabella in his arms all over again but a boy this time. This little boy was a part of Annabella, an extension of himself and a part of Anwa too. His heart burst open with joy and misery all at once.

Anwa should be here.

The random thought slammed into his gut.

The buried grief assaulted him without warning. It gripped his heart and threatened to take him back to that dark place so long ago. Nath wouldn't allow it. He was happy. He had his daughter and his baby grandson. He had a booming fishing business, a beautiful house and a stable life finally. Nathan had it all.

But there was still a noticeable hole in his heart. Some days it felt like a gaping hole, an endless dark pit that threatened his sanity. Most days, he just buried it, and it was fine. This is life, after all, he told himself. People die; we all die. It's inevitable. Nath glanced down at the blue and brown beaded bracelet on his wrist. He still wished Anwa could be here, even though it was not possible.

He kissed Mike on his small forehead; the boy was completely at peace in his arms. Nath hugged the boy's tiny body to his chest. He loved this boy so much.

Nath sat down in the rocking chair gently, still singing softly. He felt so peaceful with his little grandson in his arms like everything was finally getting better; everything was making sense.

The sun began rising slowly, scattering rays into the dark room. Nathan felt his eyes droop closed as he slowly fell asleep with Mikey in his arms, a pillow on his lap for added security. He kept nodding and awakening himself, afraid that the baby would squirm out of his grip, or he would involuntarily lessen his hold on the child.

Finally, he jerked himself awake, put the baby in the bassinet and came back to his guest bed. He laid down, gazing at the dark ceiling with the rays of early morning sunlight streaking in. He felt the painful hole in his gut. After all these years, it was still there. He stifled the tears, not allowing them to come. It's been eighteen years, he told himself. Nobody wants to hear of your grief anymore. Nobody wants to hear that you're still mourning a dead wife from when you were a young man. Nobody wants to see a grown man cry. He held everything in for so long because he couldn't let anyone see him shatter to pieces. He was a man, after all. There were enormous expectations of males; to be strong, to build the community, to survive, to never appear weak or vulnerable.

It's the past, and this is the present, his inner self chastised. Live your life and take care of what you have. You have so much to be grateful for today.

But Anwa is still gone, his heart argued.

Yes, she is gone; Nath agreed. Anwa is gone.

The reality sunk in again as if it was a neatly stitched wound that had somehow accidentally ripped open. Most times, he would purse his lips and fight the tears, but this time, he didn't know what it was, whether it was the baby, the early morning dawn or Annabella being a mom, but it all rushed over him. The circle of life was forcing its way into his heart, opening up the wound he had so carefully stitched together. Tears flowed down his cheek like waves from a river falling down a waterfall. He sat up on the bed with his head in his hands and sobbed, the grief racking his body.

Anwa should be here; he kept thinking. He fingered the blue beaded bracelet on his wrist. He wore the bracelet all the time. He rarely took it off. He felt his emotions burst out of control.

Old memories of the cabin, fishing, laughing, and Anwa's naked body flooded into his mind. He was powerless to stop it. He thought of the first day they had met, their first kiss, the first time they made love, her pregnant body and being inexperienced parents together, holding baby Annabella in their arms. It was all too much to hold back. Nath cried heavily, letting it all out, grieving almost like he was transported back to those days so long ago. His heart hurt so much. The pain cut deep and severe. Too much for a beating human heart to handle, he thought. So many times he wanted to let his grief wash over him, but so many times he held it back for fear of ridicule, shame and judgement. It had been so long ago, but the wound was still there, bleeding ever so slowly. He sometimes wondered how his heart just kept beating, regardless of the events he endured, events he had little control over.

It was a miracle that he had lived this long.

But he knew why.

He had a reason to live. He persevered for his daughter, Annabella.

And now, little baby Mike.

Nath wiped his eyes with the back of his hands.

He was their rock. He had to be. He was the pillar of strength that they could rely on always.

And he would continue to be that pillar until a ripe old age; because his love for his daughter and his grandson was so powerful, it made his knees weak. The force was akin to the same intensity that he had once loved his beloved Anwa.

Nath lay down, rolling onto his side and whispered a silent prayer that he would always be strong and always be here for his family. He would stand tall and be the strong man everyone needed.

He closed his eyes, drifting off as pleasant visions of Anwa floated into his unconscious mind, dreaming of a time long ago when his heart pulsed strongly with romantic love, and his arms held the love of his life.

CHAPTER 7

"Dad!" Annabella said, shaking him awake. "Wake up, Pabbi!"

Nath squinted his weary eyes open. "What is it?"

The baby's cries filled the small house again. "He won't stop crying!" she said pleadingly. "I tried feeding him and changing him. I rocked him, burped him, nothing is working again. Do something, please. You're good with him."

"Okay, okay," Nath mumbled. "I'm getting up." He had been staying over most nights to help with the baby over the past two months. Occasionally, he would go back home to catch up on his sleep for one or two nights but would feel the urge to return. He had just arrived this evening, and the baby was crying again. He wasn't quite sure what he did right with the boy, but whatever it was, it worked. Nath picked up the screaming baby from the bassinet and propped him onto his shoulder, gently patting his back rhythmically again. The boy straightened his body fiercely, resisting the hold, screeching at the top of his lungs, but Nathan held him firmly on his shoulder, patting his back gently but firmly. He walked out of the bedroom and into the living area, humming a lullaby, swaying and patting, consistent with the motions and singing softly, never breaking the rhythm once.

Finally, Mikey eased himself more onto Nath's shoulder, his muscles relaxing. A small burp escaped from Mike's mouth.

"That's all you've got?" Nath said softly, chuckling. "All that noise for a teeny burp?"

Mike let go of the grip he had on Nath's shirt collar and slowly allowed his body to be lulled into a pleasant sleep.

Annabella watched them both. "I don't know how you do it," she said. "But you seem to be the only one that can get him calmed down when he is screeching like that."

"He's just gassy," Nath replied.

"I don't know," Annabella countered. "Hey, by the way, where did you go the other day? I thought you had gone to work, so I went to the fishing store, but you weren't there. I asked, and nobody knew where you had gone. The boats were still tied up, so you weren't fishing."

"I was spending time alone," Nath replied vaguely.

"Spending time alone?" Annabella said, inquiringly. "Where? You always say that."

"Just wandering with my thoughts, that's all," Nath replied.

"I get worried when you do that," Annabella replied. "You've been disappearing like that since I could remember. Where do you go? You said there were wolves in the forests. I hope you aren't putting yourself in danger."

"I'm fine, sweetie," Nath replied. "Don't worry about me. It's you we should be worrying about now. How have you been feeling? Do you feel like you have recuperated from the childbirth?"

"Always changing the subject," Annabella retorted. "Yes, I am feeling well. My belly has shrunk in size considerably, and we might try for another baby soon."

"So soon?" Nath asked incredulously.

"Yes," Bella replied. "I want a big family, Dad. I always have. I appreciate your help with Mike, and please continue to help with the next baby and every child afterwards."

Nathan laughed, "I'm here for you, sweetie. Always. You know that."

"Good," Bella said. "Ok, we need to get some more clothing for the baby. Ivan wants to find some fabric for sale at the Saturday market. Could you please watch the baby for a while?"

"Sure, sweetie. Go. I will be here."

"There are large bottles of breastmilk in the cool room," she instructed him. "The baby bottles are in the drying tray." Bella stretched her neck up and kissed him on the cheek. "I love you, Pabbi. You are the best dad ever." Grabbing her boots, she walked to the front door, as Ivan held out her coat. She wound each arm into the sleeves and opened the door.

Ivan nodded at him. "Thank you, Nath. We won't be long. We just need some time to escape. We appreciate you being here for us."

"Go," Nath said, chuckling. "I'm not going anywhere."

They closed the door, and the room grew instantly quiet. Nath was at peace with the world today. His emotions felt more centred and serene; Nath felt like he was a necessity. It felt good. The grief was gone, buried for the time being. He liked being in this space; it was much easier emotionally.

Nath lay down on the sofa, stretching his long legs out. He relaxed and felt his eyelids close heavily.

He listened to the usual house noises, a little creak here, crickets chirping outside and the normal sounds of a quiet home. Then he heard a strange noise that didn't belong. His mind drifted off to sleep, then awakened abruptly. He was certain that he had heard a small gurgle. So imperceptible that he shouldn't have heard it.

His eyes bolted open.

Nothing. Silence.

Was he overreacting? It was probably nothing, although the hairs on his forearms stood up, alarming him.

Nath jumped from the sofa and rushed into the bedroom. He bent down to look in the bassinet, and he couldn't see the baby! He panicked.

Electric jolts coursed through his body as his adrenaline took over.

The baby had somehow rolled the blanket over his head! It looked like Mikey had buried himself under the blankets; something was very wrong.

Nath quickly removed the blanket and whisked the baby out of the bassinet. There was vomit on his face, and he was visibly choking.

Nath panicked. What was he supposed to do?

He needed to get whatever it was out of the baby's mouth. His small face was turning a light shade of blue.

Nath did what his instincts told him to do. Use gravity!

Nath flipped the baby over, so his head was facing downwards and firmly slapped him on the back. Nothing. With his heart racing, he did it again, harder this time.

A sudden gush of vomit sprayed onto the floor, Nath patted the baby's back and flipped him over. Mikey coughed weakly. Nath held him towards his face to see if anything else was lodged in his mouth. He searched and found nothing. He turned the boy face down on his lap and slapped Mikey on the back again. Another regurgitated stream shot out onto the floor.

Nath's heart jumped into his throat as he pulled the infant upright to his face.

Mikey opened his eyes, looking confused and then screeched loudly, crying with a ferocity like none other.

Nath smiled, relief flooding his body. That was the best screech he had ever heard in his life! His nerves calmed slightly, but his hands still shook.

Mikey cried loudly as the colour returned to his small face.

Nath pulled him onto his shoulder and patted his back again. Mikey screamed, coughing up phlegm, the cries reverberating through the house.

Nath's heartbeat hammered in his chest from the adrenaline, the fear still gripping him. What had just happened? He had almost lost his grandson, that's what. He held onto the tiny baby firmly and said a silent prayer of thanks as his heart flipped over.

Mikey visibly calmed down and relaxed onto his shoulder. Nath gripped his grandson and thanked the gods for being able to rescue him in time.

He could not even comprehend losing another loved one. He just couldn't. It was beyond his emotional capacity. The walls he had built were too high to overcome; after losing Anwa, he felt so incredibly broken. Falling in love was like a tunnel that he simply could not enter again. He was not capable of it; the boundaries of his romantic heart were insurmountable. Naturally, he had replaced his empty romantic life with family love. He poured everything he had into his family; they were his only lifeline to peace and harmony. The thought of losing any member of his family frightened him with an intensity that was most probably abnormal.

Mike burped lightly and slumped onto Nath's shoulder. Nath felt a surge of love for this little boy like he was connected physically and emotionally with this tiny human being. Mikey couldn't talk, and he couldn't walk, but Nath knew at the bottom of his soul that if he could, Mikey would be running into his arms and thanking his granddad for saving his life.

Tears welled in Nath's eyes as the release of adrenaline left his body slowly, and the afternoon sun streaked past the clouds, filtering beautifully into the bedroom.

Annabella came home and panicked when she heard the news. She slept fitfully, tossing and turning at the slightest noise.

She awoke at 3 am when Mike began to fuss. His cries filled the room, but this time, she cuddled him like crazy, shushing him as he latched onto her breast. Bella smoothed her hand along his bald head. "You know something, Mikey," she murmured, as she watched him suckling. "You have a really wonderful granddad, and he loves you more than anything else right now. You're a very lucky boy, my son. Very lucky."

Annabella slumped onto the back of the bed while her baby suckled. Her body relaxed, while the hormones released throughout her veins.

She whispered to her baby, her voice groggy, "What do you think the future holds, Mikey? Do you want lots of brothers and sisters? I know that I always did. But my momma died. I was never given a choice." Annabella grew quiet and nodded her head to the side, sleep taking over soon. "I will try to give you the biggest family that I can, my sweetie. I will try my best to always be here for all of you. I will never die young, sweetie. That's my promise to you."

CHAPTER 8

Nath held his grandson's hand as they made their way to the dock. The boy's smaller toddler legs wouldn't go fast enough, so Nath picked him up effortlessly and lifted him onto his shoulders as Mikey giggled and yelped happily.

"Afi!" Mikey squealed, using the endearing Icelandic slang for grandpa. "Where are you taking me?"

"We're going fishing, my boy!"

"Yippee," Mikey shouted.

Nath smiled as he bounced down the road with Mikey on his shoulders. It was only another two blocks; they would arrive at the boats soon. Mikey was growing heavier and heavier. At three years old, the boy was taller and heftier than he looked. He already had a baby sister. Her name was Katya. Annabella was currently pregnant with another child as well.

Nathan chuckled to himself. His daughter was certain about her future and determined to have many children. He was deliriously happy about it. He had always wanted a large family, so he was thrilled to have his only daughter expanding the family so quickly.

"Are you going to teach me how to fish?" Mikey asked, pulling on Nath's ears as he hummed happily on Nath's broad shoulders.

"Yes," Nath replied. "But you can only watch. When you get older, I will make you a rod."

"Will you teach me to hunt too?"

Nathan laughed, "You are too young for hunting!"

"Aww," Mikey cried. "I think it's cool those guns you have in your cabinet."

Nathan scowled, "And if I ever catch you touching any of them, I will spank you and make you wish you never got near them."

"I won't! I won't!" Mikey replied. "I just think they're neat, that's all. Can you show me when I'm older?"

"I can do that, Mikey," Nath responded, smiling. "But today, we're going to try fishing!"

Nath arrived at the dock, placing Mikey down, holding his hand and entered the fishery warehouse. Nath scuttled around, searching for fishing supplies. He found nets, rods, several fishing pants, some hats and a small fishing box. He gathered everything and handed the hats over for Mikey to carry.

Mikey happily shared the load. The little boy hummed while they walked. He laughed at everything his grandpa said.

They reached the boats. Nath picked the midsized wooden boat. He put all his supplies in the vessel and grabbed Mikey, lifting him swiftly into the air with a whooshing sound and placed him squarely in the boat, leaving the little boy giggling madly.

Nath laughed along as he unravelled the rope from the dock tie.

"Settle down, Mikey," Nath cautioned. "We're setting sail. Be careful not to rock the boat. You remember our swimming lessons, right?" Nath set the sails as the boat began to drift quietly away into the harbour.

"Yes," Mikey answered gleefully. "I remember our swimming lessons. I can swim now!"

"Yes, you can," Nath replied. "But let's not have to use those emergency skills too soon." Nath pointed to a large round piece of cork. "That funny round cork cylinder is your life preserver, okay? I want you to hold it the entire time that we are on the boat. Pick it up and just hug it, please." He watched as Mickey picked up the cork cylinder as instructed and hugged it comically. Nathan grinned. "No joking. You must hold onto it the entire time. We are on a boat; there is always the danger of man overboard. I want you to stay in the center of the boat, Mikey. No standing either."

"Yes, Afi," Mikey said loudly, keeping his butt firmly on the seat near the middle, hugging the cylinder obediently. "I will behave! I promise!"

"Wonderful," Nathan said, as he steered the boat out, keeping them close to the shoreline.

The morning sun rose over the horizon as the clouds parted. The bright orange rays splayed over the calm lake as the boat slipped through the ripples.

Mikey fought his tendency to squirm. He watched his grandpa untie sailor's knots and then retie them; he found everything Afi did intensely interesting. He wondered how Afi learned all of these boating and fishing skills. He even knew where to fish, Mikey mused. "What kind of fish are we going to catch?" Mikey asked.

"Good question!" Nathan replied. "We might catch some pike, whitefish and carp. Some are bigger fish than others, some are tastier than others, and some we just through back into the lake."

Mikey laughed, "You know a lot about fishing and boats. Did your Afi teach you all this when you were young?"

Nathanael laughed, "I learned to fish in Iceland with my father when I was little like you. When we came to Gimli, though, we didn't know where to fish or the best ways to catch lots of fish. We were starving."

"What happened?"

"I met my wife," Nath answered. "She taught me how to fish here. We even figured out how to ice fish in the winter together."

"You had a wife?" Mikey asked, incredulously.

"Yes," Nath replied. "Your grandma."

"Oh," Mikey said, his brow furrowing. "Mamma doesn't talk much about grandma Olason. She did tell me I had another grandma, but she died."

"That's right. Her name was Anwa," Nath said, his eyes drifting along the watery horizon. "She was the love of my life."

"How did she die?" Mikey asked.

"She died from smallpox," Nath replied. "There was an epidemic that erased large settlements here, and she was one of the victims. Your momma was only a baby; she never had any memories of Grandma Anwa, only some weathered pictures and stories."

Mikey stopped smiling, and his brow furrowed. "That's really sad, Afi," he said.

"Yes, it was sad," Nath said. "But, I learned something."

"What's that?"

"I learned that life goes on no matter what bad things happen," Nath answered. "You learn to endure, no matter your grief or your troubles, life always continues."

The boat sloshed loudly through the water, splashing the waves up against the side of the bow. Nath and Mikey sat quietly, observing the beautiful scenery while the waves rhythmically slapped the stern.

"I would have liked to have two grandmas," Mikey said. "She was a fisherman?"

"Yes," Nathan answered. "She was the best fisherman on this side of the lake."

"Oh, wow," Mikey said. "I didn't know that. Who taught her?"

"Her brothers and stepdad," Nathan said. "She grew up in a native reserve with many extended family members. She was Swampy Cree."

"Oh!" Mikey said incredulously. "Wow!" Mikey's face changed as he focused on a thought. "So does that mean I am part Swampy Cree also?"

"Yes, it does," Nathan answered. "You are a smart boy."

"So, I don't have to pretend to be Indian?" Mikey shouted gleefully. "I am part Indian already!"

Nathan's face darkened. "Don't ever call her Indian. Or yourself. You are 1/4 native," Nath said quietly.

"Oh," Mikey said. "Sorry." Mikey's brows furrowed again, trying to understand. "Is Indian a bad word?"

"I think it is," Nath replied somberly.

"Okay," Mikey said. "I will never say that word again."

"Good," Nathan said. "Now, let's fish. I see a spot that often has schools of fish." He steered the boat to an area approximately 75 feet from a rocky shore.

Mikey smiled gleefully, obviously excited to finally be fishing with his grandpa. "Yippee," Mikey shouted and jumped up, dropping the cork at his feet.

"Sit down!" Nath chastised immediately. "No standing on the boat! I cannot take you out again if you stand. And never drop that cork again! It's not safe."

"Okay, Afi! Sorry!" Mikey obeyed, immediately sitting down and hugging the cork.

"Good," Nath nodded as he pulled the boat closer, let the sails out and shuffled around the vessel for the anchor. Finding it, he lifted the heavy anchor overboard, gently lowering it into the water as Mikey watched wide-eyed and fascinated.

"What is that for?" Mikey asked.

"It's an anchor to keep the boat from drifting off," Nath answered.

"Oh," Mikey stated simply.

Nath pulled out the fishing rod, hooking the live bait on and swung the line out into the lake. The line sailed into the air and finally plopped into the water with a small splash.

Mikey was staring intently, calculating every series of movements, absorbing everything his grandpa did.

Nath noticed Mikey's impressionable eyes captivated by the bait, the rod and everything that he did. Nath smiled sweetly, "We put live bait on so the fish will bite it."

Mikey grinned happily. "You are the best fisherman in Gimli now!"

Nathan laughed, "Maybe. You're sweet. I love you, Mikey."

"I love you too, Afi."

Later that night, Nathan laid Mikey down to sleep, kissed him on the forehead and shuffled into the kitchen for a quick drink. Annabella had asked Nathan to take Mikey for the weekend. They were overwhelmed with their daughter, Katya, a rambunctious two-year-old that was intent on tearing up the household. To add to the burden was Annabella's swollen tummy; she was suffering from a lot of back pain lately. This baby was due in one month's time, and Nathan had agreed to take the two toddlers for a week while Bella and Ivan adjusted with the newborn.

He would do anything for his daughter. She was the only woman in his life, and he was perfectly fine with that. Nath had met several women in town that looked at him with that intriguing glance up and down. He sometimes caught women staring at his physique or his eyes. He was confident that he was still rather attractive.

Nathan sometimes wondered why he didn't find any woman intriguing enough to pursue. Most days, he was certain that he would never love another woman romantically again.

And he was slowly coming to terms with that. Nath had his daughter and his grandchildren to love. That was enough.

As he lay down on his bed, pulling the covers over his naked body, his penis responded from the friction. He instantly hardened, creating a tent in the blankets. He grimaced. His body had other ideas.

He looked up at the ceiling, then slowly closed his eyes, imagining a shadowy woman on top of him as he masturbated himself to sleep.

CHAPTER 9

Her naked body slid on his chest, and her large round breasts squished deliciously on his pecs. She moved her hips rhythmically onto his groin, moving his penis this way and that inside of her. He could feel his control vanishing; he would not be able to hold on any longer. It had been so long since he last saw her. He felt so elated that he somehow had her in his arms again.

Something confused him; something was wrong. He wasn't sure what, but it was like he could feel her on top of him, but he couldn't touch her. Every time he reached up to grab her breasts, he couldn't reach her.

She leaned over to kiss him, and her face was so beautiful.

He began to cry with joy. The tears ran silently down his cheeks as he tried his hardest to perform for her, to please her. Nath wasn't sure if he would ever see her again, so he had to seize this opportunity and make it the best for them both.

Her body was lush and soft. Nath grabbed her buttocks, but she somehow started disappearing. He didn't understand why. He reached up for her buttocks again, and she began to fade away.

Then Nath remembered.

Anwa was dead.

He bolted upright in bed, sweating and his heart pounding. He wiped at his eyes, and they were wet with tears. Nath felt a terrible emptiness settle in his heart, but part of him was happy that he could still have those wonderful dreams once in a while, allowing him to relive the happiest moments of his life. It was like a tiny window opening up in his subconscious, and he was able to smile and be happy again. Even if it was only a dream, he cherished it.

Someone was banging on the front door.

Nath snapped out of his memories and pulled his pyjama bottoms on.

The banging on the door got harder. A voice shouted, "Nathan! It's Viktor. Annabella needs you; open up!"

His heart pounded urgently, and he raced to the door. He yanked open the front door, dishevelled and ragged. "What is it? Annabella? Is she okay?"

Viktor stood there, shuffling nervously from one foot to the other. "Nath!" he shouted. "Yes, Annabella is okay, but she delivered the baby this morning. Just like that! I came by to pick up the tools that I left behind when I was working on their house expansion, and she sent me to get you. She needs you to come and pick up Katya."

"A girl or a boy?" Nathan asked, his heart still pounding.

"Another girl!" Viktor shouted, his voice laced with anxiety. "They named her Natalie."

"Okay, okay," Nathan said calmly. "Stop shouting at me!"

Viktor laughed and hugged Nathan. "Hurry, please!"

Mikey awoke from the commotion and crawled out of bed. He padded across the room and grabbed Nathan's legs, hugging them.

Nath reached down and mussed his hair. "Hey, Mikey," he said. "You have another baby sister!"

"I do?" Mikey said incredulously.

"Yes, you do," Viktor replied happily. "Her name is Natalie."

"We have to get ready quickly and go to your momma's," Nathan said. "You and your sister Katya will be staying here for a week while grandma Kozak helps with the newborn, and then we will switch one week on and one week off. You will live at your other grandparent's place too, while I go help with the newborn."

"I want to stay here, Afi," Mikey said softly.

Nathan mussed the boy's hair again. "Aww," Nath said. "You're sweet. We'll see."

"I will be good, Afi," Mikey said. "I promise. I like staying with you."

"Okay, we'll see," Nath replied. "Get dressed. We have to go."

Katya pulled on Mikey's ears intermittently as they walked back to Nath's house. Nath waved her away, pointing at the sunset, attempting to distract her. The sun lowered over the bushes in the distance, reflecting a wonderful kaleidoscope of colours against the sky and lake. Pinks and purples amazed the kids; they jumped and skipped along the road, pointing out the different colours.

"Look at that one! It's light purple," Katya said, quite impressed with herself that she knew her colours.

"No, it's not," Mikey argued. "It's red. Not purple."

"You're wrong!" Katya shouted. "It's purple!"

"Red!" Mikey shouted back.

"Purple!" Katya yelled.

"Red!"

"Purple!" Katya said, stomping her feet.

"Enough!" Nathan said sternly.

"Well, which one is it, Afi?" Katya asked. "Purple or red?"

"It's both," Nathan answered. "Now enough fighting."

Katya skipped behind Mikey, then slyly pulled on his right ear.

"Ouch!" Mikey yelled, anger bubbling up. He lashed out at his annoying sister and pulled her long hair.

"Afi!" Katya shouted indignantly. "Mikey pulled my hair!"

"He pulled your hair because you pulled his ears," Nathan responded, grinning to himself.

"Well," she said softly, rubbing her scalp. "Now, my head hurts."

"I'm sorry that your head hurts," Nathan stated. "Don't pull your brother's ears."

"He started it!" Katya shouted.

Nathan scooped Katya up in his arms. "It's time for a grandad ride," he said, placing her on his shoulders and grabbing onto her small legs.

She giggled intensely, "Giddy up, Afi!"

"I want a ride too!" Mikey shouted.

"You are next," Nathan responded.

Mikey pouted. It was so unfair, he thought. Katya was always so much trouble. He walked faster, trying to get ahead of everyone. He was delighted to be able to spend the next week with Afi at his lake house. His grandad's home was closer to the sand, the boats and the lake. He wasn't happy about having to share it with Katya, but he knew that sometimes grown-ups made decisions that he couldn't be negotiated.

He shrugged his shoulders, "Is it my turn yet?"

Katya stuck her tongue out at him as she rode on top of Nath's shoulders.

"Two more minutes," Nath announced. He bounced into a trot as Katya giggled infectiously.

Nath laughed along with his granddaughter as they trotted down the street.

Mikey ran to catch up.

Nathan looked down at the boy, "Do you know that you got into just as much trouble when you were younger too."

"No!" Mikey said.

"Yes, you did," Nathan said. "But it's okay because you know why?"

"Why?" Mikey asked.

"Because it's normal," Nathan answered, pulling Katya off his shoulders and whisking Mikey up next. "Even your Momma was a little trouble maker when she was young."

Mikey smiled up on top of Nath's shoulders. He could see everything up here! "I love it up here, Afi!" Mikey squealed. "You can see the entire world!"

Nathan laughed wholeheartedly, grabbing Katya's hand to make sure she didn't run off. She tugged at his hand, but he maintained a good grip. "I'm going to cook you both some oatmeal treats, with dried fruit and maple syrup," Nath said. "You'll like it. Yummy for your tummy."

"Yay," Katya squealed.

"You can help me, Katya," Nath said sweetly.

"I am a good cook!" she said gleefully.

Nath laughed, "I am sure you are!"

Nath jumbled the keys in the lock, placing Mikey down and swinging Katya over the steps leading into the house. "Wow," Katya exclaimed. "You have a big house!"

"He built it himself," Mikey exclaimed proudly.

"With Viktor, Kristjan and Aron's help," Nathan corrected. "It takes a community to build a home."

Nathan pulled the oatmeal from the cupboard and placed the ingredients on a small kids table for Katya to mix everything. "Here's the maple syrup, dried berries and some crushed hazelnuts." Nath placed each ingredient on the small table along with several measuring cups. "Start with the nuts and berries. Then we will add the maple syrup and oatmeal."

Katya focused intently on the task at hand, trying hard to prove to Nath what a good cook she was. It was endearing. Nath smiled warmly and helped her with the measurements. Once they had measured everything, they stirred it all with a large wooden spoon.

"It's so sticky!" Katya squealed joyfully.

Nath laughed, "You're so cute." He tapped her nose as she giggled sweetly. "Now we add the oatmeal," Nath instructed, holding the bowl up and mixing the oats into the larger bowl.

Katya smiled and hollered at her brother, "Mikey! We're making oatmeal treats!"

"Girl stuff," Mikey mumbled, as he played intently with several building blocks.

Katya stuck her tongue out at her distant brother.

"Katya," Nath warned.

"He didn't see anyways," Katya whispered.

"It doesn't matter if he didn't see," Nath chastised. "What matters is how you treat others. If you always treat your brother badly, he will always treat you badly right back."

Katya pouted.

"Okay, let's wash our hands," Nath instructed. "We're going to form the oat treats into flat bars with our hands."

He held her up to the washbasin and cleaned her hands with soap. Nath poured water over her tiny palms, then patted them dry and kissed her hands. Katya giggled cheerfully and squirmed, trying to get out of his grasp.

Nath laughed and tickled her. "Okay, let's finish these bars and I'll show you how to bake them on the woodstove!"

CHAPTER 10

The last few days were so busy he almost didn't hear the warehouse door chime. Nath rushed to get the fish salted before the kids tore apart the fishery. He was bringing them to work every day, and every day Mikey and Katya grew antsier. "Garth! Can you go to the front for me?" Nath yelled.

"No problem," Garth replied as he made his way through the warehouse.

Nath eyed Katya as she attempted to crawl up the fish stacks. "Katya! Get off of there immediately!"

Mikey ran to the rescue, grabbing Katya off the fish stacks. She squirmed wildly against him. He lost his balance, teetered, and they both fell back, Mikey landing on his butt.

Mikey burst into tears and screamed at his sister.

Nath rushed over to the toddler altercation, just as he noticed Garth heading to the front.

"Katya!" Nathan hollered, scooping her up and strained to hear if it was a new customer coming into the shop so late in the afternoon. The last thing he needed right now was another order.

"Can I help you?" Garth asked as the front door closed shut.

A poised lady approached the front counter, adjusting her hat. "I was told that I could find Nathanael Olason here," she said smugly.

"Oh," Garth replied. "Yes, he is here. He is just busy in the warehouse at the moment."

Mikey's screams filtered through the warehouse into the front. "She's always causing trouble, Afi!" Mikey shouted indignantly.

The woman grinned. "You have children here?" she said, adjusting the large white upturned hat that framed her pretty face.

"Yes, Nath's grandchildren," Garth replied. "He's been awfully busy most of the week," Garth said, looking towards the back. "I will go see if he can spare a moment. Can I tell him who it is?"

"Oh, yes," the woman said, waving a gloved hand in the air. "My name is Katrin."

Garth disappeared to the back and approached Nath.

Katya was in a full-blown temper tantrum, kicking her legs and shouting on the floor. Mikey was running around the fish stacks with his hands on his ears. "I can't hear you," Mikey chided, singing. "La de da de da."

Garth grinned, "Go to the front, Nath. There is a lady here to see you. I will take the kids for a bit. It looks like you need a break!"

Nath ran his hands through his thick hair wearily. He hardly had any grey hair and no bald spots yet. He was lucky, he knew. Lots of men in their early forties didn't fare so well. "A lady?" Nath asked.

"She said her name was Katrin," Garth answered. "Someone that you know?"

Nath immediately felt a jolt. "Katrin?" he said questioningly. The first woman he had ever kissed? It couldn't be. They had kissed back in Kinmount before the settlers had travelled to Gimli. Katrin and her family had chosen to stay in Winnipeg. He had never heard from her again, which was fine because he had never really felt very interested in her. He couldn't quite remember why; there was something about her he didn't particularly like.

"Yes," Garth answered. "That's what she said. Why? Who is she?"

"Nobody," Nath said quietly. "It's alright. I will speak to her. Watch these kids like a hawk! They are getting to be a handful."

Garth laughed, "Go talk to the lady. I got this."

Nath poked his head into the front store area; Katrin had her back to him. She wore a long white Victorian style dress with a pink sash around the waist. The wide-brimmed bonnet tied to her head had lilacs in it along with several ribbons. It was the current style of city women, not so much with the country folk. To Nath, it all looked quite silly; wearing a garden on top of your head was just not natural.

"Katrin," Nath said. "Is that you?"

Katrin turned and lifted a delicate hand in the air. "Yes," she said. "It's me. You haven't changed much, Nath. Still, the rough settler."

"I have grown much older than when we last saw each other," Nathan pointed out.

"Yes," Katrin replied, smoothing her dress nervously. "We both have."

Nath eyed her suspiciously. He remembered why he wasn't that interested in her before. She was one of those people that always had an agenda. "What brings you to Gimli?"

"Good question," Katrin replied. "I could lie and say that I had relatives here or other business, but to be honest, I wanted to see you, Nath. I would like to catch up on things."

Nath smiled. "That's sweet. I'm a bit busy with my grandchildren right now, but maybe we can catch up sometime later."

"Great," Katrin said, moving a lock of hair from her face. "I can come back at five o'clock. Maybe we can have dinner?"

"We might be able to do that," Nath said slowly. "I would have the kids, though. They're a bit rambunctious." As he said it, he regretted it. He didn't really desire to have dinner with Katrin. He wasn't sure if it was just him or that she was actually an unlikeable person. Nath felt his inner voice chastise himself. He hadn't gone on a date since Anwa died. It would be good for him to sit and chat with a female. She was obviously interested in him. She had come all this way just to see him; the least he could do was have dinner with her.

Katrin smiled smugly. "Wonderful! I will be back at five o'clock then. We will have some fresh fish for dinner, I suppose? That would be delightful."

"Yes, we could certainly have fish if that's what you would prefer." Nath stood awkwardly, waiting for her to leave. "Well, I really do have to get back to work. I will see you later then."

"It was nice seeing you again after all these years, Nathanael," she said longingly. "I look forward to having dinner with you." She walked to the door, then paused, awkwardly waiting for him to open the door for her.

But Nath had already disappeared into the back. "See you soon, Katrin," he shouted from the back.

She wrinkled her nose in distaste and pulled the door open for herself. He would change soon enough, she thought.

Mikey jumped on the front counter happily, running from Katya. "Ha! I told you that you couldn't catch me. I'm too fast for you."

Katya burst into tears and fell to the floor, sitting on her buttocks, wailing.

"Mikey!" Nath scolded. "Try not to provoke your sister."

Mikey looked at him slyly. "She started it."

"According to you, she always does," Nath said, a slight grin crossing his lips. He pulled Katya up and patted her back while she hugged him fiercely. "Let's close up. I have a lady friend that will be joining us for dinner tonight. Try to be on your best behaviour."

Katya raised her head. "A girl?"

Nath cleared his throat. "Yes, a girl."

"Who?" Mikey said loudly.

"Her name is Katrin. I knew her when I was just seventeen. We're just going to chat about old times and talk about what's happened since."

"Are you in love with her?" Katya asked loudly.

Nathan laughed. "No, not at all."

"Then why are you having dinner with her?" Katya asked.

Nathan frowned, his brown eyebrows curving. "Good question," he answered. "I think she may have just invited herself."

"Is she pretty?" Katya asked.

"Yes," Nath replied.

"Then why aren't you in love with her?" Katya asked, her dark brown eyes glowing with toddler intelligence.

Nath laughed hard, coughing as he answered. "Beauty is not the only thing that I like in a woman. There are many other qualities that are attractive to me."

"Like what?" Mikey asked, joining the curious discussion.

Nath put down Katya. "Well, I have only really been attracted to one woman in my life, and that was your grandma Anwa." He rubbed his beard thoughtfully. "The things that I found attractive about your grandma was her vivacious spirit, her beautiful thick wavy hair and her kindness. There were many other things, but those were the most alluring things about Anwa."

"I saw a picture of you and grandma Anwa, holding mommy when she was a baby," Katya stated. "Grandma looks a lot like momma."

"Yes," Nath said softly. "She was a beautiful woman."

Mikey jumped off the counter, happy that this girly discussion was concluding. "So, what don't you like about Katrin then?"

"I truly don't know," Nath said thoughtfully, then stopped his train of thought as the front door chimed.

They all looked at the woman standing in the doorway.

"Katrin," Nath said, nodding to the kids. "This is Mikey and Katya, my two grandchildren."

"Delightful to meet you!" Katrin replied happily. "Shall we go?"

"Yes," Nath said, packing up a bag. "Let's go."

They all shuffled out of the fishery, while Nath locked up.

A few hours later, they all sat at the large table in front of the wonderful lake view window. Fish, potatoes and corn scattered the table, mostly half-eaten. Mikey had eaten well, devouring everything but making a huge mess. Katya was picking at her food, sometimes playing with it more than eating it. Katrin had grown quiet as the kids made a mess of themselves and the food. She ate quietly and almost stonily. Nath wondered what he had said or done, although part of him didn't really care.

"Mikey," she said softly. "You will need to learn table manners if you are to grow into a gentleman like your grandpa."

Mikey scowled. "I don't want to be a gentleman. I will be a fisherman or a hunter."

Katrin chuckled, "Not if you want to marry someday."

Mikey frowned, obviously confused. "What is she saying, Afi?"

Nathan coughed. "I wouldn't pay much attention to that talk, Mikey. You are only three years old. You will grow into a man someday, Mikey, and then you will become the kind of man that you want to be. It's best that way."

Katrin lifted her nose slightly.

Nath realized that he might have offended her, but he didn't care. She was not his wife and had absolutely no say in raising his grandchildren with values and integrity.

She put her fork down and wiped her lips with the napkin. "It was a delicious meal, Nathanael. Thank you."

"I'm sorry that I don't have any dessert, but the kids ate all the oatmeal treats," Nathan said, squinting his eyes menacingly at Katya.

Katya pouted. "I didn't eat them all!"

"Yes, you did," Mikey said indignantly. "I only had four!"

"That's most probably why you weren't eating your fish," Nath said.

Katya's eyes welled up with tears.

"Ah, come here, Katya," Nath said, holding his arms open.

She jumped into his lap and buried her face in his collar.

"It's alright," Nath said. "We will make more tomorrow."

Katrin stood up and began clearing the table. "I will clean up the dishes while you put the kids to bed."

Mikey stood defiantly. "We have to go to bed early?"

"I am going to agree with Katrin this time, kids. Yes, it's time for bed."

"Aww," Mikey whined.

"No complaining," Nathan stated. "Let's get cleaned up for bed." He stood with Katya, still clinging to his chest. She wrapped her legs around his waist as his strong arms held her to him. "Come, Mikey."

Mikey stubbornly followed them into the bedroom. "Why does she talk like that?"

"She's from the city," Nath stated as if it was an obvious answer. "She's not a country person like we are. City folk value different things, I guess."

"Well," Mikey said, lowering his voice. "I don't like her," he whispered.

"I know," Nathan said. "But she's our guest for the night, so please be polite." Nathan began changing Katya into her pyjamas. "Come on, let's get ready for bed."

Mikey pulled his sweater off roughly, getting it all tangled up somehow, but he finally removed it successfully and yawned as he laid down on his bed. "Goodnight, Afi," Mikey said, opening his arms for a hug.

Nathan hugged both kids and tucked them in, closing the door quietly.

Pots and pans clanged in the kitchen as Katrin cleaned up the mess they had left behind. She was a good woman in that way.

"Let me help dry," Nath said, grabbing a towel.

"Oh," she said, smiling. "Certainly."

Nath dried a few pots and pans, replacing them in the proper spots in the cupboard. "How did you like the fish?"

"It was delicious, thank you," she responded.

"What time are you heading back in the morning?" Nath asked.

"I am not sure," she replied. "It depends."

"Depends?" Nath asked. "On what?"

"On you, I guess," she replied.

Nath looked at her, quite shocked. What was she saying?

"I came here to see if you were interested in reigniting what we had many years ago," she said boldly. "I know you lost your wife so long ago and have spent decades being alone. I talked with your aunt Anita in Winnipeg." Katrin paused, nervously wiping the kitchen counter. "We had something once. I haven't really fallen in love as you have. I never had children or married. I would like to fall in love one day."

Nathan was flabbergasted. He didn't know what to say. He should be flattered that Katrin had made a journey just to see him and that she was bold enough to ask him outright. Instead, he felt the same feeling that he had felt back when he was seventeen. No matter how pretty she was or how forward she was, he didn't feel attracted to her. He wondered if it was him or if it was just his broken heart speaking too loudly. He concluded that it was most likely a bit of both.

"Katrin," Nath started. "I am sorry. I don't know how else to say this." Nathan looked at his toes and wondered which right words to use. He never felt like this with Anwa. He always felt comfortable with her, never nervous or put on the spot. "I love that you came out here to visit me, and I feel flattered that you made the journey to take a chance on me. But, Katrin, I don't feel the same as you."

Katrin's face changed. Her eyes went dark, almost mean. She was silent for a few moments, absorbing the rejection. She squared her shoulders and spoke angrily. "You don't have to say anything more," she said, stabbing the words at him. "I obviously wasted my time." She grabbed her shawl and her bag, swiftly opening the door.

"Katrin," Nath said apologetically. "You can stay here until morning. I will sleep on the sofa. There is no need to rush out into the night. I am a gentleman."

She turned back, with her hand on the doorknob, her face turning an angry rose colour. "You are no gentleman, Nathanael," she spat. "You will never have a refined lady like me. You will only ever be accepted by the less savoury types of women. Good luck with your remaining lonely years of grandparenting."

The door slammed behind her loudly. The door frame shook with the ferocity of her rejected anger.

Nath stared at the door as he heard her furious footsteps stomp down the deck, and then he heard something else; her sobs filled the night air. Her footsteps quickened as she ran to the horse carriage, most likely looking for her driver.

Nath slumped onto the sofa, still staring at the door. What was his problem? He had a pretty available woman, his own age, throwing herself at him.

And everything in his body had said no.

He held his head in his hands for several moments before finally standing up and shuffling to bed. He pulled the covers and climbed in, looking at the blue and brown bracelet on his wrist, running his fingertips smoothly over the beads.

Every moment of this strange day assaulted his mind, making his brain twist and analyze every little thing. Any man would be attracted to Katrin. She was pretty, bold and available, but something was menacing about her. He couldn't quite put his finger on it, but it was there. It always had been; she hadn't changed. He knew it back then, and he knew it now. But he was also certain of something else too. Nath believed that he would never meet another woman; this was the end of the road. This was as far as his love life would ever get. He hugged his abdomen and curled up on his side. He was doomed to be a single grandfather for the rest of his life. No one would love him, as Anwa did.

The branches snapped, his large feet crashing through the bush. The deadwood and wild bushes didn't stand a chance at the mercy of his angry steps. The branches caught on his shoulders, ripping his shirt and tearing at his skin, sometimes even drawing blood.

He shrugged them off.

The night engulfed him and shielded him, both friend and foe. The only sounds were the crickets and frogs, sometimes the occasional pack of wolves howling together. He should be scared, but he was not. He had killed wolves before a long time ago in another world, it seemed. His life had changed so quickly after that world had ended.

It was okay, he told himself. He was a man. He was stronger than most. He had lived through so much hardship and pain; he was one of the survivors.

But tonight, all he felt was the pain.

His heart beat faster and faster as he neared the area. His emotions were quickly bubbling up to the surface; he could feel it. He was getting close.

His footsteps quickened, and the branches scratched him relentlessly. He simply waved them away like minor irritants on his quest to reach his destination. The deadwood was all over the forest floor, but he knew the way; he had travelled this path many times before. He skirted several fallen logs and balanced his feet on the uneven ground, obviously knowing the way.

He must be careful, he told himself. He wouldn't want to trip and be a meal for the wolves tonight. Blood dripped down his arms from the sharp branches, and his mind momentarily told him to be aware of the danger. He stomped more carefully through the bush, feeling it coming. He told himself to focus on his steps. He tried not to hurry, but it was urgent. He needed this. It was long overdue.

He reached his destination. It was dark, very dark. The trees were swaying with the wind, and grey shadows played with his eyesight. Everything was so very black here.

He stopped in his tracks. Then he allowed it to wash over him, and that's when he felt his heart split open, releasing a zoo of caged emotions. He felt the tears cascade down his face; he cried heavily, in torrents, it seemed.

He looked up, his eyes swollen and shook his bloody fist at the sky. "Why?" he hollered angrily, his voice echoing through-out the forest.

Then just as suddenly, his body convulsed, overcome with emotion, he curled up, and his voice grew hoarse, almost weak. "I don't understand," he croaked.

The night air blew a gust of wind through the trees as if to answer.

But the answer was not in the trees. It was silent; nothing but the night, the wind, the crickets and the sound of his own breath.

CHAPTER 11

"Afi!" Mikey shouted gleefully. "Come on, hurry up." Mikey grabbed the horse's reins and threw the saddle on his horse, snatching the gun sack onto his shoulder.

Nath pulled the door closed to the barn and led his horse out. "Now, you be careful with that firearm, Mikey. Remember the safety rules!" Nath pulled his own rifle bag over his shoulder and mounted the horse.

"Yep," Mikey said as he swung his long legs onto the saddle with a confidence that only a ten-year-old could have. His matted hair was longish, but his eyes were bright and joyful. He was a handsome young boy, uncannily close to Nath's very own looks as a youngster. His dark blonde hair was thick and wild, his eyes a captivating blue and his long legs were growing faster than the rest of his body. If they laid photographs side by side, nobody could tell whether it was Nath or Mikey. The resemblance was astonishing.

Mike had begun spending more time with his grandad, often staying over at Afi's place instead of momma's. He loved his momma, but since the arrival of his brothers, Jon and the youngest brother, Vlad, along with his two sisters, the house became seriously overcrowded with kids.

"Which way are we going?" Mikey asked enthusiastically.

"Towards Willow Point," Nath said, pointing to the south. "There's a clearing where the deer herd. Anwa showed it to me on our second date." Nath laughed.

"Hunting on a date?" Mikey asked, chuckling.

"Yes," Nath answered. "Back then, all of us Icelanders were just lucky to survive. Anwa had shown us where to catch the fish and where the deer hid. She also taught me archery."

"Really?" Mike said excitedly. "I wish I knew her. She sounds like an awesome grandma."

Nathan laughed. "We were just seventeen back then. But yeah, she was an awesome woman. Much more of a woman than anyone I've ever met."

"Is that why you never remarried?" Mike asked. He caught the brief look of sorrow that occasionally crossed Nath's face, and he looked shamefully down. "I'm sorry, Afi."

"No need to be sorry," Nath replied as he led the way onto the horse road alongside the lake. "I haven't had much interest in women, to be honest. I have Bella, you and all the rest of my grandkids. That's all I need."

Mikey frowned. "But didn't you ever want to fall in love again?"

"Sometimes," Nath answered. "But it never happened. The one thing about love I realized is that you cannot make it happen; it just evolves on its own. If you have to force it or it doesn't feel right, then it is best not to pursue such things."

Mike held the reins firmly while the horses followed in single file through the bushes. He hugged the warm animal with his legs, staying firmly on the saddle. He had a burning question in his mind that didn't make sense to him, but part of him wondered if it was a nice thing to say or not. He blurted it out without thinking much about it. "So, you would rather stay lonely then?" Mike asked.

Nath rode silently on the lead horse, thinking. "Good question, boy," Nath replied. "I don't really want to be lonely."

"But if you don't want that, then why are you staying alone?"

Nath nodded thoughtfully; it is probably best to be honest with the young boy. "Because I can never replace Anwa. She was the love of my life."

Mike looked at the trees crowding the horse trail in front of them. "That sounds really sad," he said.

"It is," Nath said. "But it is also just the way life works out sometimes. I have just accepted that I might be alone forever, and that's okay."

Mike tilted his head to the side, inquiringly, as if he thought of something important, then forgot. He shrugged his shoulders nonchalantly. "Maybe you should just stop thinking like that," he said.

Nath trotted silently through the bushes. The boy might be right, he thought. But if he accepted that he would not be alone forever, then he would also have to admit that another woman could fill Anwa's shoes. Any notion of distancing from his memories of Anwa made his insides churn. He simply could not do it. But the boy was just a child; he didn't have any knowledge of the complexities of adult emotions.

Regardless, there was something about the plain words Mike spoke that made him ponder. A tiny voice inside his head told him to listen.

Nathan shrugged and continued leading the way into the bushes; he slowed down and disembarked, tying the horse to a tree. He looked up and momentarily gazed at the clouds, appreciatively. The sun was rising higher in the sky as the shadows of dawn changed into daylight; the streaks of sunlight danced between the trees. He motioned for Mike to tie his horse to a tree and held two fingertips to his lips, gesturing to be quiet.

Mikey nodded and did as instructed.

Nath pulled his gun bag out and removed the rifle, placing it on the bag. He grabbed Mike's bag and pulled out Mikey's gun as well. He wanted to show Mike how to load the weapons. The boy would not be shooting today, but he would be practising and observing while Nath aimed and shot the animal.

Mikey had relentlessly pestered him for almost six years to teach him hunting before Nath had finally conceded. He discussed it with Annabella, and they all agreed that he would be allowed to go hunting when he was ten years old. On his birthday, Nath heard nothing but repeated requests to go hunting. He told Mikey they would go once the snow began to melt.

Mikey had waited rather impatiently, insistently reminding Nath almost every day to go hunting with him.

Nath didn't quite understand the boy's fascination with rifles, but he knew hunting was a survival skill that was necessary for his grandson to learn, and he loved spending time with Mikey.

"Grab the bullets, Mikey," Nath instructed.

Mikey dug in the bag and pulled out the box of bullets, handing it to Nath with a gleam in his eyes. "Here," he said.

"You are loading the weapon, not me," Nath said, picking one up and showing him which direction they went in. "These rifles are breechloaders." He showed Mikey how to open the breech. "Now, you do it with your rifle."

Mikey opened the breech as instructed and placed the bullet into the chamber, looking up expectantly, waiting for further instructions. Nath showed him how to close the breech, and Mikey respectfully obeyed.

"Perfect," Nath said. "Make sure the safety is on." Nath pointed to where it was located on the rifle, instructing him firmly to the importance. "And remember, never point a gun at a person or wave it. Hold it steady and be very careful with it."

Mikey nodded, dutifully making mental notes of safety importance.

"Good. Now you're going to learn how to handle the weapon." Nath picked up his own rifle and switched weapons with Mikey, making sure the boy had the unloaded gun. Nath stood firmly, his feet planted parallel with the weapon and grasped it with both hands.

Mikey picked up the unloaded rifle and imitated his grandad with the gun held firmly in his grasp.

Nath stood. "You hold the rifle steady when you are stalking prey for safety and to aim quickly," he instructed. He held the rifle firmly in front of him, one hand on the grip and the other one near the handle.

Mikey followed the example and immediately stood firmly with the weapon, as shown.

Nath placed the loaded weapon carefully down and walked over to Mike. "I am going to show you how to aim. When you are ready to shoot the deer, we will do it together, but for now, I just want you to learn how to aim." Nath pulled himself behind the boy, wrapping his arms around Mikey's shoulders and grasped the weapon. "You see that small nick standing out on the gun. That's the sights. Close one eye and concentrate. That will be where you are shooting, but we also have to adjust for gravity depending on the distance and even more adjustments are made at extreme distances for wind drift. But today, we will be fairly close to the herd, so we may only need to adjust for gravity."

They practiced several times on aiming, choosing holes in the trees as imaginary targets. "Hold the gun with one hand under the grip and the other near the trigger. This is an unloaded gun so we can practice."

Mikey held the rifle steadily, exactly as Nath taught him. Nathanael smiled; the boy was picking up on this fast. Mike aimed at a small squirrel and pulled the empty trigger. "Bang," he whispered as the tree animal scurried away. He motioned to the distance where he could see some movement in a clearing. "Is that where the herd is?" Mikey asked.

"It sure is," Nath answered.

Mikey narrowed one eye and bent down, aiming with the tip of the rifle towards the herd.

"We are much too far away," Nath stated. "We will be going closer."

Mikey nodded, peering down the sights, delighted in his new superpowers at shooting. Nath motioned, and Mikey stood, grabbing their gun bags, heading closer towards the herd. "Could we still shoot from this distance with these rifles?" he asked.

Nath grabbed the loaded rifle into his hands and joined Mikey. "Not with very much accuracy, only an experienced marksman can hit something from that far away."

"What is the range with these rifles?" Mikey asked.

"Two hundred yards with good accuracy," Nath answered. "There is less accuracy the farther away you are."

"Are there any other guns with better accuracy?"

"Yes," Nath replied. "There is a Ross rifle I have been looking at lately. I've heard it has a range of six hundred yards."

"Six hundred yards!" Mikey exclaimed.

"Shh," Nath chastised. "We need to be quiet. We don't want to scare the herd away."

"Afi," Mikey whispered. "Six hundred yards is a lot."

"I agree," Nath said. "I was thinking of buying one when they become more readily available."

"Could we go shooting with the Ross?"

"Yes, of course. Once I get one," Nath answered.

"You should buy it, Afi," Mikey pressured.

"We will see," Nath replied, chuckling.

Nath moved in front and led the way into the bush, walking more slowly as they neared the position he favoured. The very same place Anwa had taken him so many years ago. He waved for Mikey to come and motioned with his two fingers that there was no talking.

Mikey nodded and crept silently into the bush.

The herd of deer was a group of four bachelors with a young buck in the lead. Some were only a year old; others looked like they were about to become territorial and leave the group soon. One of the larger bucks was nodding it's head up and down. The other youngsters were backing away, except one. It was evident that the buck was in an adolescent fighting mood. The rogue teen looked up, fake charged and then stopped.

The larger buck nodded and started stomping.

Nathan crouched in the bush. Nath silently pulled the loaded gun and motioned Mikey to crouch down beside him. He whispered in Mikey's ear, "I am going to take the larger buck. Now, I want you to pay attention to every little detail." Nath stood firmly with one hand under the wood part of the barrel and the other cupping the trigger mechanism. "There is going to be a strong recoil from the shot I'm going to take. It will threaten to push you back and lose control of the rifle. I will be pulling the weapon into my body, planting it firmly into the solid part of my shoulder, not too high, or else it could slip. I am focusing on keeping the weapon within my control and keeping a firm grip on the barrel. Watch my shoulder placement and my stance. I want you to replicate that. Now go over by that tree and aim in the same way that I am. Pretend you are the one shooting. I want your feet planted strongly and your shoulder ready to push back against the recoil." Nath nodded for Mikey to go.

Mikey silently moved to the tree, watched his grandpa and then steadied himself with the rifle. He held the wooden barrel just as his grandpa did and slipped his finger in the trigger hole. Mikey glanced forward several times, adjusting his stance and pulling the weapon firmly into his shoulder. Mikey narrowed an eye and aimed with his sights on the deer. The forest grew silent; even the birds stopped chirping. The adolescent male deer looked up suddenly as if he sensed something. Mikey kept his aim on the larger deer. It looked like he was readying a charge on the adolescent male.

Nath's gun fired loudly, cracking the morning air.

Mike didn't even flinch.

The herd scattered crazily. The youngsters fled in a blur of brownish leaps to the right. The adolescent male bounded away in the same direction, fleeing with a panicked fury. The larger male fled too, disappearing in the opposite direction. At first, Mikey couldn't believe his eyes. What happened? Had Afi missed?

Nath cursed and gathered his bag. "Hurry, bring your gun sack," he said. "I'm almost certain that I hit him. He must be wounded." Nath rushed out into the field towards where the deer were once standing.

Mikey swung the gun bag over his shoulder and raced after his grandad. "I thought you had hit him too. What happened?"

"These old guns aren't the greatest for accuracy," Nath responded. "Next time, we will use bows and arrows." Nath knelt in the half-melted snow mounds looking for the hoof tracks of the larger male. "I believe this is his track." He pointed into the forest to the left. "Let's find him." Nath ran into the bush with Mike close behind.

"Afi," Mikey shouted. "I think I saw blood in the snow."

"I saw that too," Nath said. "I definitely hit him. We have to find the injured buck, but we need to be careful; he will charge us if we get too close."

Mike ran with Nath following the tracks until finally they slowed down and started walking. The blood was appearing more and more as they neared. They could see the trail left on the patches of old crusted snow, the blood increasing from drops to bloody hoof prints. "We are getting closer. Quiet," Nath whispered.

They both looked around the wild forest as the wind gusted through the trees. The birds were quiet again. Mikey could feel the stillness creeping into his body. His intuition told him they were closing-in towards the injured deer.

Nath motioned to be quiet and pulled the gun across his arm. He crouched in a bush and motioned Mikey to crouch beside him. There was a rustle in the bushes to their right; the lake was to their left. The deer had run a long way towards the water. The waves crashed into the rocks, muffling their noises.

Mikey scanned the trees and focused on the area where he could hear movement. He squinted one eye and focused until a calm came over him. Then he saw the deer. Mikey could only see the buck's neck and head; the remainder of the animal's body camouflaged in the bush. Mikey pointed.

Nath's eyes followed his grandson's arm all the way to his fingertip. He blinked and focused again, trying to spot what

Mikey had seen. He exhaled slowly and tried to release the adrenaline that was coursing through his veins. He blinked again, narrowing one eye.

Then he saw the buck. It was only 30 feet away.

Nath crouched his shoulder over the butt of the gun, lined up his sights and aimed for the larger part of the animal's neck. He held the barrel steady and exhaled slowly.

He fired the weapon.

The crack echoed throughout the forest as the bullet whizzed directly into the deer's neck. Blood spurted into the air as the buck fell gracefully onto the ground.

Nath and Mikey rushed over to the animal, both men breathing heavily with adrenaline. They crashed loudly through the bush until they neared the animal.

They got him! The buck was dead.

Mikey smiled gleefully. "You got him, Afi!"

"Yes, we did," Nath said. "But you're the one who spotted him. Good eye, Mikey!" Nath laid down the gun bag and pulled out his hunting knife and began gutting the deer. It was a gory mess, but Mikey never once turned away. If anything, the boy was intensely interested, as if he was mentally remembering every single detail.

CHAPTER 12

The arrow whizzed through the air, then cracked into the tree trunk, splitting the wood. The feathered arrow pointed out of the tree as Mikey ran to grab it out. He grasped it firmly and pulled hard. Nothing budged. He wiggled it, pulled, wiggled, and it still wouldn't budge.

Mike cursed. "Lost another damn arrow!" he shouted at the tree.

It sliced too deep into the wood, he thought. This was good because it meant that he had started developing sufficient strength in his pull on the bow, but it was bad because he lost an arrow in practice today.

Nath shouted to him from the bushes. "Good shot!" he said exuberantly. "You have an incredible aim, Mikey."

"It's Mike," he corrected, glancing briefly at his grandad as he pulled his bow up and aimed into the forest, searching for another tree. "Not Mikey anymore, Afi. I'm fifteen, and I'm as tall as you now. I want to be called Mike. My friend calls me Mike, so does momma."

"Okay, okay, Mike," Nath replied grinning. The boy was growing into a man. It made him feel so proud. Mike was a kind, young man but also stubborn and willful as a rock, just like Annabella and possibly himself. Nathan chuckled at the memories. "I want you to pick a tree this time and mark it first. I want to see how accurate you can shoot."

Mike lowered the bow, smiling. "Okay, let's do this." He scanned the forest looking for his target, something far enough away to impress his grandad but still be attainable.

The trees were healthy but barren; the only sound in the forest was the echoing wind. It was a cold spring with the sun warming up the land slowly, the snow melting under their feet. They had been out practicing all morning already. Momma would be angry that they disappeared for days again. He would give her lots of hugs when he saw her afterwards.

Mike spotted a narrow tree 50 yards away. He placed down the bow, rummaged in his sack and pulled out a brightly coloured rag.

"I found one," he said. "I'll be right back." Mike ran into the bush, leaping expertly over the fallen logs, the orange piece of cloth flying behind him in his hand.

Nath watched as his young grandson sailed effortlessly through the forest. He smiled proudly. The boy was at home in the woods as if he was born to do this. He had taught Mike how to aim, stance, technique and every little thing that Anwa had taught him. He was surprised by how quickly Mike absorbed everything. He wondered if it was his teaching, his love for the boy, or if it had absolutely nothing to do with him and everything to do with the inborn talent Mike had. The boy had developed an obsession for aiming, weapons and all aspects of hunting. Nath felt immensely proud of his grandson, but another little part felt like he was spending too much time hunting with the boy. It was Mike's favourite pastime, and Nath loved it also, so it was natural for them both, although they limited hunting to just enough food for their family and friends. Today was just aiming practice and archery. They had enough deer meat for the week; they wouldn't be hunting today.

Mike lifted the cloth towards the chosen tree in the distance. He wrapped it around the narrow trunk and tied it securely. Mike stood back, followed his eyes back to his shooting position, analyzing the difficulty and probabilities. He nodded and ran back to his grandad. His long legs and youthful male energy carried him effortlessly through the forest. He felt so confident lately. His legs had grown quite a bit in the last year. He was as tall as Afi, maybe even a tiny bit taller, he thought. His beard had started to grow in on his chin and upper jaw but was spotty everywhere else. He felt like a man. It was a great feeling. He started making decisions and stuck to them. Afi had taught him to be a man of his word, and he was. If he couldn't complete a project or be somewhere at a specific time, then he simply would not commit to the task, but if he was sure he could do it, he was always there. He never cancelled and never promised anything that he wasn't entirely sure that he would do. There was an undeniable comfort in knowing that he was in charge of his destiny, and he was determined to develop his stake in this life. He would be someone great; he could feel it.

Mike landed with a solid two feet a few yards away from Nath, wiping a stray lock of dark blonde hair from his eyes. Mike's blue eyes pierced through the trees as he positioned his feet shoulder-width apart, standing firmly.

The boy looked so much like Nath when he was young that it was eerie. It was like looking in the mirror but with 37 years difference. Some older people, even mistakenly called him Nath! They both laughed when that happened. He had the steel determination of the Olason's too, sometimes to the point of being difficult with others. The boy will learn, Nath thought. He would find out how to balance his wilful nature with fine negotiation skills.

"Watch your stance," Nath said, reminding him. "Keep your shoulders up and strong."

Mike picked up the weapon and turned 90 degrees from his target, placing his feet facing towards Nath and aligning his sight along his outstretched arm, aiming at the tree. He raised the bow and placed the arrow against the bowstring.

"Nice form," Nath commented, watching his grandson intently.

Mike nodded confidently and squared his shoulders, looking down the arrow at his target. He closed one eye and focused. Fifty yards was the farthest he had ever shot an arrow, and he didn't want to fail in front of his grandad, but he was sure he could do it. His aiming skills had improved considerably in the last few months. He was practicing often, and it showed.

He breathed in slowly and steadily, calming his nerves.

"Remember what I told you that grandma Anwa said," Nath whispered. "Be one with the land. Breathe it in and exhale it out. Become your surroundings."

Mike closed his eyes briefly, inhaling slowly. He opened his eyes during the exhale, the wind blowing gently throughout the forest. He could feel the wind breeze lightly through his longish hair. He closed one eye, aiming the arrow expertly on the orange clothed target. It was quite a distance away and on a narrow tree, so it was more challenging than he thought. He second-guessed himself for a brief, fleeting moment, then discarded the random thought as gibberish. He would nail that target.

He released the pointed arrow. It whizzed through the air, flying forcefully towards the target.

They both held their breath for that split second.

The arrow slammed into the orange cloth, sending shreds of orange into the air.

"You did it!" Nath exclaimed.

Mike beamed and ran to the target as Nath snatched their bags and followed. Mike jumped over the fallen logs and sailed through the forest. When he reached the target, he ceremoniously pointed at the arrow and laughed. "Dead on, Afi!" he shouted, as Nath ran to catch up.

"You have some great marksman skills, son," Nath congratulated from the bushes. He ran lightly, catching up moments later and hugged his grandson. "Good shot, Mike."

"Fifty yards, Afi!" Mike hollered proudly.

"Impressive," Nath replied. "Now keep honing those skills. Increase your range to 70 yards with the arrow and even more with the rifles. The more you challenge yourself, the better you will get."

"I will!" Mike shouted excitedly.

Nath patted him on the back. "We need to go soon. Your momma will be upset that we've been gone for so long again."

"Ok," Mike said, packing up the bow and slipping the arrows into his back pouch. He lifted the bag and followed Nath out of the forest. "Afi?"

"What?" Nath replied.

"When are we going hunting again?" Mike asked. "With a rifle, I mean. I think I'm ready to shoot a deer on my own now."

"It's your birthday soon," Nath said. "We will go out after your birthday."

"My birthday isn't for another two weeks," Mike argued.

"Keep practicing your aim with the arrows," Nath countered. "Your birthday will be here soon enough."

"The boy is a really good shot, Bella," Nath said. They had been arguing all afternoon about Mike's birthday gift.

"He hunts with you all the time," Annabella said. "He barely does anything else."

"He goes fishing with you sometimes," Nath pointed out.

"True," Bella replied. "We did go ice-fishing just last week."

"I heard you pulled in twenty fish!" Nath exclaimed.

Bella smiled proudly. "Yes, we even caught some pickerel!" She bent over the sink and rinsed the potatoes and carrots they had brought up from the cellar earlier. "It was a nice break from all the children."

As if on cue, Jon and Vlad came running into the kitchen at full speed.

"Hey!" Bella hollered. "Watch out, you two!"

Both boys had sticks and were pretending to be swordsmen. They screeched and laughed at each other, obviously to the adults around them. Jon leaned forward for the kill, and Vlad unexpectedly jumped out of the way, crashing into a table. The teapot teetered, and Nath jumped up, grabbing it quickly.

"Enough!" Bella shouted, sending the boys to their room. Her finger pointed angrily, and they obediently scurried to their bedroom. She waved her hands in the direction of their fleeing forms. "These boys will be the death of me, Pabbi!"

Nathan chuckled, "You're a wonderful mother, Bella. They'll grow up soon enough, and you'll be wondering where the time went."

"You are probably right," Annabella replied. "Look at Mike. He's already turning sixteen!"

Nathan nodded in agreement. "He's a strong-willed teen," Nath said. "Just like you were."

"He spends more time with you then he does over here," Bella said indignantly. "But I know that you've always had a special bond with Mikey, and I'm grateful for that."

"You can't call him that anymore," Nath pointed out.

Bella giggled. "Oh, You mean Mikey?" she said. "Yes, you're right. He corrected me the other day too." She threw the potatoes in a pot of boiling water and pulled a freshly caught fish onto the counter, cutting it into fillets. "Are you staying for dinner?"

"I would love to," Nath replied. "But I can't. I'm going into the city to pick up Mike's birthday gift."

"That's an extravagant present, Pabbi," Annabella said. "Isn't there anything else you could get him?"

"It's something he really wants, Bella."

"I know," Bella replied. "I wish he would take up another hobby other than hunting all the time."

"He's a perfect shot," Nath stated. "He's better than me. Even with these old guns, the bows and arrows, too. He is talented at this. I know it's not what you'd wish for him to be talented at, but it is what it is." Nath stood and hugged his daughter, kissing her on the cheek.

"Ok," she said. "Meet us back here tomorrow night for his birthday party. I am making a cake."

CHAPTER 13

Mike adjusted his hunting cap as he crouched in the bush, stalking the rabbit. He stayed completely still, waiting for his opportunity. There was a slight breeze, and it lifted his longish hair from his ears. The rabbit sensed something, his furry head turning ever so slightly, his eyes looking back, assessing the threat.

Mike slowed his breathing, trying to blend with his environment. He didn't dare move; the bow was already stationary in his hands, aimed and ready to fire. He flinched involuntarily; the rabbit suddenly realized the danger.

The animal shot out of the bushes in a full sprint just as Mike's arrow whistled through the air, connecting through the chest of the small animal, spurting blood and stopping the rabbit dead in his tracks.

Mike smiled and straightened. Perfect shot! He ran over to the rabbit, pulled the arrow out, sliced the body open, gutting it and then slung the gamey dinner into his sack with the rest. Momma would be happy to have a large rabbit dinner, he thought.

The bushes snapped in the distance; Mike froze. He listened intently. It was not a deer. It wasn't a bear either; those bruins tended to crash slowly through the bush. He peered through the trees, but it was too far away. The steps moved intently, one after another. It was human, he thought, immediately letting his guard down.

"Mike!" Nath shouted from a far distance.

"Afi!" Mike hollered back.

"Your momma wants you at the house," Nath hollered, cupping his hands around his mouth, propelling his voice to carry better. "Come, you've been out in the bush all day."

"Okay," Mike shouted back. "I'm coming. I caught three rabbits for dinner tonight!" Mike leapt through the bushes towards where he estimated his grandad's voice was standing. The sun was bright this afternoon, shining into the forest, making it difficult to see because of the intense glare. Mike continued to run nimbly through the woods, his playground, his peaceful place.

He could smell and hear his grandad before he could see him. His estimates were right. Nath stood twenty feet to his right by the widened horse road.

"It's your birthday, Mike," Nath said, holding his arms out to Mike as he approached. "We have a big surprise planned for you."

"I know," Mike replied. "That's why I wanted to get enough rabbits for dinner tonight."

Nath slapped him gently on the back. "Three rabbits?" he said. "That's really good. I could only manage one of those. They are too quick and wary for me usually."

"They never knew what hit them," Mike said, smiling proudly, his hands splattered with blood up to his elbows. His sack was streaked with blood, and it dripped down his back. Mud smeared his face, and his hair had a few small twigs entangled in the longish blonde ends.

"You're a mess, boy," Nath stated, patting him on the shoulder. Mike was as tall as he was now. The boy was growing into a man. "You need to clean up. You have blood all over you."

"Ah, it's alright," Mike said, clearly not troubled that he was a dirty mess.

"No, it's not alright," Nath said. "It's your sixteenth birthday. You need to clean up. Rinse off and wash up at my place. Let's go."

Mike bounded through the forest, but Nath kept up well, always staying within a few feet. He was getting older in age numbers but not physically. His shoulders were amazingly strong, even bigger than when he was in his twenties. His hair was slightly longer but well kept. Nath still combed it and thought it suited him quite well, framing his face handsomely. His legs were muscular now as well, and he kept pace with the young boy amazingly well.

Mike leapt over a log, and Nath followed.

"Pabbi!" Mike shouted excitedly, looking back. "I'm sixteen today!" He laughed, spiritedly, as they raced through the forest.

"That's right, my boy," Nath said, gleefully, as they neared the old horse road connecting to the town of Gimli, the same road that he had walked many times when he lived out at Willow Point in the early settlement year of 1875. The leaves had overgrown most of the paths, and the branches snagged his clothes, tearing them here and there. The past seemed so long ago but yet so close to his heart still. Wounds ran deep, he thought. He would always feel the pain in these woods. They existed within him and through him. The scars of his past would forever be here. He could not erase them. He just needed to try to live with them.

"We're almost home!" Mike shouted as their footsteps touched the sand, and the landscape turned into beachside. He didn't hesitate to call his grandad's place home because to him, it was. He spent more time with his grandad than he did with anyone else. He had his own room at Afi's, his own private space.

Nath shouted at his grandson as he flung the front door open. "Mike! Hand me your pack and the rabbits. I don't want that bloody mess in the house. I will hold them while you clean up." Nath grabbed the sack, while Mike scurried inside. "Hurry up," he shouted after Mike's retreating form.

He heard the bathroom door slam. Nath turned away, looking over the chilly horizon and sat down on the step with the bloody sack in his hands. He opened the bag and inspected the rabbits. They were all cleanly shot with arrows, all through the heart. Amazing, Nath thought. The boy was better than just a good shot. He was becoming an expert.

Nath pulled the rabbits out and placed them in another sack, so Mike's clothes didn't get all bloody again. Nath wrung out the blood from the old sack and placed it in the shed to be washed in the future. Mike would definitely need those sacks again. He was the one that brought most of the meat home now.

"Finally!" Annabella exclaimed breathlessly. "I was wondering if you were even going to show up for your own birthday party!"

Ivan laughed heartily, "Our young man made it!" He wrapped his arm around his wife's waist lovingly and kissed her on the cheek. "Your momma made a cake for you! You'll love it!"

Mike broke into a huge smile that encompassed both sides of his cheeks. "Look what I brought for my dinner!" He held up the bag as everyone looked at the contents.

"How many rabbits are in there?" Annabella asked.

"Three!" Mike exclaimed proudly.

"You said you were going to get some rabbits for dinner," Annabella said, happily. "But I was only expecting one! Three is excellent, Mike." She grabbed the bag and took the game to the kitchen washbasin.

A knock sounded at the door, and everyone swung around to see who it was.

"Come in," Ivan shouted.

Viktor walked in with his wife and several grandchildren, along with a taller young man, the same age as Annabella.

Annabella shouted with glee and rushed towards the door. "Joshua!" She crashed into him happily and hugged her old childhood friend fiercely. "You made it!"

Joshua had aged more so than Annabella did. His hair was thinning already, but he had the same robust look as his father Aron. He hugged her back, fiercely. "You haven't changed one bit," Josh said. "Still a ball of energy."

"Oh," Annabella replied. "I spend a lot of that energy raising all my kids!" She paused, cheerfully. "It's so good to see you again. We are cooking rabbits for dinner tonight. Mike brought home three!"

"Good hunter, that boy of yours," Joshua responded appraisingly.

Mike smiled proudly. Josh slapped him on the shoulder. "Happy birthday, kid!"

"I'm not a kid!" Mike said, laughing. "I'm almost an adult soon."

"True, true," Viktor said, smiling. "All of us old folk here can't believe you're sixteen now! It seems like we keep getting older, and your age progresses too quickly. Our brains can't keep up!"

Everyone broke out in raucous laughter.

"Is everyone here?" Nathan asked.

"Yes, I think so," Joshua said. "My dad and Kristjan are in Riverton today; they couldn't make it. My wife is sick at home today, but my kids came. They are still outside. Wait, I'll get them. Darn teens, I thought they were right behind me!" Joshua turned back and left the house, shouting names into the fields. "Daniel! Isa!" Footsteps crashed through the bushes as they came out of hiding. "What are you doing?"

"Hide and seek!" Isa, a cute blonde girl of twelve years old, replied.

"She was too hard to find again, Dad!" Daniel shouted indignantly. His blonde hair was almost identical to his sister Isa's, but he was much taller. The boy was fifteen years old and over six feet tall already. Daniel ran into the house, straight towards Mike.

Mike's eyes lit up, seeing his close cousin and friend. "Danny! You made it!"

"Of course!" Daniel said excitedly, slapping him on the shoulder. "I wouldn't miss your birthday, Mike."

Nath hugged his grandson's shoulder affectionately and stood proudly beside Mike. "Okay," he shouted into the room. "If everyone is here now, I have a surprise I'd like to give Mike now."

"A surprise?" Mike asked, his brow creasing bewilderedly. "What kind of surprise?"

"A gift," Nath stated.

Everyone in the room fell silent.

"A special gift," Nath said dramatically. "Wait. I'll go get it."

Mike was utterly perplexed. He looked at the others in the room, and it seemed that everyone else was just as confused. What kind of gift would be so large that you would have to leave the house to get? "What did you get me?" he asked, laughing. "A horse?"

Everyone laughed excitedly. Mike noticed his momma was silent, though. He wondered if she knew what the gift was. She smiled and nodded at Nathan as he left the house.

"Afi?" Mike said questioningly. "What could possibly be so big that you have to go outside to get it?"

"One minute," Nath shouted from outside. "I am covering it up with a blanket so you can unwrap it."

Annabella beamed happily.

"Momma!" Mike shouted. "You know!"

Bella laughed. "Yes. Don't worry! You'll love it," she said, her eyes gleaming.

Nathan stomped into the house with a long object in his hands and a thick striped Hudson Bay blanket covering over the top. He walked up to his grandson and held it out to him. "Lift up the blanket, Mike."

Mike had absolutely no idea what this was, so he ceremoniously threw the blanket up and over the long object.

He gasped.

The brown oiled wood on the long barrel shone back at him. The rifle was approximately thirty inches long. It was the longest rifle he had ever seen. The barrel had wood almost all the way to the end, but the last six inches was black round steel muzzle. At the end was what looked like a screw, but it wasn't. It was the front sight, a small iron squarish plate with a triangular screw-like projection. Mike ran his hand lovingly across the smooth brown wood surface. Along the top, the barrel was brand new and had a straight-pull bolt action chamber, and a rectangular iron piece that was flipped down. Mike immediately knew what it was. It was the rear sight, which he would position his aim.

He looked at his grandad.

Nath nodded.

Mike picked the rifle up, flicking the rectangular sight up and braced it on his shoulder, looking through the two sights. He aimed it through the kitchen window and into the wilderness. It aimed wonderfully, almost too accurate.

Mike's heart beat loudly in his chest.

The Ross M-10 rifle was actually in his arms!

It must have cost Afi a fortune. A tear welled up in his eye, and he swallowed it down. He was not going to cry like a baby on his sixteenth birthday. Love for his grandpa overwhelmed his emotions.

Mike slowly put the rifle down on the sofa.

The room was silent except for a few gasps.

Mike hugged his grandad tightly. "Thank you, Afi!"

Nathan hugged the boy back, feeling the raw emotion emanating from his grandson.

"I can't believe you bought me a Ross M-10," Mike said quietly.

"You know that it's the Ross?" Nathan asked incredulously.

"Oh, yes," Mike said, nodding. "It's the hunting version of the military issue Ross MKII." He let his grandad go and looked him in the eyes. "I have been dreaming of this rifle, Afi. Thank you so much. You have no idea how much this means to me."

Nathan smiled, "I do, son. I do." He rummaged in another sack and pulled out a small box. "Here's the bullets too."

Mike held his hands out and felt the weight of the bullets in his palms. He sensed that something significant was happening today as if his path was shifting in a unique direction for the rest of his life.

"You're the best grandad, ever," Mike said, choking back the tears.

The family continued with the celebrations all night until everyone was so exhausted that they just fell asleep wherever there was a spot. Some people slept on the sofa, some on the floor, but Mike was wide awake in his old bed, staring at the ceiling in the dark with his rifle by his side.

He would learn everything about his gun. He would learn how to clean it, oil it, aim it, and he'd take care of it for the rest of his life, maybe even hand it down to his children someday. He felt so grateful to have such a thoughtful gift. It meant so much to him, and his grandad knew it.

He would make his grandad proud one day, he thought.

Chapter 14

His hair stuck to his wet face as he lifted his head up. He had fallen asleep again. He felt surrounded by the darkness again, both a comfort and a danger. One day, a wolf might decide to pick a fight with him. He should be more prepared.

The frogs croaked nearby as he shook himself awake. His dreams were vivid and clear; the pain would never end. It would always stay rooted inside him. There was no escape; there were no reprieves. It was always there, like some dull knife in a wound, better to leave it there than disrupt the blood flow.

His back ached from sleeping on the floor. His dirty hand fluttered to his backside as he groaned in pain.

He looked up at the ceiling, listening to the forest swaying outside the flimsy walls, the wind howling through the trees. The waves were angry today, crashing loudly onto the shore. Nature was all around him, begging him to find peace.

He felt lost, like he was on a quest, searching for elusive answers but, somehow, they were always out of his reach. The only reply in the silence of his mind was his own thoughts, staring right back into his soul.

The rain-soaked branches hung down towards him; he did not dare flinch. It had been raining for weeks. June was the rainiest month out here. The heavens had opened up, releasing a torrent of tears, filling valleys and raising the level of the lake considerably. This was the first semi-dry day since the beginning of June. He stepped quietly in the bush, a slow calculating stride; he knew where he was going.

The group of does were in the clearing spaced well apart from each other, all enjoying the rays of the warm sunshine after the gloomy several weeks of rain. There were four does and three fawns, the youngest ones staying close to their mommas. The last doe was an older deer, you could tell by her stance. She also didn't have a fawn, likely the grandparent of the younger fawns. Mike watched as the older doe stepped into the bush away from the others. She was still healthy and robust, but the area had been over hunting male deer lately; a change was necessary.

Mike set up in the bush, slowly and methodically. He pulled his Ross rifle out of the bag, flipped the sight and loaded it with bullets. The wood barrel was still smooth and oiled nicely. He had taken meticulous care of his weapon in the past year. He had just disassembled it and cleaned it last night.

He glanced at the herd while he found a good vantage point in the bush. He pulled the weapon up to his shoulder and settled the weight of his shoulder into the barrel snugly. He looked down the sights. The doe was foraging away from the group. He noticed a recent injury on her leg, possibly a barbed-wire fence. Farmers had just recently started erecting the pointy wire fences to keep their livestock in, although sometimes deer wandered inside the properties.

Mike rested his elbows on a pile of deadwood, staring down the barrel of his rifle. He moved with the doe, waiting for her to move to an ideal position. The wind breezed lightly through the trees. It was a beautiful early summer morning. He could smell the wet grass; it filled his nostrils with a wonderful homey scent. He was happy and content here; it was home. But he started feeling a yearning for something else, a larger purpose, a bigger destiny. He wasn't sure what it was, but it pulled stronger than anything else in his life. Mike wasn't overly concerned about girls as much as his friends were. There was something out there for him. What or whom it was, he didn't know, but it tugged at him, pulling him into the unknown.

The doe turned her head lazily and looked directly at him, unseeingly. Mike froze, not moving an inch. The doe stared in his direction for several minutes then turned away, continuing to munch on the grass. Mike relaxed and let out a deep breath.

He narrowed his eye into the sights and crouched his shoulders into the weapon. The doe turned sideways for a perfect shot.

Mike breathed slowly and held his finger on the trigger for a multi-second. Then he pulled the trigger, pushing back into the recoil.

The bullet cracked into the air, slicing the branches along its path. The bullet slammed into the doe's heart. She fell instantly.

The other deer looked up in alarm and leapt away in a frightened frenzy.

Mike straightened and ran to his kill. He crashed through the grassland, bushes and trees until finally reaching the fallen deer. He had shot at over 200 yards. He looked at the bullet entry; it was a direct hit to the heart. The doe had died instantly.

The Ross rifle had a highly effective sight, making the aim with great distances easy. Mike laid his rifle in the bag, rolled up his sleeves and pulled out his hunting knife. He knelt by the corpse and went to work, field dressing the animal right there in the grassland. The blood covered his hands and elbows within minutes. He continued for several minutes until the job was completed. The bloody mess was all over his clothes and the grass. He lifted the carcass onto a burlap bag and slid his catch for the day towards the footpath. He would tie it to the horse as he rode back into town. But first, he needed to clean up. Blood had spattered on his face and his teenage beard. It was all over his shirt as well.

Mike pulled his kill towards the lake and stopped short of the sand, listening in the air for any predators or other humans. There were none.

He stripped his shirt off and held it as he removed his pants, socks, underwear, everything. The day was progressively becoming hotter. He felt the beads of sweat forming on the back of his neck. The cool water would be a welcoming relief. He stepped naked to the shore.

Mike rushed into the water and dived in. The water parted to allow him entry. The waves splashed beside him in currents as his growing masculine body spliced through the calm surface. He swam out until he was chest-deep.

Mike washed his body, rubbing the blood off and rinsing his hair. Twigs nestled in his hair, and he frustratingly gave up trying to get them out. He scrubbed his hair, his chest, his face and every body part. It felt incredibly satisfying to cleanse his body. It didn't happen too often; he washed only twice per week.

Mike straightened and gazed towards the middle of the lake; the sun shimmered back at him, glinting on top of the calm waters. He inhaled the fresh Lake Winnipeg air, smiled and then dove into the lake strongly with his shoulders, sending the water swooshing around him as he swam in the murky lake. He moved like a fish underneath the surface for several moments and then bobbed up with the slightest splash, continuing swimming at great speed out into the open waters. Mike felt so free and wild in the open seas. It was exhilarating and exciting; he loved the rush of testing his strength and agility. Similar to hunting, it gave him a sense of physical mastery.

His long slim body slipped through the water easily, the lake parting for him as if welcoming him back. Mike decided that he would swim more often, at least once a week, and he would swim nude more often too. It was harder to swim with clothes on, he thought, but it did have the added effect of cleansing his garments at the same time. He would rinse his clothes in the water after his swim, he mused.

The water was cool but calm. Mike dove again and resurfaced multiple times, feeling the lake caressing his skin. He rejoiced in his newfound freedom of his country, his kill and his growing skill. This wasn't the first time he had shot a direct hit at 200 yards. The accuracy of the Ross rifle was amazing. Combined with the years of aiming practice, Mike was proud of his newly sharpened skills of marksmanship. He was always a good shot, he knew, but with the Ross rifle, he was uncannily accurate.

He swam up to the surface and floated briefly with his toes to the sky. He looked up to the clouds overhead. Something extraordinary was waiting for him. He was not sure what, but he could feel it. It filled him with a longing for purpose and passion.

Mike shook his head, the water spraying everywhere. He walked calmly out of the lake, his naked body dripping wet. He pulled his shirt to the water and rinsed it fully, wringing it out.

He unrolled the shirt and pulled it back on, stretching it over his developing muscles. His biceps were getting larger, and his chest was broadening. Things were not as heavy to carry anymore, and it felt good to rely on his physical strength.

He grabbed his underwear and pants, sitting on an abandoned beach rock, and pulled the clothing over his long legs and large feet. He pulled on his boots and relaxed back onto his hands, breathing in the crisp morning air. Mike smiled.

This was his land, his world, now. Wherever life led him from here on, he did not know, but what he did know was that it would be of his own choosing.

He felt this with a certainty like none other. He might look like his grandad, act like his grandad, even have some of the same nuances, but something tugged in his mind. He felt it like a fire in his belly, growing with every breath, every exhale.

Afi may have taught him everything he knows, but Mike Kozak was going to be his own man; he was going to blaze his own path, without fear and without hesitation.

PART THREE

1914-1917

CHAPTER 15

It was late June, and Gavrilo Princip was in Sarajevo. He had a mission to complete. Soon everyone in the world would know his name. He was a patriotic assassin planning an attack along with a group of six other like-minded Serbs and Bosnians. Politics enraged Gavrilo. He felt so inflamed about it that his anger would sometimes get the better of him. His life was meaningless without his rage. Tuberculosis had begun in his body; it would eventually kill him anyways. This was his purpose; this was his path in life. He was determined to make it count.

But the next day went horribly wrong. One of his associates threw a bomb at the imperial motorcade only to have it bounce off the car and explode seconds later under the wrong vehicle! Gavrilo was dismayed. After all the training they had gone through with the terrorist group, The Black Hand, years and years of grooming himself to this day ending with a day of utter failure. They had been instructed to commit suicide after their deeds were done, and Gavrilo was committed to doing just that, but if only he could find the opportunity.

He slumped in a café, wondering what to do from here. Their plan was falling apart. The motorcade had left unscathed, and the Archduke had delivered his speech, even angrily noting that he came to visit and was attacked with bombs, making a mockery of their efforts.

Gavrilo felt hopeless and hungry. He ordered a sandwich and brought it to the small table just as several motorcars rumbled down the street.

He gazed out at the motorcade and couldn't believe his eyes.

Archduke Franz Ferdinand and his wife, Sophie, Duchess of Hohenberg, were in the motorcade barely ten feet away. He abandoned his sandwich and walked swiftly out of the café, directly to the motorcade. The adrenaline pumped through his veins. This was his chance to be a hero. He took three more strides until he was miraculously only five feet away! Pulling his firearm from his coat, Gavrilo aimed directly at the imperial couple. Anger bubbled in his throat as his pistol fired. He felt the recoil as two shots rang in the air. Nobody even knew what was happening; he had stunned them all. One bullet slammed through the air, entering the Archduke's neck, sending blood spraying as onlookers gasped. The other bullet blasted into the Duchess's abdomen, sending her flying back, grasping her bloody stomach. He glanced around; everyone was still stunned.

He had done it! He had succeeded where everyone else had failed.

He quickly turned the pistol to his own head. Suicide would be quick and painless. He looked to the sky and fingered the trigger to his head.

He felt a heavy arm on his wrist. Then a commotion engulfed him. A man wrestled with his arm. Gavrilo didn't understand what was going on. The man was strong, grabbing Gavrilo's wrist and wrestling him to the ground. Several policemen piled on top of him, pinning him down.

Gavrilo wasn't allowed to finish his suicide, but he had succeeded in killing the imperial heirs; for his ideals and the future of his people.

It was the 28th day of June 1914. Gavrilo was immediately arrested and imprisoned for the murder of Archduke Franz Ferdinand and his wife, Sophie.

Several weeks later, on July 23, Austria-Hungary issued an impossible ultimatum to Serbia.

The Serbian government must accept a list of impossible demands from the Austro-Hungarians. Baron Giesl von Gieslingen, the ambassador for Austria-Hungary to Serbia, held the note in his hand. No nation would ever submit to these demands, he thought. His hand shook slightly as he delivered the ultimatum to the Serbian government.

Serbia would never eradicate the Black Hand nor destroy anti-Austrian propaganda. And that was just the start of the demands. It was a stern ultimatum like none he had ever seen before.

Gieslingen had packed his bags this morning to leave the embassy, finalizing his plans to depart. He knew Serbians; he knew their passions. Serbia would never submit to these terms.

The Serbian government had 48 hours to respond to the ultimatum.

Two days later, Serbia refused to submit. Gieslingen was right.

On July 28, 1914, Austria-Hungary declared war on Serbia, starting a catastrophic world war.

The Great War had begun.

In the late fall of 1915, Canada, being part of the British Empire, had been recruiting soldiers country-wide, including the 108th Overseas Battalion in the Selkirk area. News had spread quickly across the Interlake region that the 108th Battalion was enlisting men from the areas of Gimli and northern Hecla.

Annabella and Ivan had prospered over the last few years as farmers and fishermen, raising their children to help with the family farm as most landowners did and bringing home fish weekly.

Mike chose to live mostly at his grandad's home, sometimes drifting back and forth from Nath's place to Annabella's. He helped with the fishery every day, and they still hunted together often.

Nathanael loved all of his grandchildren immensely. He took care of the other four grandchildren, too, allowing them to stay overnight periodically and shatter his quiet life with chaos. It was a small inconvenience in exchange for a wonderfully large extended family; he felt so grateful to Annabella and her five children. His heart felt pasted together, piece by little piece, with family love. Annabella would always be his baby girl, and Mike would always be his baby grandson. Every day seemed, outwardly, to grow better and more bearable. There were still days when his mind drifted off, imagining what was and what could have been.

Nathan had long ago accepted Anwa's death, but his heart still felt damaged, as if no amount of repairs could restore it to what it was before. The love from his family kept it intact and beating strong every day, and he was extremely grateful for that.

He thanked the stars for his family every night. He couldn't imagine his life without his daughter and grandchildren.

Nathan lifted the pen and dipped it in ink, musing upon his life so far. He didn't need anything else, he told himself. This was everything he needed. He tried not to think about Anwa too much, but some days the pain gripped him and refused to let go. Those were the days when he realized how broken he really felt inside. Every woman he met just didn't understand him, so he just gave up on courting females. Most men didn't understand his pain either, so he locked the door to his emotions. Occasionally, the dark thoughts took over his entire being; those were the moments that he escaped, seeking solace with the memories. Nathan absentmindedly slipped his hand over the blue bracelet on his right wrist. His fingers lightly smoothed the native beads as his mind wandered.

The front door opened. He looked up as Mike walked in. The boy had grown up into a formidable man, Nath mused. Mike was over six feet tall with broad shoulders and a muscular chest; his arms and legs were thin but strong. He was proud of the man Mike had become. He was a warm, gentle soul but with an eerie hunter instinct like no one else. He was a good man that most people looked up to and rarely challenged. The entire town knew he could shoot a deer at over 300 yards now. Mike's Ross rifle was still his prize and hung on the wall in his bedroom at Nath's home. Nathan smiled as his grandson walked over.

"Can you grab those stacks of salted fish and bring them in the warehouse, Mike?" Nathan asked while he continued writing in the ledger sheets, filling in the entire day of entries.

"Sure, Afi," Mike said warmly. He left to the front of the warehouse, grabbing stacks of the heavily salted fish and brought them into the back. His grandpa could still probably do all this physical work, Mike thought. The older man was still in incredible shape, nothing even close to what people's perception of what a grandpa should be. After all, 57 was supposed to be old these days. His grandad looked ten years younger; so did his momma. The Olason's had good genes, he mused thoughtfully.

Mike loved his grandad with all his heart and was always available to help. He carried load after load of the salted fish into the warehouse, as Nath continued tallying the entries. Nath had been working non-stop, trying to get everything stored before the winter grew colder. The snow would be falling soon. The days were getting shorter, so they had to work extra hard to get everything stockpiled before it was too cold to be outside anymore. Well, except for the ice fishing. They went out in large groups now, with all their ice fishing equipment and hauled back prize fish, larger than ever seen before.

When Mike stepped out to grab the last few stacks of fish, he noticed a tall, uniformed man walking by.

The man was noticeably muscular and strong. He had markings on his uniform cuffs of a high-ranking officer. He noticed Mike fumbling in an attempt to load all the remaining stacks in his arms. "Here, son," the man said, rushing over. "Let me help you with that." The tall man grabbed the remaining four stacks with ease, leaving Mike with only two.

"Thanks," Mike said. "Follow me; they go into the back of the warehouse this way." Mike led the way, winding past many nets and boating equipment, until they reached the back, stacking them onto the tall columns against the wall. The man followed dutifully behind Mike, chatting quite friendly and amicably.

"Are you one of the local fishermen here?" he asked.

"Oh, yes," Mike answered, laughing. "My grandpa was one of the original founders of the fishing industry here. He owns this warehouse."

"Oh," the man laughed heartily. "So, you have been doing this all your life?"

Mike laughed. "Yes, pretty much," he said. "Fishing is in my blood. I love it here; it is our way of life. But I have to say that sometimes I wonder if I would like to do something else." Mike chuckled as he grabbed the last stack from the man. "Thanks for the help, by the way. What's your name?"

The man straightened and offered a friendly handshake. "My name's George Bradbury," the man said. "And you?"

"Mike Kozak," he replied, shaking George's hand. "I can tell you are in the army. What rank are you?"

"Lieutenant Colonel," George replied.

"How do you like it?" Mike asked.

"I love it," George said, laughing. "It's in my blood; it is my way of life. But I've always wanted to try fishing too."

They both burst into raucous laughter. "Well," Mike said. "I will have to bring you fishing one day. But you will have to show me some of the barracks. I've always had a keen interest in all kinds of machinery and weapons."

"I can do that," George replied.

"What brought you this way, Colonel?" Mike asked curiously.

"I am here with my staff, who are looking to buy fish for my growing Battalion in Selkirk," George replied. "The locals told us it's worth the trip to come to Gimli."

Mike laughed, "Well, you found the right place! How many of these stacks do you want?"

George sized up the younger tall gentleman. "I can buy them from you?"

"You sure can," Mike smiled.

"Okay," George said. "We will need roughly enough to feed 800 soldiers for a month. Although, we only need enough to give them a break from the standard army fare so we can use an estimate of two meals per week for one month."

Mike's face lit up in a huge smile, his blue eyes glinting intelligently. "Ok," he said. "I believe fifty of these stacks would be a good start. Do you have a horse and carriage?"

"Yes," George replied. "We just corralled them down the street. I can go fetch them and the Quartermaster now."

"I will go with you," Mike said. "We are just closing up for the day. You will be the last customer." Mike waved at his grandpa. "Afi, I'm just going with this friendly fellow George to get the horses and carriage to load him up with fifty stacks of salted fish. I will be right back."

Nathan waved him off, smiling at their good luck. Fifty stacks were a lot of fish to sell.

Mike smiled and continued out the door. He turned to George as they walked down the street. "So, tell me, do you have enough vegetables and grains as well? My father is a local farmer at the edge of town. I could help you with that as well."

"That would be great, actually, yes, please take me there," George replied, shaking Mike's hand. "I'm glad we met."

"Yeah," Mike said. "So am I."

Nathanael wasn't keen on his grandson making such close friends of the Lieutenant Colonel. For the past few weeks, Mike had travelled back and forth to Selkirk, bringing food and supplies to the soldiers. The money was great for both families, but it was worrying Nathan. He knew Mike had an adventurous spirit and a fascination with weapons. He remembered when he had taught his young grandson how to dismantle the guns, clean them, oil them and reassemble them. Mike's eyes had gleamed with interest. It was a complicated process but one that any good hunter needed to know.

Mike had his M-10 rifle hanging above his own bed, although, in the last few years, he had also collected several other rifles and an impressive array of bows, arrows and hunting knives. He stored everything in a locked gun closet hanging on the wall at Nathan's house. Nath had always encouraged his grandson's interests, but now he thought maybe it was a mistake. Mike had taken a sort of obsession with guns, collecting them and taking great care of them. It was wonderful in many ways, to have such a formidable passion, and Nath continued to encourage it; although something tugged inside Nath's heart. He didn't want his grandson to be interested in joining the war. Just the thought put a cold fear in the pit of his stomach. He didn't even want to consider the possibility.

Nathan mused over this as he gazed through the large front window. The lake churned waves onto the beach as the wind picked up. He still loved his Gimli. He had worked so terribly hard to build a stable life here.

After New Iceland had become part of Manitoba, the railroad completion in 1906 changed everything. Gimli was now open to travel; it was no longer an isolated northern community. The railroad provided easy transportation. The farming and fishing industries were still going strong, but now a massive influx of tourists began holidaying in the area. Gimli developed into an unusual tourist town, attracting many people to its sandy shores and hot summers. It seemed that the rest of the country had discovered what Nathan knew all along; that Gimli was indeed something special.

The front door opened abruptly, snapping Nathan out of his thoughts. Nath turned his head to see who it was.

Mike closed the door forcefully, obviously exuberant about something. "Hi, Afi," Mike immediately said. "Guess what?"

"What is it, my boy?" Nath asked, smiling.

"I met a woman today," Mike said, grinning from ear to ear. "Her family is also Icelandic and Ukrainian. Her grandparents left Gimli for Winnipeg during the smallpox epidemic."

"Yes," Nath said. "I did see large groups of Icelanders leaving before the quarantine and afterwards. It was almost like a ghost town here for many, many years afterwards. The Olason's even discussed leaving, but we stuck it out. My Pabbi died early from a weakened immune system when your momma was only 10 years old. He struggled with his health for many years after contracting smallpox. He was never really the same after that dreadful disease. It is a shame that you never got a chance to meet your great-grandpa before he passed away. But at least you had time with your great grandmas Marg and Bea. Life is short, Mike. All of us eventually die, and so did they. But at least you had the opportunity to spend some years with Anwa's momma. She was a good gentle soul. Anwa got her kind soul from her momma. Bea was lucky; she was one of the very few Swampy Cree natives that didn't perish."

Mike walked into the kitchen and hugged his grandpa. He loved the old stories of the past. It made him feel so lucky to be alive, right here, strong and breathing, with all this land, forest, fishing and everything in-between. His relatives had brought such wealth to this land. "I am so grateful," Mike said. "If it weren't for what you and your family had done, we wouldn't be here right now."

"That's right, Mike," Nathan agreed. "But enough about that! What about this girl you've met? What's her name? How old is she?"

"She's 26, Afi," Mike said, excitedly. A curious smile crept onto his face, and he felt his cheeks get warm. "Her family just moved here a few weeks ago, taking over Yuri's old farm. After Yuri died, his sons had struggled to keep it going. Aron and Julia's family had already moved out, too busy with their own farm, so it was eventually passed down to her family as an inheritance. It is just her mom, herself and her younger brothers that relocated here, trying to salvage the farm." Mike was beaming, his eyes had lit up, and he was talking animatedly. "Her name is Vira, Afi. She has the most beautiful blonde hair. I just crossed paths with her on the way here. She's really nice!" Mike beamed.

Nathan smiled. "Well, then you must talk to her more," he said. "Find out more about her."

"I will," Mike said, the tone suddenly changing in his voice. "I just don't want to get her too excited, though. I'm not sure if my plans include a woman in my life right now."

Nathan looked up, alarmed. "Why would you say that?"

Mike's eyes softened as he sat down close to Nath on the sofa. "I have to tell you something. I have been trying to put everything in words so you'll understand."

Nath felt his heart drop into his stomach. He took a deep breath. "You can tell me anything," he said, hoping that it wasn't what he thought it was.

"I've been thinking of joining the 108th Battalion," Mike said softly. His eyes closed briefly. "I'm sorry, Afi. I know you never wanted to hear this. I don't know what to say, but I feel pretty strongly about it. The Great War needs men like me."

Nathan's heart banged loudly in his ears. His pulse quickened, and his head started to hurt. He lifted a few long fingers to his temples and rubbed them gently.

"I'm sorry to disappoint you," Mike said.

Nathan felt a weariness descend upon him. He wasn't even sure how to respond, what to say to his beloved grandson. Nath was hoping he would become a fisherman and take over his business. He was deathly afraid of losing his grandson to war, and now the worst was happening. Talks of mandatory conscription would have taken him anyway, but it still wasn't law yet. They still had a few more years. He wanted his grandson safe and for him to continue the legacy of the Icelandic fishermen. He was disappointed, sad and fearful. His guts twisted up in all sorts of knots. He knew that, as a grandparent, he had to let Mike live his life the way he wanted to, to follow his passions and evolve into his own identity. He felt defeated and weak. It wasn't something he wanted, but he knew he had to support his grandson's decisions. His emotions, his feelings weren't what mattered right now; it was what Mike wanted. It was his life. It was his path, his purpose.

Nath rubbed his eyes, leaning forward, his head in his hands. "Mike, I want you to be happy. I hope you know that," Nath said quietly. "If it means that you will find your passion in the army, then it is your path. I don't like it. I don't want to lose you, Mike. I've lost too many loved ones, too much tragedy and too much anguish for one person to have to deal with in a lifetime. If I had my choice, I would want you to stay in Gimli, take over my fishing business and marry a nice girl here in town, like Vira." Nath abruptly looked up at Mike. "But the whole point is, it's not my choice, it's yours."

Mike sat silently, letting his grandpa's words sink in. He stood and walked to the window, pulling the curtains to the side. The sun was setting, looking out onto the lake, the reflection mirrored a beautiful array of purple and pink swirls onto the eastern sky. It was always a breathtakingly beautiful sunset, even looking towards the east; there was something about it. Gimli was a perfect little paradise. He loved his home. He knew that he would return here after the war. He was tough and determined. But there was always the possibility that he could die or be injured, of course. Part of him wanted to stay, find a woman and fish just like Afi said, but then another part of him wanted to improve his skills, see the world, the ocean, Europe and the places where his ancestors originated. He was an excellent marksman. He knew how to hunt; he knew weapons exceptionally well. Better than anyone in the area. He would be an immediate asset to the Great War. What good was it if he stayed here and cowered anyways? Any woman that he built a life with may not have a good life anymore if they didn't win the war.

"I will return from the war, Afi," Mike said finally, staring at the sunset. "This is my home. I love it here." He turned and faced Nathan. "I will take over your fishing business. I will marry a girl. I will do all of that. But first, I must fight for our freedom. You know as well as anybody how accurate my aim has become. You taught me, Afi."

"I know," Nathan nodded solemnly. "Grandma Anwa taught me bows, arrows and hunting knives. I taught you guns and so much more. I remember the first time I took you out hunting. Your eyes were round and open, absorbing everything. It's in your blood, Mike. I knew it then, and I know it now."

"Yes," Mike said, smiling. "I remember." He walked up to Nathan and put both his hands on his grandpa's shoulders, bending slightly to meet his eyes. Nathan looked up as Mike stared into his identical blue eyes, their identical faces, one young and one much older. "I am tough as nails, Afi," Mike said. "You made me that way. I will be back. And I will do everything I said I would do. Just like you did when you landed at Willow Point. I have the Olason determination; it's in my blood. I won't disappoint you, Afi. I will return."

Mike saw Vira the next day. She was walking along the beach by herself. Her blonde hair shimmered in the sunlight, making her look like an angel. Mike smiled at the thought.

"Hey, Vira," he called, running along the sand towards her.

"Mike!" she said, stopping in the sand, turning her head around, waving for him to catch up. "How have you been?" she shouted across the beach. "I noticed that you've been quite busy lately. Are you making another trip to Selkirk?"

"Yes, I will be going to Selkirk again to deliver another order for the Battalion towards the end of the week," Mike said breathlessly, as he reached her, slowing to a walk. "The fishing is hectic this year. The fish stocks are high, and the demand is even higher. It is a good profitable situation for everyone." He walked closely beside her as they both shuffled along the shoreline. Mike cocked his head to the side and smiled sheepishly. "How have you been, Vira?"

"I've been alright, although I'm somewhat overwhelmed with the farm right now," she said, wearily. "There is so much to do. My mother knows a great deal about farming, but unfortunately, my brothers are young and stubborn. They don't help as much as I thought they would. I suppose it's a big transition for all of us."

"Do you come from a family of farmers?" Mike asked.

"Yes, somewhat," Vira said, the wind blowing her wavy hair over her face. She lifted a hand to swipe the locks behind her ears. She was a tall, gangly woman, only a few inches shorter than Mike. She wore a peasant dress, although it hung on her slim frame. She had a chiselled face, with a strong square jaw and medium length light hair. Mike thought she had a unique prettiness about her, distinct from the other girls in town. She was different. He liked that. "My grandparents were both Icelandic. They settled just outside Winnipeg during the small-pox epidemic. They did some farming, but they weren't overly successful, so they chose to breed livestock instead. My parents were the farmers; my mother's side is Ukrainian and has extensive knowledge of growing wheat and vegetables. When she met my father, they helped my grandparents with the livestock and purchased some land adjacent to them, growing wheat and vegetables. They were very successful; then, they gave birth to me, then my brothers, raising us to work in the fields. Several terrible things happened in succession after that, changing everything."

"May I ask what?"

"Several devastating storms ravaged the land, ruining our crops two years in a row. It was tough recovering. Then the unspeakable happened." She looked down at her shoes. "My daddy died soon after my youngest brother was born. I was sixteen," she answered softly.

"I'm so sorry," Mike said. "How did he die?"

"A farming accident," Vira answered. "After his death, being the eldest, I naturally became the head of the household. My mother was mourning and was having difficulty keeping up with everything. Someone had to get all the work done."

"But you were only sixteen!" Mike exclaimed.

"Yes, I know, although there was no one else," Vira explained. "My mother was very distraught, and my brothers were still quite young."

"I'm sorry, Vira," Mike replied. "Sometimes, bad things happen to good people. I lost my grandma to smallpox before I was even born. I never knew her. My grandad taught me lots of things that he had learnt from her in those early days. It feels like her spirit still lives on within us."

"What was her name?"

"Anwa," Mike replied.

"That's a beautiful name," Vira responded.

"She was a beautiful woman, just like my momma," Mike said.

"Your momma is Bella, right?"

"Yes," Mike answered. "Do you know her?"

"No, but I've seen her in town," Vira said. "She is a very stunning woman."

"So are you," Mike stated simply.

Vira blushed briefly, her cheeks turning a light shade of pink. "Thank you," she said, looking down. "I'm not anywhere as beautiful as your momma, though."

"I think you're very beautiful," Mike said easily.

"Thank you, Mike," she replied bashfully.

Mike glanced over at her. She was blushing and staring intently at her shoes. He didn't want to make her feel uncomfortable. "So how are you dealing with the move up to Gimli?" Mike asked nonchalantly. "I heard your family ended up inheriting Yuri's farm. Are you related to Yuri in any way?"

"Yes," she replied. "Yuri's daughter Sarah is my mother's second cousin. She inherited Yuri's farm, along with the surviving siblings. But Yuri lived to an elderly age, so all his children had been older too. The farm declined rapidly, and the siblings struggled to keep it afloat. Sarah and her husband stayed and helped as much as possible, but she fell quite ill with a painful case of gout and asked if we could take it over six months ago. We saw it as an opportunity for change and agreed. We sold our land near Winnipeg and made the big move to Gimli."

"Are you still the head of the household?" Mike asked, genuinely interested in this woman's history. She fascinated him, and he wanted to know everything he could about her.

"Yes, unfortunately," Vira replied. "My brothers are older and stronger now; they are taking over a lot of the heavy work, so that's a relief, but I still seem to have to organize everything."

"Oh, I see," Mike said, thoughtfully. "Do you enjoy farming?"

"Yes, and no," she said, laughing. "It's the only thing I know. I would like to do something else one day. I love the water here. I love swimming and boating. It's quite beautiful out here." Vira tossed her hair to the side; the wind caught it and blew it strongly across her face. She curled the errant locks behind her ear, her eyes glinting. "What about you? How long have you lived here?"

Mike laughed. "I was born here," he exclaimed, rubbing his young beard. "All I know is fishing and hunting. My parents are farmers, but I chose to spend most of my time with my grandpa Nath; he's Icelandic too."

"Oh," she said, smiling. "What a coincidence! Was your grandmother Icelandic too?"

Mike grinned, "Actually, my grandmother was Cree, so my mother is part Icelandic and part native. My father is Ukrainian."

"Oh, my!" Vira exclaimed. "So, you are Icelandic and Ukrainian like me! With a bit of Cree mixed in for spice."

They both laughed wholeheartedly. Mike laid his hand along her shoulder gently while they talked. "Yes, I do have some spice," he said jokingly. "That is for sure."

Vira chuckled and grabbed his hand, pulling him along the shoreline. Mike followed happily, kicking the sand up with his shoes. They wandered closer to the water, letting the waves wash the seawater almost to their feet. A few times, Vira jumped as the waves threatened to engulf her shoes. Giggling, they finally removed their footwear and socks, immersing their feet into the water. Vira reached down and grabbed a ball full of wet sand, then stood with it dripping from her fingers. "It's so mushy and soft. It feels so nice."

"I used to make sandcastles," Mike said. "When I was little. I would shape them and ball them, make forts, battlements, rivers and gorges. All right here at this beach."

Vira smiled, balling the sand into both her hands. "Show me," she said.

Mike grinned mischievously. "Alright," he said. He knelt in the sand, scooping up a large mound, then moving his hand along to form a gorge. "Bring that sand ball here, and we can start making the castle, or maybe the turrets, yes, the turrets, first."

Vira knelt on her knees with him, handing him the sand ball, then pulling a large mound of sand in a circle around the castle.

"Hey," Mike said. "You're good at this!"

They both laughed and continued building the sandcastle, complete with battlements, turrets, rocks and sticks. They worked together as a team, letting each other take the lead periodically, adding some personal touches on the turrets, bridges and castles. They laughed and thoroughly enjoyed each other's company for hours. Soon enough, they noticed that the sun was quickly setting, and the sky was turning darker.

"We should clean up and get home," Mike said, washing his hands in the lake. "I need to pull the fishnets in early in the morning. So, I must get to sleep soon."

"Oh, yes," Vira said, agreeably. "I need to get home too. Oh my, the time went by so quickly!"

Mike walked back with her across the sand. "Can I see you again, Vira?" he asked.

"I would like that," she said, grasping his hand one last time.

Mike smiled and walked her back to the farm; their hands joined. When he stopped at her front door, he pulled back and touched her on the cheek. "It was very nice spending time with you."

"Yes, it was," she agreed, as she slipped into her house, smiling.

The door closed gently, and Mike turned back to Nath's house alone. His heart was pounding, and his head felt light. He felt like skipping! He liked this woman; he really did. But he wasn't going to say anything, not yet. She would be upset that he was planning to fight in the Great War. So, it was better to just be friends for now. Just friends, he thought.

CHAPTER 16

Annabella knocked on Nath's door quietly. "Pabbi? Are you home?" She peered into the window and saw a figure moving around the house. Soon, the door creaked open, and Nath poked his head out, surprised. He wasn't expecting anyone. Seeing that it was Bella, he opened the door wide.

"Come in, sweetie," Nath said. He noticed right away that something was amiss. She had been crying. "What is it, Bella? Are you okay?"

Her eyes were red, and her cheeks swollen with tears. "My baby is going to war."

"Aww, Bella," Nath said softly. "Come here." He wrapped his arms around her and pulled her in close. "Mike told you that he was joining the Battalion; I'm sorry, sweetie. I feel the same. It's a shock."

"I don't want to lose him, Pabbi," Annabella said, sniffling through her tears.

"Neither do I," Nath responded, hugging her tight. They embraced for several moments, leaning on each other for support.

She pulled back and looked up at her father. "Why?" she asked. "Why do things like this have to happen? Why couldn't he choose to be a fisherman? He's so good at it. Or maybe he could be the town rancher?"

"I asked myself the same things," Nath responded, looking out over the lake.

They both fell silent, sharing the pain of possibly losing a loved one.

After a few moments, Bella broke the silence. "What answers did you come up with?" Bella asked. "You said you asked yourself the same questions."

Nath cleared his throat, arranged his thoughts, then spoke softly. "Everyone has a path in life. It's not always what we think it'll be. Sometimes it's wide; sometimes it's narrow, sometimes it encompasses the world, through many different countries. I had a worldly path leaving Iceland to come to Canada; then, once I arrived here, I narrowed it. We all have our own lives and make choices every day about how we live it. You chose to marry and have a large family. I didn't want you to leave. Every inch of my body wanted to keep you at home with me. But what would that have accomplished?"

Annabella looked up at Nath and nodded. "I would have never had any children at all."

"Exactly," Nath said. He pulled a lock of her hair behind her ear like he often did when she was young. "Mike has his own distinct path too. You must let him choose it."

"I know," Bella said, tears welling in her eyes again. "But he might die, Pabbi. It's war. He'll be going to war. Lots of young men die. I can't lose him, Pabbi."

"I can't lose him either," Nath said solemnly, grabbing her shoulders and hugging her tightly again. "I don't know what else to say. I don't want to lose him."

Nath steered the boat towards the dock while Mike gathered the nets inside the vessel. The sun was high in the sky. When they had started, it was just peeking over the lake horizon, an orange ball of light. It was a long morning of hard work, but they had completed so much, both sharing a satisfying feeling of accomplishment. He was grateful to spend the morning with Mike, even if it was work.

Nath jumped out to anchor, while Mike began unloading the days catches from the nets. It was a good year for fishing. Not all years were prosperous; some years, it seemed that there was no fish at all. This year there were more fish than the town could eat.

Nath anchored the boat to the new wood stump on the dock. It had flooded last year, and the storm had destroyed everything again, so the town had come together and built a new pier to replace the old worn one. They were both proud of the new marina and treated it as such.

Mike rolled the nets up, pulling the fish into the baskets. Nath carried them into the shop. A young male employee came running up to him. "Mr. Olason," the young man said. "I don't have time to pick up the mail for the day. I have to go home and tend to my sick mother. Is that alright? It's urgent; I have to go."

"That's fine," Nath said. "Go. I will get the mail." He waved the young man away, telling him to hurry.

Nath turned back to the boat and shouted at Mike from across the pier. "I have to go to the post office sometime today, so let's finish this day's catch quickly. Jacob said he had to leave early."

"Oh, okay," Mike replied, rolling the nets up.

"I'm going to miss not having you around," Nath said. "You are the most reliable man here."

"I won't be gone right away," Mike replied, smiling. "I still don't know. I will enquire when I'm at Selkirk at the end of the week. Probably won't happen immediately."

"Ok," Nath said. "Your brother Jon will have to take your place while you're gone."

"Good idea. He would probably like that!" Mike replied. "I will ask him tonight. Vlad is still too young, but Jon is 16. He has done some work for you before. He would enjoy getting away from the farm."

"Sounds good," Nath said, picking up the remaining baskets. "Ok, I will take in these last baskets and head over to the post office. Could you please tend to the shop?"

"Of course," Mike said. "I will be here."

Nath stepped into the post office. It was a trading post, imports, exports and a postal office all in one. The first post office had been in Arnes, serving as a link to the outside world, but now there were post offices in most towns. Gimli had one in the trading post. Nath walked in and waited patiently in line.

It was a busy day. Towards the end of the week, it grew busier, and on Mondays too, everyone hoping letters from relatives would come in after the weekend. Nath had been expecting a letter from a business in Winnipeg, requesting a large shipment of fish. He needed to organize when he was going to take the boat into Winnipeg again. The line up was long, and it was frustratingly slow. He overheard the woman in front of him, saying that it was a long wait today.

"Excuse me," Nath said politely to the woman. "How long have you been waiting?"

The woman turned her head to look at him. "About 20 minutes so far," she said. "I don't know why it's so slow today; usually, it isn't. I need to hear from my parents. They are still back in Michigan."

Nathanael smiled gently, taking in her warm voice and her long dark blonde hair. She had a lovely confident stance, strong but still feminine. Her eyes were bright green, and her hair fell to her mid-back. It was wavy and thick. Her face was oval and quite stunning, with a strong chin.

She spontaneously smiled at him. He smiled back. "Michigan, you say?" Nathan asked. "Is that where you're from?"

"Yes," she replied, her eyes darting from the woman in front of her to Nath. "I just moved here. My parents are still back in Michigan."

"Oh," Nath said politely, keeping the conversation going. "How do you like it in Gimli?"

"It's quite beautiful, actually," she said, smiling. "I was born here. It's more beautiful here than I thought."

Nath smiled back at her, his eyes creasing in the corners. She was a very attractive woman. Something about her made him want to know more, which was strange, he mused. He hadn't been interested in any woman for a very long time, over 30 years. The failed date with Katrin had sealed his bachelor's life. He would never find a woman to fit in his life, and he had long ago accepted that. It was not because of his age or looks; he was still quite an attractive man, even in his 50s. He was very fit and muscular, with a full head of hair and only a small sensual speckling of grey; most people mistaking his age to be ten years younger.

"Do you know what Gimli means in Icelandic?" Nathan asked.

"Yes," she replied. "It means paradise."

Nathan cocked his head to one side, smiling.

"Did I surprise you?" she laughed, her eyes twinkling.

"Yes," Nath said, grinning ear to ear. "You did. Are you Icelandic?"

"Yes, I am," she said. "My parents were both Icelandic settlers. We left Gimli when I was very young; I really don't have any recollection of this area at all. Except for pictures and drawings that my parents had."

"Interesting," Nath said. "My parents came here with me, and I stayed. When did you leave?"

"My family left after the terrible smallpox," she said. "I was born shortly after the epidemic quarantine had been lifted. We lived in the countryside near Arnes though, far from most civilizations. My parents were immune." She nodded thoughtfully. "So that means you survived the smallpox epidemic as well."

"Yes, I did," Nathan said, solemnly. "Actually, I had contracted the wicked disease. But I lived."

"Oh my Lord," she said. "That must have been horrible. I'm so sorry. I heard most children died."

"Yes," Nathan responded. "Many people died. I was eighteen at the time."

The line moved up, and the pretty woman shuffled lightly forward. He caught a whiff of her scent; she smelled like flowers. He inhaled unconsciously. It was so pleasant to smell a pretty woman again, he thought.

"So," Nathan said. "What brings you back to New Iceland?"

She immediately laughed, a soft sultry chuckle; he liked her voice. It was soothing somehow. "Oh," she said. "I haven't heard anyone call it New Iceland for many years. Only the first settlers called it that. My mom and dad called it New Iceland too." She looked briefly down at her shoes. "I came back because I needed a change. I lost my husband a few years back."

Nathan looked down at the top of her head. "I'm so sorry," Nathan responded. "What did he pass away from?" He coughed politely and stumbled over his words. "You don't have to answer. If I am being too intrusive, please accept my apologies."

"It's alright," she said. "He died of pneumonia."

"Oh," Nath said. "I am sorry for your loss, Miss."

"It's Maria," she said. "My name is Maria."

Nathan's hand floated up gently, lifting her hand and gently kissing the top of her knuckles, in the customary gentleman greeting. "My name is Nathan," he said. "It is a pleasure to meet you, Maria."

"Yes," Maria replied, her hand tingling from his touch. "It is very nice to meet you as well, Nathan."

The line moved again, with them both shuffling their feet forward. "Looks like the line is moving now," Nathan said, glancing down at the curve of her waist and hips.

Her eyes darted and caught him looking. She smiled and gazed away briefly, then turned back. "Have you lived here since you immigrated?"

Nathan smiled knowingly. "I am actually one of the original settlers. We landed at Willow Point, not too far from here. The rest of my family immigrated with the Large Group."

"Oh my," Maria replied, her green eyes twinkling. "That is quite the story. I heard about it from my parents. Didn't the flatboats crash on Willow Point?"

"Sort of," Nath replied. "We had no control over the boats. They just floated wherever they wanted. We were blown into Willow Point. Some crashed, but no one was seriously hurt."

The line moved forward again. Now Maria was next in line. She smiled. "I would love to hear more," she said. "I always heard the stories, but my parents came with the Large Group. I have never actually met one of the original settlers. I heard half of them perished in the first cold winter."

"Yes," he said, straightening his shoulders. "We had help from the native people. That's what saved us." Maria was looking up at him with a keen interest in her eyes. "I would be delighted to share my stories with you."

"I would love that," Maria said. "I can take notes and share your first-hand accounts with my students."

"You're a teacher?" Nathan asked, smiling. He was impressed. She was educated and pretty.

"Yes, I am," Maria replied beaming. "I teach at the school, history, English and some Icelandic too."

"You speak Icelandic?" Nath asked, incredulously.

"Yes," she said. "My parents raised me in a very strong Icelandic household. That was my first language. I have since forgotten some of it, but I work at speaking it as much as I can."

Nathan smiled and switched to Icelandic. "You are unique."

"Ah, thank you," Maria said, responding in Icelandic. "I always enjoy the chance to speak my native tongue."

"Next, please," the postal clerk shouted.

"Oh," Maria said in English. "That's me. Well, hopefully, I will see you again soon."

"You can visit anytime, Maria," Nathan replied, smiling broadly. "I own the Olason fishery to the right of the dock."

"Okay," she said, glancing back as she walked up to the teller. "I will drop by soon."

"I look forward to it," Nathan said, politely. He smiled broadly again. His heart felt funny like it was fluttering. He hadn't felt that feeling in so long that he wasn't even sure what it was. There was a time, long ago, that he had this weightless happy emotion, but it was buried under years of sadness. He recognized something about this emotion; he wasn't sure what, but it was like he knew something wholesome about it in his heart. It was odd, he thought.

"Next, please," another postal clerk shouted.

Nathan approached the teller and collected his mail. He placed all the letters in his mailbag, turned to go and noticed Maria was already gone. He frowned disappointedly. Oh, well, hopefully, she will stop by for that history chat, he thought. He stepped out onto the main road and glanced down the street. He saw her walking towards the market in the center of town. Her dress flowed freely behind her, creating an illusion of care-free freedom. He smiled. He liked her.

Nathan walked back to the fishery, with a very small, almost imperceptible, lightness in his step.

Mike was tired today. He had helped his grandfather clean up the shop all day. Mike wanted to visit Vira before leaving for the Selkirk barracks on Friday, but he was physically exhausted. He slumped on his grandpa's sofa with a beer in his hand. He often hid the alcohol in the house because of rumours of the pro-hibition coming to Manitoba. He sipped the rare cold liquid and gazed thoughtfully at the horizon. He liked Vira but felt hesitant to create any bond with her yet. He was making plans in his mind to leave for the Great War. He was going to talk to George on Friday. If they accepted him, then he would join.

Part of him felt apprehensive, and part of him felt sad for his family; they would be so worried. But the biggest part of him felt absolutely compelled like something was tugging him to his destiny. A place to finally utilize the skills he had honed all these years. It felt like all the pieces of his life were aligning; it was all beginning to make sense.

He certainly didn't want to fall in love with a woman right now.

He didn't know what to do. Mike wanted to see her again. He felt drawn to her strength, her character and her kind nature. He really liked her. His attraction to her was potent.

But the pull to go to the Great War was stronger.

The door opened, and Nathan walked in, kicking his shoes off and letting the door slam behind him.

"Hi, Afi," Mike said, casually, his arm on the back of the sofa.

"Hi, Mike, thanks for all the help today," Nathan said. "I appreciate everything you do."

"No problem, Afi," Mike said, staring out into the distance.

Nathan washed his hands in the kitchen and grabbed a beer for himself. He sat down on the other long sofa, staring out across the horizon with his grandson. "Penny for your thoughts?" Nathan said.

"Ah," Mike replied. "Just thinking about Vira."

"And?" Nathan prompted.

"I was supposed to see her tonight or tomorrow before I go to Selkirk," Mike said, throwing his head back.

"So, then what are you doing here?" Nathan replied, taking a big sip of beer.

"Ah," Mike said. "It just doesn't feel right. I like her, Afi! And I don't want to fall in love right now. I might be going to the Great War. It's not right."

"Oh, I see," Nathan said, taking another long swig of beer. Nath swallowed and stared thoughtfully at the sun setting for several minutes. "Well, maybe it's not right to avoid her either. Maybe it's not right to deny yourself some happiness. You could be honest and explain things to her. Tell her that you are going to the Great War, and you feel that it's better if you were both just friends for now."

Mike smiled, happy for the advice. "Yes," Mike said. "You're right. I will be honest."

"Okay," Nathan said, smiling. "What are you waiting for then? Get out of the house."

"Alright," Mike said, chuckling. He threw his legs over, sitting up. Mike drank the rest of his beer in one long swallow. He stood determined, put his shoes on, said goodbye and left the house.

As soon as his feet hit the sand, he saw her, about 100 feet away. It was strange how coincidence happened like that; he mused. She was walking along the beach near the pier. Her feet shuffled in the sand, and her hair blew forward over her face. He ran to catch up to her.

"Vira," Mike called after her, laughing. "Funny meeting you here again."

She smiled sweetly. "Mike," she said enthusiastically. "You live right near the beach, right? I would probably bump into you all the time when I'm going for a walk."

"Yeah," he replied, smiling back. "Sort of, I live unofficially with my granddad. My mom and dad live on farmland just outside Gimli."

"Oh?" Vira said. "You farm as well?"

"No," Mike said. "Not really. I fish mostly and hunt. I tried farming, but it was not in my blood, I guess."

"That's how I feel some days," Vira said.

"Rough day again?" Mike asked.

"Yes," Vira said, smiling weakly.

"Ah, I'm sorry," Mike said. "Do you want to talk about it?"

"Not really," she replied. "I'd rather go on a boat ride than talk, to be honest."

Mike laughed. "You're serious?"

Vira giggled. "Yes," she said. "I haven't been on a boat for a long while. It's such a beautiful lake."

"Okay," he said. "Let's do it. I can ask Afi if I can take out the small boat. It is calm enough, although it can be chilly this time of year. It is October."

"Are you serious?" Vira said, smiling. "You can just take a boat out?"

"Yeah," Mike said. "Let's go ask my granddad." He grabbed her hand. "Come on."

"Okay," Vira said, her face brightening. She followed him to the big house on the sand. "Such a beautiful house!" she exclaimed.

"Yes," Mike said. "The entire family helped build it many years ago. I think it's the biggest house in Gimli."

They walked through the sand, Mike leading the way, through some bush to the back of the house, still aimlessly holding her hand. He opened the door and shouted. "Afi!" Mike called.

"What is it, Mike?" Nathan shouted back, then suddenly appeared on the back deck. "Oh, hello," he said, noticing Vira.

Mike looked back at her, noticing that their hands were still together. "Afi," Mike said. "This is Vira."

"Hello, Vira," Nathan said, waving.

"Hi, Mr. Olason," she said politely, waving back.

"Afi," Mike said, letting go of her hand briefly. "Can I take out the small boat with Vira? She wants to go for a boat ride."

"Yes, definitely," Nathan answered happily. "Go, have a nice time. Come back before the sky turns dark, though."

"Yes, for sure," Mike said. "We will just go out for a brief boat ride." Mike turned to leave and shouted back. "We will be back soon! Thanks, Afi."

"No problem," Nathan replied, smiling and closing the door.

Mike gestured for Vira to follow him. "This way," he said. She stepped quickly to catch up. He looked back and grasped her hand again. It felt so good to hold her hand, he thought. They trudged across the sand, Mike clasping her hand firmly.

Within a few minutes, they had reached the dock. Mike walked around the back of the factory and found the small fishing boat, enough space for two maybe three people. "It's small, but it will do," he said, releasing her hand. "Grab the other end, and we will slide it in the water." Vira did as instructed, and the boat slid gently into the water. "Okay, you get in first," Mike said.

He watched as she lifted her farmer's dress and stepped in. She had nice strong legs, he noticed. He gently held her hand as she boarded the small sailboat. Mike pushed the boat out onto the water and quickly jumped in, unfurling the sails. They began drifting onto the lake. The wind started blowing as they drifted farther out. He removed his jacket and draped it around Vira's arms. She looked up at him, her eyes saying something, he wasn't sure what, but there was definitely a message in her eyes. "Thank you," she said.

Mike pulled at the sails and tied several sailor's knots. As he did this, the wind immediately caught the sails, propelling the boat across the water. The wind blew straight into their faces. "You need to get on this side of the boat," Mike said loudly, gesturing to the side he was on, patting the seat beside him. "We need the weight of our bodies to balance the boat, or the boat might tip."

The wind was loud. It howled in their ears, muffling any conversation. She rushed to the other side of the boat, as instructed. Mike leaned out, sitting on the edge of the boat, and she joined him, unsteady at first. He noticed her hesitation and immediately grabbed her waist, pulling her in close.

The boat sailed out rather quickly. Within 10 minutes, they reached the middle of the lake. The wind blew harder here, changing the direction of the boat. Mike used the rudder to steer and then relaxed the sails a bit, the wind no longer hitting them at full speed. He steered the boat around, pointing out towards the other side of the lake. "That spot over there is where we lay the nets," Mike shouted, pointing in the distance. "And over there is the route we take to get to the northern parts of the lake, but we are careful not to go too far north. The lake gets violent and has killed fishermen in the northern areas."

They had to shout at each other to be heard over the wind and the sails. He grabbed her waist firmly to ensure her safety. Vira easily accepted his touch. Mike felt so comfortable and excited; he had never taken a girl out on a boat. It was fun being spontaneous with her!

He glanced over at her, and she was smiling broadly. Her face lit up, and her eyes shined with something special. He didn't know what, but she looked quite happy.

She laughed heartily and shouted over the wind noise. "Mike," she called. "I love this! Thank you so much."

Mike laughed. "My pleasure, Vira," he said. "Anything to make that beautiful smile overtake your pretty face."

She beamed proudly, holding onto the boat's edge, with the wind blowing in her hair. Mike thought she looked like an angel. He smiled back, enjoying the happiness emanating from her.

Dusk was quickly descending onto the lake, showering the sky with dark blue and light purple hues, the clouds reflecting all the colours like a painter's masterpiece. Mike slowed the boat, flapping the sails and drifted. He laid back onto the rails staring at the picturesque dusk. "Isn't it beautiful?" he asked.

"It's breathtaking, Mike," she said, admiring the sunset. "I had no idea it was so beautiful and freeing out here."

"Yes, it is," Mike said, pulling her in close again, as they gazed at the dusk silently, just absorbing the beauty. After a long while, finally, Mike spoke. "I like you, Vira," he said, turning to look at her. "I want to do this more. But I am going away soon."

"Where are you going?' she asked, confusion clouding her face.

He turned to look at her, gazing directly into her eyes. "The Great War," he responded solemnly, bracing for her reaction.

"Oh," she said, a hint of disappointment in her voice.

"I really like you, Vira," Mike said. "I just don't know what else to do. I would like to stay friends for now until I know more. Are you okay with that?"

Vira looked up at the sky, all the purples and pinks beginning to grow darker. "I guess so," she said. "I really like you too. As long as you come back to Gimli."

"Oh yes," he said. "I will be back." Mike moved his hand farther around her waist. He squeezed her gently towards him. "I have lots to come back to."

Vira smiled. "I like you, Mike," she said.

"I like you too, Vira," Mike said, as a gust of wind caught her hair and blew it all over her face. Mike instinctively lifted the locks off her face, his hand briefly staying on her cheek. He slid his hand slowly down her jaw, then grasped her hand again.

"We should turn back soon. The wind is picking up." He bent forward and pulled the sail taught again, tying knots. The boat responded immediately, picking up speed. "Promise me something, Vira," he said.

"What?" she asked, holding her own locks out of her face.

"Don't worry about me," Mike shouted, steering with the rudder in the back of the boat. "Just don't, no matter how long I am gone; know that I will be fine. I will be back."

"Alright," she said. "I will try."

Mike steered the sailboat back, paying close attention to the wind direction as the boat sped back to shore with the wonderful kaleidoscope of colours shimmering all over the sky above their heads. Vira watched as the dusk slowly started slipping into the night until finally, they arrived at the dock. The night sky began absorbing the sunset and quickly turning everything into a dark bluish colour, the colour of night. He helped her out of the boat and anchored it, pulling her hand with his along the beach. Finally, halfway to the house, he stopped and turned, looking into her eyes in the falling darkness. Mike opened his arms and wrapped them around her strong slim shoulders, resting his head alongside hers. Vira slipped her hands comfortably around his waist and inhaled his manly scent. They stayed like this, hugging each other for several minutes, swaying slightly in the descending darkness.

The moment felt so special like it was something he would remember and long for. Finally, after a long moment, they broke the embrace and walked back to the house.

He wanted to kiss her so badly but stopped himself. He could not allow himself to fall in love right now. He had a war to win.

CHAPTER 17

Mike watched the clouds curling into the sky as they loaded the covered wagon with fish and vegetables for the long ride to Selkirk. Hopefully, it doesn't rain, he thought. He grabbed more vegetables as Nathan, Annabella and Ivan helped him load the wagon. Even his younger brothers and sisters came out to help load the carriage. They all came together as a family wishing him well. Nobody was happy about his decision to join the forces, but it was his passion, so they grudgingly supported him. Nathan jumped onto the riding seat and hollered at Mike to hurry up.

"We need to leave before 8 am," Nath complained. "We have a lot of work to do, and I still need to return back to Gimli with the horses and carriage. Let's go."

"Okay, Afi," Mike answered as he grabbed his cloth bag with his personal items, throwing it in the back of the carriage.

Annabella watched her son and felt tears forming in her eyes. She may never see him again, she thought. At that moment, Mike slammed the carriage door and turned to her. "Momma," he said softly, his arms outstretched.

Annabella rushed into his arms and hugged him fiercely. Her head buried into his shoulder as her silent tears dropped onto his arms. "Stay safe," she said. "Be smart. Think twice, and oh my Lord, come back home alive, my son."

Mike hugged her tightly and kissed the side of her cheek. "Momma," he said. "Don't worry. I will be back. I am the product of two courageous settlers. I will survive; trust me. They need men like me."

Annabella pulled away, wiped her eyes and smiled. "I know," she said. "You are a courageous soul. I love you."

"I love you too, Momma," Mike responded softly. He kissed her on the cheek again.

As he jumped into the riding seat beside Nathan, Annabella rushed forward with something in her hand. "Oh," she said. "I almost forgot. Vira brought this sealed letter to the house last night. She wanted you to open it when you got settled in the barracks."

"Oh?" Mike said, surprised. He held his hand out and accepted the letter; it was wrapped in fine paper with a seal. "Interesting. I will read it once I get settled. If they accept me, that is."

"Oh, they will accept you," Nathan replied. "That is certain. They wouldn't let a good marksman like you get away."

"Thanks," Mike said, laughing. "I hope so." He turned his head back to his family one last time. "We have to go, Momma, Pabbi, brothers and sisters. I love you all!" He waved as the carriage lurched forward, and the entire family waved back.

Mike felt his heart lurch with the carriage; he loved his family so much. They meant the world to him. He didn't want to cause them anguish or heartbreak, but now he felt his own heartstrings pull. He would miss everyone.

But it was something that was calling for him. The Great War needed men like him.

The road was long and bumpy. The November winds had started, and a chill in the air brought the whispers of winter. Clouds obscured the sun, but it was dry today; no rain and no snow. Not yet, anyway. Nathan and Mike chatted along the trip, talking about Mike's expectations and what he wanted to do within the Canadian Expeditionary Force.

"I am interested in rifle shooting, Afi," Mike said. "You know that. Any post that utilizes my marksmanship, I'd be thrilled to do; riflemen or a sniper would be ideal."

"That would be perfect for your skills," Nathan replied. "You have an uncanny accuracy. Anwa was a perfect marksman too. You seem to have the best of all of us."

Soon the road veered into the outskirts of Selkirk. They lumbered on towards the Red Feather Farm, nicknamed from all the large chicken barns on site. The barracks sprawled in the distance, getting closer and closer as the horses clopped their hooves rhythmically.

"Are you sure about this, Mike?" Nathan asked. "You don't have to. Talks of conscription started but enlisting is not mandatory yet. We could just drop off the fish and vegetables like any other day."

Mike thought about his grandpa's words briefly. It was true; he had not told George yet of his plans. He could simply change his mind and go back. But he couldn't; the pull of fate was too strong to resist. "I'm certain, Afi," Mike said. "This feels like my destiny. I feel pretty strongly about defending the good in the world; the Central Powers need to be stopped, Afi. You know that. Heck, everybody knows this. Who am I to say that less experienced young men should go in my place? Who am I to say that someone else should risk their life for my freedom? I will go, and I will return."

Nathan nodded. "I thought so," he said. "Well, you were always the stubborn one. It will keep you alive. Stay that way."

Mike smiled. "I will," he replied.

Nathan nodded, accepting his decision, feeling his heart break with every jolt of the carriage. The closer they got, the more his stomach lurched into his throat, leaving Nath speechless. My grandson must not see my pain, he thought.

They rode in silence until they finally arrived at the barracks. Long chicken barns were everywhere. The largest was the mess hall and the sleeping quarters were the smaller barns. Some of the smaller barns were reserved for the higher-ranking officers. Several flags flew on high stakes, and many officers scurried about on the expansive grounds.

Four soldiers manned the guardroom. One of them immediately stepped down from his position, inspected their credentials, and another inspected the wagon. When everything was deemed safe, they were allowed in. The horses rumbled onto the mess hall, where all the food was being prepared. As they neared, Mike shuffled excitedly in the riding seat. Nervousness and anticipation had his body primed for the unknown. His forehead began to sweat, and he ran several opening phrases through his head that he would say to George. He had become quite close friends with George, sharing tea and discussing the Great war. The Colonel was an intelligent man, and Mike looked forward to their chats. But today, the chat would be different.

The horses stopped in the back of the mess hall, and Nathan jumped off, opening the covered wagon. Mike proceeded to the door. As he grabbed the handle, it opened suddenly, startling him.

It was Lt. Col. George Bradbury dressed in full uniform. "Oh, son!" George said excitedly. "You surprised me. You have brought us some much-needed food. Come, I will show you where to put it." George looked up and noticed Nathan's large form carrying a large stack of fish. "Oh, you brought a strong helper today?"

"This is my grandpa, Nathan Olason," Mike said, introducing them. "Nath, this is Lieutenant Colonel George Bradbury."

Nathan nodded, his hands presently occupied. "Pleasure to meet you, Colonel," Nath replied. "Where would you like the fish to go?"

"Oh," George replied. "Right this way to the kitchen." George walked them both into the mess hall to the back of a massive kitchen, rows of camp sinks and hot stove ovens. Several cooks were already preparing for the lunch rush. Nathan placed down the stacks of fish, then returned with Mike to gather more. When they came back to the wagon, George had directed several soldiers to help with the stacks and hauling it in. With five strong men working, the wagon was unloaded in no time.

George thanked Mike for making the journey, and the Quartermaster paid him. "I need to give this money to my grandpa," Mike said, as he made his way back to where Nathan stood by the horses. "He will be taking the horses and wagon back today."

"Oh?" George replied, confused. "Are you not going back with him?"

"I am hoping not to," Mike answered. "I would like to enlist with the 108th Battalion."

"Today?" George asked incredulously.

"Yes," Mike said. "Today." Mike handed the money to Nathan and grabbed his cloth bag from the wagon.

George looked at him, sizing him up. "You are a confident, young man, Mike Kozak," George said. "What skills will you be bringing to the 108th Battalion?"

"I am an excellent marksman," Mike said. "I have been hunting since I was a small boy. You'll see. I will be a definite asset to the Great War. I wouldn't be here otherwise."

George laughed, "Son, welcome to the 108th Overseas Battalion of the Canadian Expeditionary Force. Come with me; I will show you to the Recruiting Office." George waved at Nathan.

Before he followed, Mike turned around briefly. "Give me one second," Mike said, then he ran back to his grandpa and hugged him warmly.

Nathan held his grandson tight. His emotions rose quickly to the surface, threatening his eyes with tears. He swallowed it back. "Mike," Nathan said, his voice briefly faltering. "You are a strong, determined man. Remember what I said. Stay stubborn. It will keep you alive."

"I will, Afi," Mike responded. "I love you. I will write often." Mike ran back to George Bradbury and waved once more, then disappeared into the barracks.

Nathan stood there alone for several seconds after, wondering if he had just lost his beloved grandson. He slumped his shoulders and climbed aboard the riding seat, grabbing the horse's reins. No reason to stick around being sad, he mused. His grandson is doing what he loves; he is an Olason. He has the strength of many generations of survivors in his blood.

Nathan cracked the horsewhip. The horses lurched on command onto the roadway carrying the empty wagon out of the barracks, as the November winds circled around their tails.

Mike was led to a training room soon after being enlisted. He had been passed down to several Corporals and Lieutenants, filling out paperwork and outfitting him with a uniform. It was now afternoon, and Mike was thrilled. He stepped into the training area.

"Hi," the man in uniform said. "I'm Corporal Stan Horacs. Nice to meet your acquaintance, Private Kozak. You missed the recruit training session this morning. I've been asked by the Lieutenant Colonel to address you individually today. You must be special. He never does this."

"Yes, sir," Mike said proudly, tipping his hat on his already closely cut hair.

"Ok, ready?" Stan Horacs asked sharply.

"Ready, sir!" Mike responded.

Stan led him to a table of rifles. There were several rifles, different makes, some which he knew, some he didn't. He spotted the weapon he wanted immediately. Stan gestured to the weapons. "You will be issued a rifle and prepare for target training. I will be issuing you a Ross," Stan instructed, gesturing to the weapon on the table. "This one's yours. I will remain here and give you orders to fire. Listen and be attentive."

Mike calmly walked to the table.

The gleaming brown oiled barrel of the new Ross Rifle MK III shone back at him. He ran his hands along the smooth wood finish and picked it up. "This is the MKIII," he said, almost to himself.

Stan replied nonchalantly, "Yes, that's her. We just received those MKIIIs. A nice accurate rifle. Do you know the rifle?"

"Yes, I do," Mike said thoughtfully. "My favourite hunting rifle is a Ross M-10."

"You'll like these then," Stan said. "Very similar. Military issue model."

Mike lifted the rifle and felt the satisfying heavy weight of the weapon in his arms. He smiled and stood at attention, his heart soaring.

Stan grinned. He instantly liked something about this man. "Alright, Private Mike. Let's see you shoot. Follow me." Stan led Mike to the shooting range.

Mike followed Stan and walked confidently to the range. He moved into position. Mike crouched expertly with the MKIII, looking through the sights, with the barrel snug against his shoulder. He waited, nothing. The far end of the range had a dugout with a reinforced wall where the targets would appear. The targets were mounted on a board in a place called the butts, an area cordoned off in the dugout for raising and lowering the targets, each board hand-operated by individual pulleys.

Mike exhaled and waited a little while longer, no targets. His instincts told him not to turn and ask if there was a problem.

Suddenly, a target appeared. It was a standard circular target being raised in the centre of the range. It stopped abruptly. Mike waited.

"Fire one round, centre target, " Stan commanded.

Mike squeezed the trigger and felt the recoil into his shoulder satisfyingly. The bullet whizzed through the air, hitting the target directly in the centre.

Stan whistled. "Good shot," he commented.

Again, Mike's instincts told him not to respond. He stayed crouched, looking through the sights, waiting, just like he did as a boy in the bush, waiting for the deer. Another target appeared, raised by the hidden soldier in the butts. It was the same plain circular target, except it appeared to the left. He waited for the command and fired quickly, hitting the target in the centre again.

Stan whistled again. "You're better than I thought," he said admiringly. "Three more. Let's see what you can do, Private Mike."

Mike moved ever so slightly; he steadied the rifle and exhaled. His eyes were trained to the sights as the next target appeared to the right this time. He waited for a brief second, aimed, judging for angle and distance, then fired when commanded. The bullet entered the middle of the circle. He steadied the rifle again and crouched, waiting for his fourth target. Nothing happened. He waited patiently. A few seconds passed, then another target moved up, the same circular target but to the far left.

"Target left, three rounds rapid-fire," Stan commanded.

Mike quickly aimed and then fired rapidly in succession. The bullets whizzed through the air, one, two, three and splintered the wood in the center of the target.

Mike felt sweat forming on his forehead but did not flinch. He imagined another deer ready to pounce out of the bushes.

Another target appeared, although it was farther away like time, in the centre but slightly to the right. Mike aimed, judging for distance and waited.

"Right centre, two rounds. Fire!" Stan instructed.

Mike's bullets hit the centre, once and then again, the rifle recoiling snugly into his shoulder. Both shots were satisfyingly accurate.

Mike exhaled slowly and remained still.

"Private," Stan said. "You have completed the training. You may stand now."

Mike wiped the sweat beads trickling down his face with his hand and placed the rifle on the weapons rack. He approached Stan. "How did I do?" Mike asked.

Stan laughed. "Where have you been all this time, Private Kozak?" Stan replied wholeheartedly. "I haven't seen anybody shoot like that in my entire military career. I mock you not! How did you learn to shoot like that, Mike?"

"My grandfather, Nathanael Olason," Mike answered. "He taught me bows and arrows too."

"Holy cow," Stan exclaimed. "So, you are an archery specialist too?"

"I guess so," Mike said, smiling proudly. "We had to hunt for our food. There was no other way. Shoot to kill or die starving. Mostly deer, some moose and many rabbits, but the rabbits I hunted with arrows."

"Well, well," Stan said excitedly. He stuck out his hand, shaking Mike's hand firmly. "Welcome to the 108th Battalion. You will be in Platoon 3 in A Company for now. We are excited to have you!"

Mike beamed. "Thank you!" Mike said strongly. "Corporal!"

"You can just call me Stan," he replied. "Apparently, I am in the same living quarters as you. Spaces have been filling up. Glad to make your acquaintance. You are definitely someone I would want watching my back." Stan slapped him on the shoulder and led them both out of the training center. "It's been a long day for you. I will show you the way to the living quarters."

By the end of the day, Nathan was mentally exhausted. Travelling back to Gimli was a slow ride, made even bumpier with the lack of weight in the wagon. The chains rattled, and the wheels creaked loudly. Several hours later, he finally arrived back into town while the sun was setting. The days were growing shorter and colder, he thought. He corralled the horses at Annabella's, hugging her fiercely, telling her not to worry, that her son was a fighter, through and through.

Nathan trudged back to the shop, tiredly. Jon, his second grandson, was sweeping the floor when he opened the door. Another male employee was stocking supplies in the back; Nath could hear the rustling of feet and shuffle of boxes. It already felt empty somehow without Mike.

Nath hung his coat up and was surprised to see the blonde woman from the post office at the counter.

Nathan searched his memory briefly, then satisfyingly remembered her name. "Maria," he exclaimed. "How lovely to see you here!"

She turned her head, looking over her shoulder. "Oh, Nathan," Maria said excitedly. "I wasn't sure whether you were going to make it back before closing. I was just about to leave. Jon told me that Mike joined the Battalion today. I'm sorry."

"Thanks," Nathan said, tipping his hat in an attempt to hide his emotions. "Mike is a tough man. I have no choice but to accept this. It is his decision to make." Nathan approached Maria and kissed her hand. "Nice surprise to see you tonight. Are you here for that history lesson?"

Maria laughed, her smile lighting up her face so beautifully. Nathan thought she looked even more attractive when she smiled. Her eyes crinkled at the sides and her dimples showed on her cheeks. She was a very pretty woman.

"Yes," Maria said. "You could call it that. Do you have a few moments? Or should I come back at another time?"

"No, please stay," Nathan said, smiling back. He was amazed at how quickly his mood had lifted just by seeing her presence in the shop. He mused about this strange emotion briefly and wondered if he had ever felt this way before. A small voice inside of him confirmed that, yes, he had experienced such elation before, many forgotten years ago. Nathan grinned joyfully as he glanced into the warehouse behind him. "Just let me get the fishery locked up and send Jon and our stock boy home. Give me ten minutes, Maria." Nathanael disappeared into the back, while Jon began packing up the front. He rummaged in the warehouse excitedly, instructing the stock boy to finish up; the boy looked at him curiously, wondering why there was suddenly a big rush.

Maria waited patiently, gazing out the shop windows, feeling her heart flutter briefly. Nathan was a very handsome man. She felt slightly nervous.

Nath finally grabbed the skeleton keys and prepared to lock up from the back as Jon gestured for Maria to follow him to the front. She followed the young man.

"Nathan is happy to see you," Jon said, smiling a boyish grin back at her. "It's nice to see grandpa interested in a female again."

Maria blushed. "Oh, no," she responded. "It's not like that. I just arrived in town, and we began talking about the Icelandic immigration and everything they had to endure. It's a wonderful story for my students, so I'm doing some research for them, and Nath was happy to help."

"Oh," Jon said. "I see. I just thought Afi looks at you differently. He's never looked at a woman like that before. Sorry, I didn't know you were just friends."

Maria smiled and nodded, finding it quite a pleasant thought that Nathan looked at her differently. It was just probably a teenage boy's misinterpretation, she thought. She glanced behind him and caught a view of Nathan bending forward, moving a few stacks of fish from the back door. His legs were heavily muscled, and his buttocks were quite round and firm. At that moment, Nathan looked over his shoulder and caught her eye. She nervously glanced away instantly, feeling a bit embarrassed.

At that moment, Jon gestured her out of the shop and locked the door behind him. "Nathan will lock up from the back," Jon said as he sat with her on the front step. Seconds later, Nathan appeared and hugged his grandson, sending him home.

"Thank you, Jon," Nathan said. "I will see you tomorrow."

"Bye Afi, bye Maria," Jon replied, as he walked away, waving.

Nathan and Maria waved back, then started walking along the beach. "Would you be interested in having tea with me? I just live right there in the first big white house."

"That would be lovely," Maria responded, as she followed him across the sand to the large home. "That's quite a big home!"

"Yes," Nathan replied. "I built it myself with lots of help from my cousins and family." As they neared the home, Nathan glanced over at her small feet and the way she delicately walked on the sand. It was so utterly feminine, and he found himself intensely interested in this unique woman.

"That's a big project," Maria said. "How long did it take to build your home?"

"One year before everything was finished," Nathan said, proudly, grabbing her hand as she walked over the pebbles surrounding his home. She delicately stepped along the stones, and her hand was so smooth in his, so very womanly. He was astonished that he was noticing such mundane things.

Nathan unlocked the back door, and they both entered the kitchen. It was considered a sizeable innovative kitchen; not too many homes even had separate kitchens, making it quite impressive.

Maria thought it was a clean and welcoming household. "You have a beautiful home," she said.

"Thanks," he said, rummaging in the cupboards for tea. He pulled out two cups and a teapot, sprinkling the tea leaves inside, then put some water on to boil.

"Oh," Maria asked, surprised. "What kind of tea is that? It looks homemade."

"It is!" Nathan exclaimed. "It has dried berries and some herbs in it. A native tea recipe from the aboriginals here."

"Oh, my," she said. "How did you get such a recipe?"

"That's a long story," Nathan said. "Maybe one day, I will tell you." He looked down, pouring the hot tea carefully into the cups. "I will tell you all about the landing at Willow Point right now, though. It is quite the story."

"Wonderful," Maria said enthusiastically.

She gazed at his handsome face as he sat down and told her the story about the Hudson Bay steamer, the flatboats and the crash landing.

His blue eyes glimmered as he detailed the account of their arrival. Nathan's face glowed as he relayed all the details of the first night he had spent on this land. She smiled and nodded, accepting the cup of tea as he spoke of the hardships he endured.

Nath's eyes lit up as he spoke of the colony's achievements in the early days, and grew darker when he spoke of the first difficult winter. Maria sipped her tea and felt something strange happening between them. Something about this man was so intriguing, so mesmerizing. She couldn't stop looking at his eyes; she felt drawn to them, sucked into his gaze. Every time he smiled, she smiled too.

Hours passed from the moment they first started talking, and it seemed like only fleeting seconds. This moment felt so incredibly special, just being able to share with someone and connect. He looked out the window and noticed the sun setting and the sky growing darker. "I'm sorry," Nathan said. "I am talking your ear off."

"No," Maria smiled. "Don't stop. I like it."

Nathan laughed. "An old man like me doesn't get to tell his story too many times," he said.

"You don't look old," Maria said. "You look maybe 45? Am I right?"

"No," Nathan laughed. "I am 57."

"Oh, my! You don't look it," she said. "You look like my age."

"I was born in 1858. What year were you born in?"

"1877," Maria replied. "Right after the smallpox epidemic had ended. It was a difficult time for people here."

Nathan's face went still. He looked into his cup of tea, swirling the liquid around. "Yes," he said. "It was a difficult time."

Maria sensed his grief. She didn't know what had happened to him, but she instinctively knew it was something heart-wrenching. She didn't push him. She accepted that this is how it was; he would tell her someday, just not today.

Nathan cleared his throat. "Well, it is getting dark, my dear. I should walk you home soon."

Nathan grabbed their coats and walked with Maria into the dark night. They both walked quietly through the shadowy streets towards her home. The night was delightful and serene. They didn't exchange many words but the calmness of the night they shared without hesitation. Nathan realized they were walking quite close together, an occasional shoulder brushing against each other, nothing distinctive, just subtle signs of comfortableness, of a shared space. The silence was not awkward; it was comfortable. It felt right. The night merged in between the shadows, separating the spaces in between their bodies but also somehow joining them. Nathan wanted to grasp her hand but felt nervous. He didn't want to scare her away.

They arrived at her front door.

"Will you join me for another tea sometime?" Nathan asked.

"I would love that," she replied, smiling shyly.

Nathan tipped his hat and kissed her hand. "Until then," he said. "Goodnight, my beautiful Maria."

Stan showed Mike the living quarters and where he would be keeping his meagre belongings. Mike sat on the small army issued bed and removed his boots, placing them on the floor. He began to unwrap his puttees, the woollen material that wrapped around his calves to his ankles. Mike laid the yards of rolled-up cloth on his bed as he removed the remainder of his clothing until he was sitting on the bed in his underwear and white undershirt. He folded his trousers and put them in the kit bag.

He stretched his legs on the bed and pulled the letter from Vira out of his cloth bag. He had forgotten about it. The day had progressed so quickly that it felt like a week full of activities crammed into ten hours.

Stan's bed was just on the other side of the quarters. Stan waved and sauntered over slowly.

Mike fingered the letter seal in his hands, running his fingertips along the top of the gluey material, wondering what she had written. Would it say what he hoped it might say?

Stan arrived at his bedside. "You have a special woman, too?" he asked.

"No, not really," Mike said, blushing. "I just met her earlier this week, but I am growing to like her."

"Ah," Stan said, laughing. "That always happens. Just when you finally make a big decision to leave, you meet a good woman."

Mike laughed. "Maybe," he said.

"I have a girl too," Stan said, smiling. "Here's her picture." He rummaged in his pocket briefly and pulled out a black and white picture, crumpled on the edges. "She's a beauty. My future wife."

Mike took the picture and examined it. The woman in the photograph was pretty; her dark hair was tied up in a tight bun, making her look serious, but somehow her eyes made up for it; they gleamed with intelligence, and her small grin was sensual, but polite at the same time. "What's her name?" Mike asked.

"Shirley," Stan replied, smiling. "What's your girl's name?" he asked.

"Oh," Mike said, grinning. "She's not really my girl. But her name's Vira."

"Nice name," Stan said. "She wrote you a letter?"

"Yes," Mike replied. "She gave it to my mother, asking her to make sure that I read it once I was settled at the barracks."

"Then she is your girl," Stan said. "Or she wants to be."

Mike laughed. "Yes, maybe," he replied.

"Okay," Stan said, turning away. "I will leave you alone to read it in private. Sleep well. You have a big training day tomorrow, very early. Be ready."

"I will be ready. Goodnight," Mike said, waving as Stan walked away.

Mike fingered the envelope again and then broke the seal. He unfolded the paper, and a scent drifted through the air of flowers and berries. It had the prettiest cursive writing. It read:

Hi, Mike,

I know you will probably be reading this while you are sitting on your new barracks bed. I suppose that it is not much of a glamourous bed, but it is a place to rest your head, and that is always a good thing at the end of a long, hard day.

You are probably wondering why I would be writing to you. It is because I want to tell you things that I was not bold enough to say in person. I think you are the strongest and most courageous man I have ever met. I admire your courage and your bravery. In the short time that I have known you, you have taught me that life goes on and you can always find little bits of happiness along the way, in the sand, on the water, everywhere; that beauty and happiness surround us at all moments of the day, all we have to do is open our eyes to see it. Thank you for this, Mike.

I enjoyed the last time we spent together on the boat. It helped me so much. I felt free, and you lifted my stresses and worries. They just effortlessly floated up into the sky while I was with you. I am looking forward to seeing you again. If it is possible to see you before you leave for the Great War, please let me know. I would like that. If not, I look forward to seeing you when you return.

Could we remain in contact and exchange letters throughout the war? I want to hear all about your triumphs and defeats.

Also, I understood what you said on the boat, and I appreciate your honesty. We can remain close friends. I am completely fine with this. I have many duties at the farm and much to take care of with the inheritance.

I do like you a lot. I just thought you needed to know that.

Be brave, and remain safe, Mike. You are the best kind of man there is. Stay that way.

Sincerely yours,

Vira R. November 9, 1915

Mike folded the paper back into a square and slipped it back into the envelope. He felt his heart soar. He liked Vira a lot. She gave him this strange kind of mellow happiness deep in the pit of his stomach, like a dozen drunken butterflies.

He stuffed the letter away in his bag and laid down, staring at the ceiling of the quarters. He smiled; he would write to her tomorrow night. He would tell her of his weapons training; she would be proud. He will write to his momma and his grandpa too. They would all be proud. He knew this because he felt gratified, loved and honoured to be here. Mike felt good about his decision. It felt right like he was on the exact path that he needed to be on, moving in the right direction at the perfect speed.

He cuddled on his side with his hands under the pillow and closed his eyes. He would do his best, and he would excel beyond anyone's expectations.

The barracks light's shone at an early 3 am. There was shouting, and everyone had to be ready in 20 minutes. Breakfast was a swiftly eaten bacon, bread and jam. He almost didn't have time to finish it.

Stan nudged him. "We have to go now," he said.

"It's still dark," Mike said.

"Best time to train," Stan replied. "Battle training today. Let's go. We are in the same platoon."

Mike and Stan hurried to the platoon. They were rushed out in a group onto the battle training field. It was snowing. The grey sky was opening up, and a steady wet snowfall sunk their boots into the mud. Every time they lifted their feet, the mud sucked underneath their boots with a pop. There were no lights, just darkness. Mike's eyes adjusted slowly. He began to make out a rough training field, with dark black trenches, stones, downed trees and lots of mud mixed with snow everywhere. There were several other faint things that Mike couldn't make out, but his instincts told him that they were important to avoid.

"You will be going through a battle," the Lieutenant in charge shouted. "There will be shots fired constantly above you, so don't lift your head up, keep down. There will be barbed wire fences, identify them and crawl underneath, you will get wet and full of mud, and you shouldn't care, because your life is in danger and you must get to the other side. There will be pointed sticks, difficult to see; you need to avoid them. There will also be four trenches along the way. You need to reach each one. Within every trench will be a box. Inside the box will be a small coloured flag. You need to retrieve all four different coloured flags. You have one pack. It is stuffed with 60 pounds of kit, including 120 rounds and a satchel with two Mills bombs. Don't lose any of it. You will have targets to shoot at; be alert to them. Try to get as many targets as you can. This is how war is going to feel like men. It's dirty, it's wet, and I'm here to prepare you. Remember, this will be nothing compared to the real thing. Be aware and listen to your instincts. You will see a white tent at the end. This will signify that you have completed the course. Good luck, men!"

Mike and Stan grabbed their packs and hefted them onto their shoulders. Mike slung his rifle over top of his other shoulder, and they assembled into the lineup.

The thick wet snow was relentless. Mike's entire body was already soaked. His infantry uniform was completely wet and hanging like a heavy weight on his body. The backpack just added the final insult.

"Go," the commanding officer shouted. A shot was fired.

Mike immediately threw himself onto his abdomen, the wet mud splashing onto his face as he crawled through the mucky snow. More shots were fired; he felt a splinter of wood crack above his head. He kept his head down. Stan was beside him, crawling in the mud nearby.

Mike moved stealthily through the snowy mud, until he reached what appeared to be two stakes with barbed wire across it. The wire was too low, and the shots were still being fired above his head; he couldn't go over and couldn't fit under it. Mike removed his backpack and placed it in front of him, pushing it under the barbed wire. It fit! Mike then squirmed underneath, digging with his hands in the soft mud until he was all the way through. He stayed flat on the ground and grabbed his backpack, squirming it back onto his shoulders.

A stationary target was in front of him. Mike aimed and fired at the target. The bullet blew a neat hole in the target's centre. Mike rolled onto his abdomen, held his rifle up, digging his elbows in and continued on through the mud. He could see a black hole silhouetted in the ground; he crawled cautiously towards it. Another target was to his left; he aimed and fired another perfect shot. Mike grinned and scuttled into the trench, his wide eyes scanning the blackness.

"You're here," Stan whispered in the darkness. "You are doing good. Keep going."

Mike searched for the box; he found it in the corner, opened it and pulled out a small orange flag. He stuffed it in his jacket pocket and closed the lid. When he turned around, Stan was gone.

Mike peered his head over the trench and assessed his surroundings. The blackness looked slightly bluish to his adjusted eyes now. He could make out another black hole approximately 50 feet away. He could also see the strange barbed fences with pointed sticks and several downed trees. He would have to go around the downed trees to avoid the bullets whizzing over their heads. Mike slid onto his stomach in the mucky snow and dug his knees in to move faster. His body scrunched up like a frog, and he propelled himself, further along, squirming around the downed trees. It took longer, but he certainly did not want to get hit by the bullets flying overhead.

Mike squinted his eyes and barely made out a target to his right. He quickly aimed and fired. His bullet hit the target's centre again. Mike shouldered the rifle and continued onto another barbed wire fence. He was moving a little faster this time. He knew what to do. He pushed his heavy backpack through first, then squirmed his body underneath. He moved his hand to his backpack as he suddenly noticed another target. He grabbed his rifle quickly and fired. The bullet entered the target's centre satisfyingly. Mike turned to retrieve his pack, and his hand sunk into the wet snow. He moved his hands around, searching for it. It wasn't there! Mike panicked, shuffling his hands all over the snowy, wet ground, blindly grasping for his backpack. Nothing. Mike calmed himself and crawled back to the barbed wire fence. He found his pack snagged on the barbed wire. He tried to unhook it, but it was stuck. Mike cursed. Sweat formed all over his collar, and the wet snow pelted his face. Mike told himself to still the panic rising in his chest and study the barbed wire. He got as close as he could and grabbed a part of the wire, pulling it and pushing the backpack in the opposite direction. He felt it loosen. A sigh of relief escaped his mouth. Gratefully, he pulled at his pack, freeing it and shouldering it.

A shot splintered the wood fence right above his ear. Mike's nerves crackled. Don't let it rattle you, he told himself.

He scurried quickly across the field towards the next black trench. He scanned the area for the next target, nothing. He assessed the trench as best as he could and dived in. What a feeling of relief a trench was, he thought crazily. He searched for the second box, found it and opened the lid, discovering only two yellow flags remaining. He felt the panic bubble up in his throat and stuffed the flag into his jacket pocket, buttoning it snug.

He peered over the trench and saw the white tent in the distance. He squirmed onto the muddy snow again, frogging through the sludgy cold dirt. Suddenly he felt a piercing pain in his shoulder. He craned his neck to see. A pointed stick lodged in his shoulder. Damn, he thought. He yanked it out roughly, wincing from the pain, bit his lip and then threw the stick away, shuffling on. Another target appeared in front of him very close; he hadn't been paying attention. Cursing, he reached into his pouch for another 5-round charger clip and reloaded. He aimed and fired at the target, another accurate shot. He continued onto the next trench, sliding in and sitting up on his buttocks. He opened the third box. There were several flags left. He smiled satisfyingly, took a white flag and stuffed it in his pocket. Mike shuffled to the edge and peered over to assess his route. A target was to his right, very close. His heart jumped into his throat. It had rattled him. Calm and focus, he told himself.

He fired his rifle, the bullet hitting the target's centre cleanly.

Keep going, almost done, he mused.

Mike squirmed through the muck, finding another barbed fence. He dug down in the snowy mud, then pushed his 60-pound pack through. Sweat beaded on his forehead. Mike wiggled under the barbed wire and grabbed his backpack. He instantly felt a downed tree directly in front of him. The ground was higher. He moved his hands along the log; it was a big tree. He kept feeling the log and shuffling his body alongside the obstacle until finally, it ended. Mike squirmed his way forward just as several shots fired overhead. Making good choices, he thought.

The final trench was near; he could see it. Three targets appeared near the black hole. Mike grabbed his rifle and fired three times in succession. All targets hit! He secured the rifle and scurried to the black trench, sliding into it like a muddy wet fish. He searched for the fourth box in the dark, found it and lifted the lid. Several flags left. Good, he thought. He shoved one of the green flags in his pocket, closed the cover and secured the button on his pocket, patting it for good luck.

Mike peered over the trench. The white tent was close, maybe only 40 feet away. He squirmed onto the mud again, instantly feeling his backpack pulling him back. Something caught on his hat. He gently felt above his head; it was another barbed wire fence! Mike cursed.

He shuffled back into the trench, unhooked the backpack and dug into the mud. He shoved his pack through quickly. He then squirmed his body through, squeezing through the tight spot. Mike felt his body clear the barbed wire and wiped the sweat off his brow.

He continued shuffling on his belly and instantly felt something odd; his abdomen felt very wet. Water seeped sightlessly into his clothing and splashed onto his face. He dipped his fingers in and peered into the dark distance. It was a small wet pond!

Mike cursed involuntarily.

He felt his way along the edge of the pond, followed it towards the right, sliding his body along the wet mud until he reached the other side. The bullets stopped here. There was no more firing, although he could still hear shots in the distance. Mike still didn't trust anything. He squirmed along the ground until he reached the fabric of the tent. He looked behind him and to both sides. His instincts said it was fine, but his training told him to stay low. He slid to the front flap and squirmed into the large tent like a wet fish. Several men were sitting on rocks; Stan was one of them.

"Welcome, Private," Stan said. "You made it. Well done. You are the fourth to make it through. Not bad for a rookie."

Mike lay exhausted on his bed. His boots were muddy as hell. He left them at the end of the bed. The whole day was challenging, but he perversely enjoyed it. The infantry filled him with a clear sense of purpose. Mike stared up at the barrack's ceiling. He grabbed an ink well, pen and paper. He thought about Vira a lot in his spare time. It aroused him and intrigued him. He wrote:

Hello, Vira,

It has been a rough two days, but I am enjoying the challenges of joining the infantry. We had our first battle training today, and I was fourth to make it through. I experienced so many different emotions during the training battle exercise; fear, frustration, panic, aloneness and sometimes a strange calm. It has confirmed to me that I do indeed need to be a part of the Great War. I have skills born in me that most others don't.

I hope you understand my passion.

I do like you as well, Vira.

I think of you often when I lie in bed at night.

I don't know when we will see each other, but we will most definitely meet again.

Until then, my best regards,

Mike K. November 12, 1915

Mike folded the parchment paper and tied it with a string. He scrawled her name and address on it; as an afterthought, he scribbled a tiny heart onto the corner. He put the letter onto his box. It would be picked up with the morning mail.

He laid his head back onto the firm pillow. His eyes searched the ceiling, his hands resting on his inner legs, realizing that his penis was rigid. He closed his eyes.

Her blonde hair was in his face; her small breasts were dangling above him. Sweat was sliding between their bodies. She looked down and grasped his penis, positioning it inside of her.

He gasped as she gazed lovingly at him with those thoughtful eyes and rocked herself on top of his hips.

Mike felt his penis twitch as the images of Vira floated in his head. He released the stress of the day, thinking of sensual Vira, her scent, her hair and her smooth skin. Mike fell asleep quickly afterwards, physically exhausted, with sexual dreams persisting in his mind all night.

CHAPTER 18

Nath went to the post office to pick up his mail again. Ever since meeting Maria there, he always went to pick up the mail now. He laughed at himself. Women have such a profound effect on men. It twists you up and makes you do things that you don't normally do. It's also the most amazing happy feeling in the world, he thought.

He was delighted that he was finally interested in a woman after all these years, but he also felt sad and confused. She was much younger than him. Almost a year younger than his daughter. He would need to talk to Annabella about it first. If his daughter said no, then he would not pursue it any further. Maria and Nath would just remain friends then.

He opened the post office door and stepped inside. He immediately saw her. It was as if no one else existed in the entire room, but of course, this was not the case. There were three postal clerks, with a homesteader at each postal window, along with two individuals in the lineup.

Maria was at the far-left postal window, talking to the clerk. She had her back to Nath, so she was unaware of his presence. She had a beautiful blue dress on, her shoulders scrunching then relaxing as she talked. Her feet shifted slightly from side to side, and her long dark blonde hair flowed so wonderfully down her back, it was almost sensual. He couldn't help but stare. She was a very beautiful woman.

At that moment, as if on cue, she turned her head, glancing sideways. Her eyes caught his. She waved lightly, her fingers floating in the air gracefully; Nath waved back with a huge grin on his face. She smiled then turned back to the clerk, finishing her business with the post office and stuffed her mail into a small handbag.

Maria left the postal window and approached Nathan. "Hi, there, stranger," she said chuckling. "It seems that this is our regular meeting place."

Nathan laughed, "Yes, it seems so. How have you been, Maria? How is your history class going?"

"Very well, actually," Maria said, smiling. "My students have a lot of previous knowledge of the Icelandic explorers and settlers, but I was still able to teach them more. Thanks to you, Nath."

Nathanael beamed, "You are most welcome. Would you like to take a walk with me? Do you have any plans today?"

"I have some time, yes," Maria replied, smiling. "That would be lovely." She slid beside him in the lineup, her shoulders straightening proudly. "I will wait with you. I was lucky; there wasn't a line up when I arrived."

"You look rather lovely today," Nathan said, smiling and kissing her hand. "The blue dress really compliments your eyes and hair."

"Thank you, Nathan," she said, smiling.

They chatted briefly until finally, it was Nathan's turn; he walked up and grabbed his mail. Maria stood proudly beside him, patiently waiting until he nodded, and they left the post office together. Her shoulder brushed against his arm several times while they walked back toward the dock. The strong November wind blew into their faces as the snow started pelting down.

"Let's run," Nath said, pulling her into a dash to the fishery. They rushed in and closed the door behind them. The warehouse was empty. They giggled like teenagers as the door slammed shut on the snowy flakes. He instinctively flicked flakes of snow from her hair. She looked up at him, her emerald eyes glinting, with a simmering desire. The draw was like a magnet, pulling him to her. He laced his arm around her waist and pulled her in close to his body.

"You must be cold," he said, removing his deerskin coat. "Here, wear this."

She accepted the coat over her shoulders. It covered her like a huge blanket, her body a much smaller version than his. "Thank you," she said. "It's warm."

"It looks good on you," he said, smiling.

She laughed, "Just four sizes too big!"

He laughed with her. Nath felt warm and comfortable with this woman like he could not do anything wrong. He enjoyed having his arm around her; she didn't complain, so he left it there. Her waist was small, but her hips curved out, sculpting a sexy figure that Nath found very appealing. "You are a very beautiful woman," he said.

"Thank you," Maria replied, looking down shyly. "You are very handsome yourself too, Nath."

Nathan smiled briefly. He wanted to kiss her, but something was holding him back. He wasn't sure what it was, but he needed to honour the feeling. He wrapped his other arm around her and hugged her close, his chin on top of her head. "Is it alright if we hug like this?" he said.

"Yes," Maria murmured warmly into his chest.

He hugged her tenderly, his arms enveloping her entire body. His smell surrounded her, and it was a pleasant smell, an attractive male scent. She relished in the feeling of being hugged so fully and completely again. It had been a long time since she had been in a man's arms. She murmured satisfyingly and exhaled out a long, cleansing breath. It was like she had been holding in her breath for many years. She felt comfortable with Nathan like she had nothing to fear.

He swayed both their bodies slightly. He murmured something and kissed the top of her head. "This is nice. I like this."

"Mmm, I agree," she said, although it came out as a mumble into his shirt.

Nath kissed her head again, delighted to have her in his arms. It felt like the dam in his heart was opening every so slightly. He pondered if everything from the past thirty years had brought him here to this moment but banished the thought, wondering instead where this woman was leading him to.

"Do you ever wonder what the future brings?" Nath said, thoughtfully, staring at the empty closed up fishery warehouse.

"All the time," Maria replied, snuggling in closer. "Some days, I wonder how much control I have over events that happen in my life and how many times I have absolutely none. When life just blindsides you, it can be surprisingly joyful."

"Yes," Nathan said, chuckling. "I was thinking the same thing. Sometimes you work so hard for something to happen. Years later, you are left wondering why you put all that energy into something that doesn't do that much for you in the end.

Then all the sudden out of nowhere, something happens, and all your plans change."

"I agree," she said. "After working so hard towards accomplishing your goals, other things happen so randomly that completely don't make any sense. But yet it somehow feels so right. You have little control over it, but somehow it just doesn't matter, you just let it happen."

Nathan kissed her hair again. "You're sweet, Maria," he said, breathing in her womanly scent. They hugged for several moments, just enjoying the physical closeness. A few times, they swayed, and other times, they just stood holding each other, propped against the closed door.

"Maria," he said, interrupting the silence. "Do you want to come with me to Willow Point in the spring? It's only four months away." He laughed.

"Only four months away!" Maria exclaimed, laughing. "Are there any houses left on Willow Point?"

Nathan smiled. "Yes," he said. "There are still a few small cabins left. There is also a small dock someone builds every summer there too."

"Sounds lovely," Maria said, smiling. "I would love to go. That's where you first claimed New Iceland."

"Yes, it is," Nathan said. "I would love to show you. But we have to go in the spring. It is too cold out there right now."

"It's a date," she said.

"Wonderful," Nathan said softly, kissing her head again.

Nathan knocked briefly and then opened the small brown door. Annabella was in her kitchen cooking a deer stew; the entire home smelled so very delicious, making his stomach growl.

"Oh, my goodness, Bella," Nath said. "That smells delicious!"

"Pabbi!" Annabella said excitedly, running to him and hugging him fiercely.

"You were always a fireball, my sweet daughter," Nathan said affectionately.

"And you were always that tough guy," Annabella said, hugging her father warmly. "I missed you. You haven't been around for over a week. What have you been up to?"

"Just closing up the fishery," Nath said. "Getting ready for the ice fishing season soon."

Annabella released her father and walked back to the kitchen. "Okay," she said. "You just let me know when you are ready to go out, and I will be there. I might bring Jon and Vlad too if that's alright."

"Of course," Nath said, following her to the kitchen and seating himself at the rough wooden table.

"Have some stew with me," Annabella said, ladling the soup into ceramic bowls.

"I would love that," Nathan said. "Your cooking always makes my mouth water."

She finished serving the soup into the bowls and carried both to the table and sat down. They both ate in silence, devouring the delicious stew.

Nathan finished first, wiping his mouth on a cloth napkin. "I have something to tell you, my sweet," Nathan said.

Annabella looked up, concerned. "What is it, Pabbi?" she asked, a worried look clouding her face.

"Well," Nathan said. "I don't know how to say this, but I met this woman named Maria. She's a teacher."

Annabella laughed and immediately jumped across the table. She hugged her father fiercely, almost knocking his empty bowl to the floor.

Nathan laughed. "I love you, Bella," Nath said, wholeheartedly.

"I'm so happy for you, Pabbi," Annabella said, her smile beaming across her face. "It's been so long for you."

Nathan chuckled. "Yes," he said. "But there's something I need you to know, and I need your blessing for it. I really do."

Annabella pulled away and looked suspiciously in her father's eyes. "What is it?"

"Maria is a lot younger than I," Nathan said.

"How much younger?" she asked.

"She's your age," he replied.

Annabella smiled warmly. "Pabbi," she said, looking into his eyes. "I am so happy that you have finally found someone that you are interested in. She could be an elephant, and I wouldn't care."

Nathan burst into a wholehearted laugh; Annabella chuckled along with him. Spurred by the infectious giggling, Bella laughed more and more. They burst into joyful laughter until tears began forming in their eyes. The fits bubbled up into their throats, and they tried to settle down. Then Nath shouted, "Elephant!" Annabella grasped her abdomen, engulfed in the laughing fit, while happy tears dropped from her eyes. Nathan stood and hugged his daughter strongly. "Thank you," Nathan said, wiping the tears of joy from his eyes. "It means a lot to me. I love you, my sweet fireball."

"I love you too, Pabbi," Annabella said, hugging her father back. "Your happiness means much more to me than a number, her age and what other people think. What you must keep in your mind is how you feel. That's what should remain the most important, always."

The snow crunched under his feet as the wind blew through the branches. He hadn't come here for a while; he had almost forgotten. He was slightly angry with himself. The twigs broke along his sleeves as he barrelled through the forest. This was his refuge, his personal heaven and his lonely hell.

The snow started falling lightly at first, then larger flakes followed, blowing wildly in his eyes. It was dangerous to be out when it was so cold, but the forest lured him, spoke to his heart, urging him to seek clarification.

He didn't have the answers. He always somehow thought the forest would give him the answers. The deer, rabbits, trees and wind would show him the path.

He sat on a log with his head in his hands, snow surrounding him in a blanket of white. He stretched his neck up at the snowy sky, the flakes landing all over his face. His eyes darted, searching for the right thing to do.

The wind blew stronger, but there was still no answer.

He pondered why. He had always come here to this forest sanctuary, and he often left feeling better. Although the clear direction and answers always eluded him.

Then he slowly realized something profound.

The answers were in his heart.

He strained his neck up to the sky, blinking.

The answers were always there. He looked down, grimacing sadly, feeling a piece being torn from him. One important answer was very clear; he was still too frightened to accept the horrible conclusion.

CHAPTER 19

M ike lay in bed, his boots on the floor and his pen in
hand. He dipped the pen in the inkwell and wrote:

Dear Momma,

Infantry life is hard, but it is so rewarding. I enjoy it immensely. Please know that I was made for this. It is in my bones. I love you dearly and miss you, Momma. Please tell Pabbi that I miss him too. I will write a separate letter to him next week.

Now that the spring thaw has come, we are planning to leave for Halifax. No definite plans, but the Battalion is hoping to get to England by the summer.

I am excited but apprehensive. I know what awaits me there is war, but I am better skilled for this than others. My training and hunting skills have prepared me for so much and have led me to where I am now.

My best friend, Corporal Stan Horacs, is confident that we will be absorbed into other Battalions as snipers when we arrive in England.

I will keep you updated.

I love you and miss you, Momma. I will be back soon, don't worry.

Mike K. March 28, 1916

Mike let the ink dry on the parchment paper. He laid back and dreamed of being back home one day, surrounded by his momma, grandpa, the forest and his new girl, Vira.

I just have to stay alive throughout this war, he thought gravely.

The early dawn was warmer than usual, the winter thawing away into early summer. It was late April, and Nathan had promised to take Maria to Willow Point today. She had agreed to meet at her place and just walk. They had developed a close friendship in the past few months, and he was thrilled to be seeing her again.

The blue beaded bracelet rubbed against his pants as he dug his hands into his pockets. He rarely thought of the bracelet anymore; it was somewhat an extension of who he was now. Some people commented on it; others didn't even notice it.

Nathan was elated. They were going to watch the sunrise together. It was an hour walk along the road through deer paths and bushes. He stepped carefully through the pre-dusk darkness, looking up at the skies. Purples and lighter blues streaked in the eastern sky, reflecting the coming sunrise.

She came out prepared. Maria had her peasant dress on and her walking boots. Her hair was an uncombed morning mess pinned up in a loose bun. She looked even more stunningly beautiful, Nath thought.

"Ready?" he said as he grabbed her hand and led the way.

"Yes," she said, smiling and walking briskly alongside his strong arms. Nath led her along the road, her hand still in his. It felt warm and quite lovely, he thought. Memories tugged at his mind, teasing him with flashes of happiness. Nath turned to smile at Maria.

"What are you smiling about?" she laughed.

Nathan smirked, "Oh, nothing. You just look so darn beautiful. It just makes me smile."

Maria's face lit up in the prettiest smile he had ever seen. "Thank you," she said, chuckling. "You're very sweet, but I truly look like a mess. In case you haven't noticed."

"No, you don't, Maria," Nath said. "You look even more beautiful in early morning disarray. Maria, I haven't felt like this in years. I haven't seen a sunrise with anyone other than my daughter for many years. I feel like a youngster."

Maria smiled joyfully and swung her arms. Nath imitated her as they walked into the wind together, swinging their joined arms happily.

This woman made him feel so balanced, he thought. He didn't have a care in the world when he was with her. He enjoyed it immensely. He looked forward to every moment with her.

Nath veered off onto a deer path, and before they knew it, they were stomping through the bush, Maria following Nath, his hand still outstretched behind him and grasped onto hers.

His grip tightened as they approached several downed trees. "Watch your step, Maria," he said, leading her through the bush.

She focused on the ground and placed each foot carefully in front of the other. Soon they came across a large pile of dead-wood. Nathan jumped over and held out his hands, helping her make it over. She smiled and accepted his help. She briefly lost balance, but he was there, with his strong grip, steadying her. She felt very safe around him.

"We are getting close," Nath said. "You can see the lake. Look." He pointed through the bushes.

"It's beautiful," she said. "The skies are getting lighter already. Did we miss the sunrise?"

"No, I don't believe so," Nath said. "But we are very close. Let's hurry."

They hiked through the bush; it became quite thick in some areas. Again, Nath helped her through the tricky spots, and she followed along happily; it gave her a strangely pleasant feeling knowing he was there for her.

"The beach is right here," Nathan said, pointing through the bush. "This is close to where we landed in 1875."

Maria looked up and saw the beach sprawled out before them. It was deserted, only a few rustic cabins remained. The beach was beautifully quiet and serene. The sand was paler in colour than the beach in Gimli, almost whitish.

"It is so calm and peaceful here," Maria said, her eyes taking it all in, as they stood on the shoreline of the beach.

"We had a lot of tragedy here," Nath said. "I don't come back here often anymore."

Maria hugged him. "I know," she said. "I heard the stories. Almost one hundred people died in the first winter. It must have been so hard. How did you deal with it?"

"I was young," Nath said. "I just took the blows as they came and tried my best to manage the events as they happened. Lots of funerals."

"I'm sorry," Maria said. She looked thoughtfully across the lake, feeling the wind blow warmly in her face. "Is this where you met your wife?"

Nathan looked at the sand. "Yes," he said solemnly.

"I'm sorry," Maria said again. "I shouldn't have mentioned it."

"It's alright," Nath said. "It is going to come out sooner or later. We were only together for just over a year. But it was the most amazing year of my life. I still remember the details. When you lose something like that, it is devastating." Nath walked to the water's edge and peered over to the horizon. "You must feel the same pain from losing your husband. Does it still hurt?"

"Yes," Maria said. "It is not as fresh of a wound anymore. I have healed, but sometimes, certain things will trigger a memory, and I will instantly crumble. But I am picking myself up quicker and quicker every time."

Nath glanced at her from the side, watching her dark green eyes glow, appreciating her words. As they walked along the beach, she spoke of her late husband; he related with bits of Anwa's story and her death.

"She died saving my life," Nath said, sadly. "When I developed smallpox, Anwa was so distraught; her parents said that while she was nursing me, she wasn't even eating or taking care of herself. She contracted smallpox from me shortly after I started improving. I understand that it was what any devoted spouse would do, but it still stings. The Swampy Cree natives succumbed much more quickly to smallpox than anyone else, and we were aware of this at the time, but we just didn't want to believe it. There was nothing I could do but hold her until she died in my arms. I lived, but she had to perish because of her love for me. Life just doesn't seem fair, and that's how I looked at things for many years."

Maria watched his eyes as she listened to his story, shuffling closer and finally hugging him tightly. His eyes were dry, but his heart felt open and raw. It felt so right talking, as if some puzzle pieces had finally been found after all these years. All they were doing was fitting the pieces into the correct spots now. They stood there, hugging each other in silence for several moments, just the sound of the waves hitting the shoreline. It was beautiful, touching and serene.

"The sun will be rising soon," Nath said. "I know a spot that we can watch it. It's a small fishing dock that I build every year, just to enjoy the solitude. Often, I come out here just to see the sunrise and fish. You will love it. Follow me."

They walked along the beach hand in hand, connected, talking about life, death and love. His soul felt electrified like someone had lit a match and restarted the fire in his heart. He was falling in love; he could feel it. And he was totally okay with it.

"Do you ever wonder why we exist?" she asked.

"I sometimes wonder that, yes," Nathan said, looking down at her hand in his. "Why does the universe spare some people and not others? What purpose do we have here on earth?"

Maria nodded in silent agreement.

When they reached the end of the beach, they both crawled up onto the high dock, walking right to the edge. The sunrise began peeking out from the horizon, scattering its beautiful orange rays against the heavy clouds, creating a kaleidoscope of purples, reds and greens. Strangely, the clouds had parted just in the exact spot where the sun was rising, as if allowing it to rise. The effect was breathtakingly beautiful. The sun reflecting against the lake and the receding storm was truly amazing. What is a sunrise without the clouds anyway?

They reached the end of the dock, took their shoes off in the warm spring breeze and sat down. Maria's dress bunched up under her buttocks, and she dangled her pretty legs over the side. He smiled and copied her, swinging their legs like children, giggling. They hugged briefly, then both leaned back on their hands, taking in the picturesque sunrise, feeling the wind blowing through their toes. The moment was surreal. It felt so right to be here with her.

Nath mused reflectively, "I wonder if sometimes we need to go through hard times in our life to get to the other side. What do you think?"

Maria looked at him, her green eyes piercing through him. "I think we never really appreciate the light or worse, sometimes we never find it, unless we've known the dark and lived in its trenches."

Nath's spine tingled as her words sunk into his heart. At that moment, he knew something as clear as he had never before. He wasn't quite sure if it was real or just his mind playing tricks on him. But he sincerely thought at this moment that he was going to be spending many years with this woman, that she was his future wife.

The blunt thought shot through his body like a strong current; he let it ride through him. He didn't resist the thought, although it momentarily confused his rational mind. Such a random idea of marriage! His heart thumped in his chest, and his hopes soared.

The revelation made his head feel light. He smiled at her while she talked, watching her lips as they moved and felt utterly happy.

She laughed. "You have the most wonderful blue eyes," she said. "I look into your eyes, and I feel you."

Nath lifted his hand to her chin and looked into her eyes, as her green eyes gazed back. "I feel the same, Maria," he said. Then he leaned in and kissed her soft lips. His hands grazed along her waist and moulded her soft body gently into his; they kissed tenderly, embracing each other with their heat. Her lips tasted slightly sweet, and she opened her mouth for him to enter. His tongue penetrated her mouth, finding her wetness. She groaned, then lifted her hands into his hair, her fingers curling into his shoulder-length waves; her touch sent shards of electricity through his spine, tingling his skin and his soul. She kissed him back passionately, while the sun rose majestically above the horizon. He leaned her back onto the dock, wrapping an arm around her head as a pillow and continued kissing this wonderful woman in his arms. It felt like heaven, the place of love that he had been waiting for all these years.

His heart thumped inside his chest loudly, as if someone had begun beating on drums. His feelings were growing rapidly for this woman. He briefly wondered if he should be more cautious, but then completely abolished the thought. He had spent the past several months befriending this woman, relating their pasts, their history, their loves, their deaths and everything in between. He couldn't resist her anymore. It was futile.

He broke the kiss, smiled at her, then kissed her nose. "You know what I was thinking?" Nath said. "I thought that it's so strange sometimes when random things happen, and you can't seem to explain it all. I wonder why that is."

"I think certain things are just better left unexplained," she said. "Maybe sometimes we just have to accept, not try to rationalize. Often things just happen, and maybe they are meant to be, and other times they are not. We need to accept the unexplainable and just leave it at that."

"You are a smart woman," he said, smiling.

"Thank you, Nathan," she said, sincerely. "I don't think any man has ever told me that before."

"No?" Nathan said, laughing. "Well, I know it to be true." He looked out onto the lake briefly, then grabbed her arms and pulled her up with his weight while he stood. "Time to go. We still have an hour to get back to Gimli."

Maria stood with him; they strolled along the dock, hands around each other's waists. They stepped off the small pier and into the sand. "You know something," Maria said. "I feel very comfortable with you like I've known you for years, not just several months."

Nath smiled. "I was going to say the same thing," he said, laughing. "I'm so glad I picked up the mail that day!"

Mike lay down on the grass after another day of training. His body was becoming adjusted to the cruel physical demands of Battalion training. Stan was there with him. They had developed a strong friendship, sharing several things in common. Stan was Ukrainian, and he had a woman waiting for him. They often spoke about the women they had left behind.

They sipped water and smoked a cigarette in the fading sunlight. They both had pens, inkwells and paper. They were both writing letters home.

Mike's letter read:

Hi, Afi,

I miss you, grandpa. I miss our chats and our friendly banter. I miss fishing with you and everything we used to do. I spent more time with you, Afi than I did with my own Pabbi. You were always there for me, for any reason, any time of the day. You would stop what you were doing just to see me, always.

I don't think you realize how much I appreciate your influence in my life. So, I'm going to tell you now. Thank you, Afi, for being the best grandpa and the best role model for me. You taught me to fish, to hunt, to shoot, archery, to cook, everything. It prepared me for what I am doing now. I know you don't want to hear that, but I am becoming one of the most skilled snipers here. And the 108th Battalion is thrilled to have me.

We received news that a train will be taking us to Halifax soon. We don't know the exact dates yet, but it will be sometime this summer. It is expected to be a long train ride. Our commanders told us to be ready to pack up our belongings at a moment's notice.

I am anxious and excited at the same time. I have never even travelled outside of Gimli or Winnipeg before, and now I will be going to Europe! It feels exciting, but I also know the reason I am going there. The danger is real, and the Central Powers must be stopped. The training that we do every day is hard, but it is preparing us for battle, which we need. We will be prepared. It is a good Battalion, with a lot of good people.

I will be back fishing with you again, Afi. I promise.

Miss you,

Private Mike K. May 2, 1916

Chapter 20

He felt a strange lump in his chest. He swallowed and looked up at the morning sky; he had felt this type of fear once before. A tear ran down his cheek. He walked into the bushes, the leaves crunching under his large feet. He made his way through the trees and shrubs, swatting stray branches out of the way. His emotions were raw, and his eyes were wet. He didn't see the log buried on the forest floor. His foot connected, and his legs flew over the log, sending him crashing onto the ground. He looked up at the sky and cursed, brushing the dirt off his pants and straightening. He continued walking through the forest; several branches scraped his arm, ripping a large tear in his light coat. He grimaced, looked down and tried to close the gaping flap on his coat arm tenderly. He was disappointed; this was his favourite coat.

He gazed up at the sky. The trees swayed at the top of the canopy eerily. The wind gusted forcefully into his face, warning him to go back the way he came.

The answer was not here.

But he knew something that the forest didn't. The fear in his heart was here. It always was. It felt like salvation at first, a quiet place to lay his head. But it slowly became his prison, the comfortable space that only he knew, and no one else would dare visit.

But someone did visit.

A few days ago.

A wonderful lady friend.

She cared about him.

He knew this, and it scared him. She easily walked with him to Willow Point. They laughed and shared such beautiful moments that his heart felt like it was breaking open.

Then he had read his grandson's letter.

Nath had only felt this fear once before, and he had lost the love of his life soon after. What was he supposed to do? There really was nothing he could do, Nath felt helpless. Mike was an adult, and he had made a decision. The Great War needed him. Nath could not feel selfish and needy at this moment. He wanted his grandson back home, but it wasn't his choice to make.

He strolled along the small path, hiking through, retracing the steps he had taken several days ago. His heart felt so confused, jumbled with emotions. He felt a throbbing love for Maria, so much that he had avoided seeing her for the past five days. His emotions clouded his head and ignited his fears. The walk they had taken that day hit him so hard, right in the gut, almost as if someone had punched him there. He hadn't even realized that he was allowing her into his self-imposed prison. It just felt so natural at the time to watch the sunrise with Maria. His feelings for her were growing incredibly strong. He didn't want to scare her away. She was the most beautiful woman in the entire town of Gimli; she could choose any man, why him?

He felt confused and immensely grateful at the same time. When they were at the dock, he had been so sure that she was his future wife! Absolutely certain! It just didn't make any sense.

Now, he just thought it must have been some craziness inside his head. He could not rationalize it. He twisted it up in his head many times, trying to make sense of it all and each time, it came up as a jumble of events and emotions.

Now, his grandson was leaving for Europe. The threat of having another family member die was real. After his Pabbi passed away, his momma had died also and, of course, his beloved Anwa. Mike was part of Anwa. Nath was terrified of losing him. The thought made Nath crumble inside.

He reached the beach and walked along the sand until he arrived at the dock. Nath stopped, turned his head back and gazed at the path leading to the pier. It was a worn, overgrown path. Nath didn't come out here too often anymore. When he was younger, he would come out here every week, be alone with his thoughts and fish, sometimes thrash angrily through the bush. It was the only outlet he had for his anger at life.

Nath looked up the path into the bush, towards the old cabin. He had fixed it over the years, funnelling his raw anger into productivity. He had removed the tent walls and built all four walls with lumber that he had chopped down. It was a crude log cabin, his old cabin, the one he had lived in with Pabbi. The same cabin he had spent the first week together in with Anwa.

He shivered as the ghosts of the past whispered in the trees. The wind blew the leaves, rustling them loudly. Nath took a deep breath and walked steadily towards the cabin. His eyes were swollen, and his heart raw. He was being pulled to the cabin with a force he could not understand. He couldn't make sense of it.

He reached the door, turned the knob, and it creaked open.

He looked down on the floor and remembered their first night together.

The snow was blowing underneath the door. It was the first heavy snowfall of the year. Anwa was cuddled in bed with him; her skin was warm; they were snuggling together, wrapped up with each other. Her smell was so sweet, like honey. The first time he saw her naked, he felt like his body was on fire. He was floating in heaven when they made love.

He was certain that was the night that Annabella, their beautiful daughter, was conceived.

Nath fell on his knees and began to cry. He tried to wipe the tears off his cheeks, but it was useless; they were coming out too fast. It wasn't the first time he had done this. Over the past thirty years, Nath had come to the forest and the cabin just to relive being with Anwa. He had missed her so terribly. It had eaten away at his soul some days. But then other days were better. The sun would shine, the fish were plentiful, but he always walked through life with a piece missing, like he wasn't a complete human. He would always come back to the cabin and the dock to fish, absorb the sunrises and eventually cry at the door. The first few years were horrific. He couldn't function very well. He ate and slept, took care of his daughter, but he walked like a zombie, just moving in and out of a world that he couldn't understand anymore. He felt cheated and robbed of his beautiful future.

As the years went on, it became easier. He became more accustomed to not having Anwa in his life. He still had his days when the grief was too much, and he would retreat here to this safe place.

His daughter began growing up also. Even at the age of six years old, she looked like Anwa. He found solace in raising his daughter. A part of Anwa was still alive and well. He loved Annabella with so much of his heart; it felt like it would burst some days.

When his grandchildren came, Anwa's memory began to fade into the corner of his heart, where deep love resides. Some years, he would only come here to the cabin once or twice, but each time he would fall down and weep.

This time was different, though; it seemed to hurt the most, almost as much as it did in the beginning.

And he knew why.

Nath stepped up and walked to the table, pulled out the old wooden chair and sat down. He pulled the inkwell out, the pen and the paper. He needed to do this; he needed to write this all out. He needed to let all his emotions free. He wasn't sure what he was going to write, so he just started without thinking or even understanding the entire meaning.

He wrote:

Dear Beautiful Anwa,

I am here to tell you about our grandson Mike today, among other things. He joined the 108th Battalion and is leaving overseas for the Great War soon. I am terrified that I will lose him as I lost you. Mike is only 20 years old; soon, he will be turning 21. He has both of our wilful spirits. He is stubborn and has a head of stone! As Annabella looks like you, Mike looks identical to me when I was young.

I taught Annabella and Mike everything you had taught me about fishing and hunting. Mike even became an expert marksman as a result. So, yes, the Great War needs him, but, I don't want to lose him, Anwa. I cannot. It would be like losing a piece of you.

The only thing that had kept me alive and breathing in this world without you was knowing our daughter and grandchildren are pieces of you, Anwa.

And I am terrified of losing them too. I know that you are in a very different world than us, but if there is anything you can do, please do it. I will pray tonight that the universe brings Mike safely back home.

I know he is stubborn and skilled enough to survive. He tells me that we will go fishing again, and I believe him. I must continue to believe him and bury all my fears and doubts.

There is something else that I need to share also.

I have fallen in love with a woman.

Her name is Maria. She is kind, beautiful, and she shares the same grief. She knows the heartbreak of loss. She was at the dock with me a few days ago. We shared so much, our emotions, thoughts on life and death; it made me tingle. The same kind of tingle that I felt with you. It scares me.

So, I have withdrawn from her to be alone.

But as I am writing this letter, it is clear what I must do.

I must ask for her hand in marriage.

I feel conflicted with my emotions because I have been so terribly heartbroken for so long, but I now realize what I must do.

I must let you go now, Anwa.

I LOVE YOU.

Love,

Nathanael Olason May 5, 1916

Nath stopped writing and just looked at the words on the paper. Could it be? The thought was both terribly sad but also comforting at the same time. He knew that Anwa would want him to be happy. He knew that she loved him with all of her being when she was alive and maybe even looked over him in spirit.

But he also knew that he could not love another woman without letting her go.

He had to. It was all so very clear to him. As if someone had just told him a special formula or a certain recipe that he was searching for all this time.

It was remarkably clear now.

The tears had dried up on his cheeks, tightening the skin on his face and beard. He stood up and gently folded the letter and stuffed it in his pocket. He grabbed some sticks and wandered outside, the door closing behind him.

Nath pulled some logs from the woodpile and started a fire in the pit. He watched the flames flicker, and the smoke swirled upwards, creating odd shapes and little puffs of clouds. The fire crackled, and embers jumped out haphazardly onto the brownish-green spring grass. He looked out at the dock and the shimmering lake. Several small chunks of ice still floated on the surface in the distance. He could make out the odd shapes, bobbing up and down, somehow being an obstruction in the massive lake but yet melting to form part of the lake itself.

His heart felt at peace now.

He unfolded the letter and silently reread it over and over again. Several tears plopped onto the paper like raindrops on a tent. Nath reread the last two lines again:

I must let you go now, Anwa.

I LOVE YOU.

The words rang in his head like an echo. Was he really letting go of Anwa today? he asked himself. It has been such a long journey to get where he is now.

Yes. He was letting her go now.

Hopefully, she could somehow hear these words, somehow feel these emotions, somehow be there for Mike in Europe. Although she was a ghost now, no longer of this earth, she hasn't been here for 39 years! Nath thought, incredulously. Has it really been that long?

He folded the letter delicately, running his fingers over the crease repeatedly.

Then he stood and placed it gently in the fire. He watched the flames engulf the letter immediately with a surge of orange heat. Then it disappeared into ashes, just as quickly as it ignited.

Nath stood by the fire for several moments, tears streaming down his face. Reluctantly, he grabbed his fishing rod and headed to the dock to catch one last fish. What would he do with the old cabin? Nath wasn't sure. He would ask Annabella what she wanted.

CHAPTER 21

Nath returned home late the next morning. He changed and put on his best suit; he straightened his bow tie and looked in a chipped mirror. He still looked quite distinguished and handsome, he thought. He was still slim and fit, his body easily mistaken for a man twenty years younger. He shined his shoes and opened the door.

Several townsfolk were out on the streets today. It was a beautiful warm spring morning, a good sign of the coming summer. Nath's shoes clomped on the dirt road. He was determined. He didn't care anymore. If she said no, then he would sulk, but he could not hold this in any longer. He knew it was the right thing to do. She would be distraught that he hadn't contacted her for over five days after their first amazing kiss, so he had to do something grand to let her know how he really felt.

He walked up to her cobblestone walkway.

Suddenly she stepped out of her front door onto the porch. She didn't see him initially; she was quietly turning the skeleton key into the lock, unaware that he was there. Nath froze, standing quite still, then smiled as he watched her fumble with the lock. She was the most amazing woman he had ever met since Anwa. He could not let this opportunity go. Her long dark blonde hair fluttered down her shoulders as she straightened, then turned to face him.

Maria's face showed surprise, then a veil of sadness and misery crossed her face. He was right, Nath thought. She had been crushed by his disappearance. He could see it in her eyes; they were saddened. Then her face changed, her brows bunched together briefly, assessing the situation, then just as quickly as it appeared, it was replaced with a small smile. The grin crept onto her lips, making her dimples show.

"Hi, Maria," Nath said nervously. "You look as beautiful as ever."

"Hi, Nath," Maria replied.

They both stood silently for several moments, a standoff of wits.

"You disappeared," Maria said.

"I know," Nath said. "I'm sorry."

"Why?" Maria asked.

"Because I needed time to think," Nath said. "Time to sort out my thoughts."

"Oh?" she said questioningly. "And what have you come up with?"

Nath smiled and took the opening. He dug in his pocket and took two large steps towards her. "I believe that I need to ask you a very serious question," Nathan said, grinning mischievously.

Maria blinked her eyes several times and felt tears of joy escaping from her eyes. She watched as he knelt down on one knee and brought his hand out in front of him.

Nath looked up at her with the sexiest grin a man could ever possess and held out a gold ring with a milky white pearl in the middle.

Maria pulled her hands to her face and started crying happy tears of joy. "Oh my Lord, Nath," Maria exclaimed.

"Maria," Nath said formally, still bent on one knee. "Would you do me the honour of marrying me? I promise you will not find a better man. I will be with you during whatever hardships happen, during the happy moments, the sadness and the joy. I will never leave your side."

Maria's face was streaked with tears; she could hardly see anymore. She carefully walked down the two steps towards him, as a small crowd gathered on the sidewalk near Main Street. She bent down in front of him and looked into his eyes. "You crazy romantic fool!" she cried, laughing. "I can't believe you are doing this!"

Several people chuckled in the crowd. A few people muttered this and that. One small teenage boy said something. At first, it was muffled, then he spoke louder.

"Say yes!" the boy shouted.

Maria leaned closer; their eyes locked. It was the most heavenly moment ever. It felt like everything clicked at this moment; everything made sense. It felt so right. She leaned in for the kiss, and their lips met. She kissed his salty lips, little kisses, then suddenly he grabbed her and kissed her harder, right in front of everyone!

The crowd cheered!

Maria giggled while he was still kissing her. "I'm not finished," he said. "Go away!" He waved his hands at the small crowd, jokingly, then continued kissing the love of his life.

When he was finished, he released her. She looked at him very closely, her face almost touching his and mouthed the word yes. He smiled. "You will have to say it louder, I think, my sweetheart," Nath said, chuckling.

She peered over his head at the crowd. "Yes!" she shouted strongly.

The crowd cheered again, a few people hugged, and several started clapping their hands.

"You crazy man!" Maria exclaimed, a brilliant smile on her face.

Nath put the ring on her finger, sliding it on delicately. "You haven't seen anything yet, my sweetheart," Nath said, smiling coyly.

Suddenly, he grabbed her legs and scooped her up in his arms. Maria shrieked and laughed.

"Give me the key," Nath instructed firmly.

Maria handed him the skeleton key.

Nath placed it in the lock, turned it and opened the door. He turned to everyone on Main Street. "You can all go home now!" he shouted, warm-heartedly. "Show's over!" He kicked the door open, then booted it closed.

She giggled in his arms. "Where are you taking me?"

He smiled and carried her across the house to her bedroom. "I'm taking you to your room."

Her eyes gleamed with desire.

They entered her bedroom. The heat between their bodies rose like a wildfire. Silence filled the room as their bodies took over the conversation. He placed her down near the dresser and kissed her lips softly, his hands still gripping her soft buttocks. Nath felt his penis respond instantly. She moaned as he kissed her mouth deeply, still grasping her buttocks. His body was pressing against hers urgently; he paused and looked closely at her face. Her emerald eyes gazed back at him with a fire so strong his head swam. "Would you like to wait until the mar-riage vows?" Nath asked, his voice cracking with desire.

"Would it be bad of me to say that I'd rather not wait?" she said breathlessly. "Haven't we waited long enough?"

That was all he needed to hear.

Nath kissed her mouth fully, attempting to remove his shirt at the same time. She fumbled with his pants while they kissed, urgency shooting like wildfire throughout their bodies. She somehow removed his belt rather quickly. Next thing Nath knew, his pants were falling to the floor at his feet.

He looked at her urgent eyes and fumbled with her dress, undoing the delicate buttons, while she ravaged his penis. She started touching it and even bent down to lick it. His entire body lit up with a surge of testosterone firing throughout his veins.

The dress finally came off, and he was momentarily stunned by her beauty. The afternoon sun was streaking through the windows; the rays glimmering off her white skin. Her large breasts rested beautifully on her chest, the large nipples shrivel-ling and pointing directly at him, pleading for his attention. He bent down in response and touched her pretty breasts, immedi-ately suckling on the right one.

Maria gasped as her body lit up with electricity. "Oh, my," she breathed.

Nath quickly switched to the left one, sucking the entire nipple into his mouth. Abruptly, he grasped both of her breasts and squished them together, kissing one and then the other. Maria's head stretched back, lost in desire. She squirmed and pushed her naked body against his, propelling them towards the wall.

His large hands travelled madly down her curvy hips and over her shapely legs, trying to feel every tiny inch of her body.

His hands were moving almost as if they had their own mind. He squeezed her buttocks and lifted her body closer. He finally pushed both their bodies backwards onto her bed, falling with a soft thump. They both laughed as they landed in each other's arms.

Nath ran his hands along her pale legs, caressing her smooth feminine skin. His hands travelled down her hips and her shapely thighs, stopping to squeeze her soft curves. She groaned and squirmed underneath him urgently, kissing and then lightly nibbling on his shoulder.

Nath grinned and then thought of something. He gently caressed her face, looking into her eyes briefly. "Maria," he said. "I never asked you before. I always assumed that you could not conceive. Do we need to worry about pregnancy?"

Maria's eyes gleamed back at him, so filled with desire and estrogen that it threatened to make his head burst. The urgency was so strong right now all he could think about was to enter her immediately. But he needed to know. He had heard that men could have babies well into their sixties. "Oh, no," she said, her voice musky and almost slurring the words. "My late husband was impotent. Not I."

Nath smiled then kissed her lips roughly. He had a strong, irrational desire to impregnate her immediately. His body was not telling him no. But neither was she, he thought momentarily.

He felt along her thighs, running his hands urgently along her smooth skin until he reached her vagina. He touched her there and found the smooth skin very moist. His penis urged him to continue. He was ready at her entrance, trying to calm his mind down and lessen the urgency, which was proving futile.

"What do you think about having kids?" Nath asked, his words muffled by his sexual desire. "Do you want me to pull out?" he asked huskily.

Maria smiled coyly. "I think having your seed inside me would be the most wonderful feeling ever," she said, her voice thick with desire. "I would be thrilled to become pregnant with your child."

Nath kissed her lips in agreement, his tongue fully inside her mouth now, her sweetness mixed with that little bit of musk, creating a heady aroma that filled his senses. "I love you, Maria," Nath said, his heart thumping inside his chest. "I've been waiting for you for so long."

"Nath," Maria said, her words getting cut short as he slid his penis inside her vagina, slowly at first, tensing at the tight walls, then finally entering her deeply all the way to the end, touching her inner cervix. She groaned heavily and bit his shoulder gently. The feeling of connectedness was incredible.

Nath stopped, with his rigid penis fully inside her, and kissed her lips lightly.

She opened her eyes lazily, her eyelids hooded and full of yearning. "I love you, Nath," she moaned quietly, almost whispering the words into his shoulder.

Her words melted into him. He moved his hips slightly back, sliding deliciously out of her while she gasped and grabbed onto his shoulders. He teetered at her entrance, then slowly entered her fully again, eliciting groans of passion from her sweet mouth.

Nath moaned as he lay on top of her, his body inside hers, connected so exquisitely. He would not have much control this first time, he knew. It had been 39 years!

Nath kissed her ear and whispered. "I cannot hold back this first time, my sweetheart," he whispered sensually. "I haven't had sex for a very long time."

She kissed his shoulder. "Don't hold back," she said. "I want your baby inside me."

That was it. His control vanished. He began pushing in and out of her rhythmically, possessed by a primal urge now. Her face was so lovely, enraptured with estrogen and desire. Her hair was in a great mess all over the pillow, and every time he pushed inside of her, her body lifted a bit, her breasts bobbing with the motion. He could feel, smell, hear and taste everything. His orgasm was imminent.

Nath felt the semen surge to the tip of his penis in a rush. He closed his eyes and tried to will it away, hoping to please her a bit longer. He stopped, feeling his penis twitch inside her and inhaled heavily.

Then suddenly, without warning, she moaned deeply, bit his shoulder, sucking on it hard as her vagina clamped down intensely around his penis, squeezing it unbelievably firm. His penis throbbed inside of her as she orgasmed around him, her juices flowing out along his scrotum. He stretched his neck out and breathed in sharply.

He thrust into her one last time. There was no way he could continue in this kind of grip. His penis ejaculated forcefully, pulsing streams of semen inside her womb. Nath groaned heavily as he released inside her. He ground his buttocks into her instinctively, trying to bury his seed as far as he could. His legs shook several times as her moans filled the room.

He was breathing so incredibly fast, and she was moaning loudly. He splayed on top of her, completely engulfing her body, glued to each other, their bodies slick with sweat. He could feel their hearts, banging like drums against each other's chests. She quivered silently, and he melted on top of her, feeling his body slowly relax.

She started kissing the bruise on his shoulder. "I'm sorry for biting you," Maria said.

He chuckled. "I liked it," Nath said, grinning mischievously.

They lay there physically exhausted for several moments, before either spoke. Nath slid onto his side and pulled her close. He kissed her head.

Maria kissed his shoulder, murmuring. She absentmindedly danced her fingers over his bicep and traced it down to his wrist. Her hands stroked the blue beads on his wrist. "That's a beautiful bracelet. So unique. I don't think I have ever seen a man wear a bracelet. It suits you. I never did ask you where you got it."

"It was Anwa's," Nath replied, his voice suddenly stuck in his throat.

Maria kissed his wrist." I know what that feels like, babe," she said softly. She cuddled into his chest and exhaled. "The bracelet is part of you. Your past, your pain; it all contributed to creating who you are now and I accept everything that made you into the wonderful man that I love."

He buried his face into her hair. Nath's heart hammered in his chest at her words. Her smell was so wonderful, like the smell of morning rain on a field of grass, and her words sounded like heaven. He wished for this day to happen for so many years. Nath wrapped his arms around her and slid her to his chest, cuddling her tight. His entire body draped around her. "I'm so glad I found you," he said, moisture forming in his eyes.

They lay like this for several hours that afternoon, the sun's rays dancing all over their sweaty bodies. They soon fell asleep, wrapped in each other's arms, their sweat and fluids combined. Maria was the woman he had been waiting for all this time, he mused. He kissed her forehead as their spent bodies fell asleep easily into a mid-afternoon nap.

Chapter 22

It was 5 am, and they were packing up their belongings. The Battalion had moved to Camp Hughes in May. They spent the summer in bell tents, sleeping on straw mattresses and training tirelessly. They received word that they would be heading to Halifax by train today. A long journey.

The trip overseas was happening soon. Mike had a strange mix of excitement, anticipation and fear wiring his body with adrenaline. They had been training hard for ten months; it was time. He packed up his belongings and rushed in line with everyone else awaiting the train.

The steam train whistled and decelerated as the soldiers nervously waited. When it had fully stopped, they received the order from their officers and began to board. Stan was right behind him.

"Time to go to war finally," Stan said. "How are you feeling?"

"Nervous," Mike said. "But ready. We've trained for so long. I feel like a slingshot, strung as tight as can be, ready to fire."

Stan laughed, "Same here."

"Did you hear back from Shirley?" Mike asked.

"Yes," Stan replied. "She's upset but taking it well. How about you? Did Vira write back?"

"She did," Mike replied. "She was happy that I was doing something that I strongly believed in although she was still quite nervous and concerned. As she should be."

"Did she tell you anything about the status of your friendship when you get back?" Stan asked.

"Yes," Mike said. "She said that she was looking forward to hugging me again. I think we will just take it day by day. We are growing to like each other quite a lot; I don't see it cooling down anytime soon. But I can tell you this; I won't be just hugging her. I'll be kissing that woman with all my heart." Mike laughed.

"That's the way to a woman's heart," Stan said. "Kiss her good." They both laughed.

The train was filling up with soldiers and equipment. The infantry soldiers chatted excitedly; there was a nervous tension in the air. Something was about to happen. Every single soldier could feel it, right to their bones.

They were going to war.

Annabella banged on Nath's door loudly. "Pabbi!" she shouted. "Are you home? Answer the door, please!"

Nath grabbed his pants and pulled them on as Maria slept soundly. It was early morning. He rubbed his beard with his palm, trying to shake the cobwebs of sleep from his mind. What was wrong, he wondered?

"Coming," he shouted back as he neared the door. He yanked it open. "What is it, Bella? Is everything alright?"

Annabella's hair was uncombed, and her face streaked with tears.

"Oh my God, Bella! What is wrong, my dear?" Nath asked.

Annabella held a letter in her hand, waving it. "I got a letter from Mike this morning," she said. "Can you come for a walk, and we can read it together?"

"Okay," Nath pulled on his coat and shoes, heading out the door with his daughter.

The September rain began falling in a gentle drizzle. A silent calm rain. The skies were cloudy and gloomy. Nath felt a chill in the air and a chill in his soul. They walked towards the beach and sat silently onto the sand, Nath's arm around her shoulders, watching the raindrops plunk into the water. Every drop disturbed the surface of the calm waters, making the lake look like tiny raindrop craters were everywhere. The wind was nonexistent.

Nath held his coat above them, shielding them from the rain, as they both read the letter, Annabella reading aloud.

Dear Momma,

We arrived in Halifax today. We are preparing to leave for England soon. Rumours are that we will be boarding the SS Olympic, the sister ship of the Titanic! I am excited. We were told to write our letters home now. The date of deployment is September 19th.

I have a strange mixture of anticipation, excitement and nervousness. I am not fearful, but I am anxious. We have no idea what brigades we will be with, when we will land and how long we will be in England.

I don't want you to worry, Momma. I love you, Mom. I will be back no matter what it takes. I promise.

Tell Afi that I love him also and dad and all my brothers and sisters.

I'll write again as soon as I can.

Love,

Private Mike K. September 18, 1916

Nath hugged Annabella as she cried into his shoulder, the tears gently sliding down her cheeks. He rubbed her back and soothed the emotions from her. "He will be alright, sweetie," Nath assured her.

"How do you know?" Annabella looked up at him, her face streaked with emotion.

"I don't," Nath replied simply. "But I trust his judgement and his decisions. Ever since he was little, he made good decisions. He's not going to change now; he continues to make good choices. He's stubborn and hardy like all of the Olason's. He has continually proven to be a very skilled soldier. So, if you combine all of this information into one thought, I would conclude that it means he will be coming back home."

Annabella hugged Nath. "I hope you are right, Pabbi," she said. "I want to believe this."

"Believe it," Nath said, smoothing her hair.

The 108th Battalion arrived in England on September 25, 1916. The men were immediately broken up and transferred to other units where they were most needed.

The Canadians were much different than the British, which shocked Mike; he had thought they would be very similar. As a result, there were many clashes between the British and the Canadians. The Canadians had a reputation of being hardy, more stubborn and sometimes insubordinate. They were physically bulky and larger men. They were mostly farmers, very hardy explorers and settlers, not willing to let something or someone take them down. The Canadian soldier also made more money than the British. Mike drew $1.10 Cdn per day, almost three times as much as a British soldier and vastly more than his enemy. Mike could not understand why they could not buy many supplies in rationed Britain, and the Brits were envious. Mike did see that many Canadians were purchasing more alcohol and cigarettes, which only fuelled the rivalry.

He quickly learned that their weapons and equipment had problems. The Ross rifle had jammed with mud in earlier battles, especially at Second Ypres in April 1915. Canadians became impatient to remedy the situation. There was borrowing, stealing and too much alcohol. The old school soldiers viewed Canadians as undisciplined, but Mike just felt that the British were battle-worn and grouchy. But he also heard that during actual battles, these clashes were not an issue. The two groups of soldiers, Canadian and British, fought side by side with a united intensity.

For many of the infantry, the Ross rifle was replaced with the British-made Lee Enfield, a bolt-action rifle that weighed about nine lbs, fired a .303 round and could kill from a distance greater than 500 yards. The rifle also had a seventeen-inch sword bayonet attached to it. Walking into battle with this large sword leading the way helped strengthen confidence. It was indeed terrifying to the enemy to be the focus of a bayonet charge. The idea of being run through with a seventeen-inch sword convinced many enemy soldiers to surrender. The Canadians and the British used this reputation to their advantage.

Mike and Stan were told they would go into the 2nd Canadian Infantry Brigade as snipers, keeping their Ross MKIII rifles because of accuracy. They were instructed to keep them as clean as possible.

The training was intense and swift. There was an air of urgency and uncertainty. Mike and Stan were not told exactly when they would be going to France, but it was imminent.

Every soldier was issued a kit; greatcoats, shirts, steel helmets, trousers and leather boots, along with pouches containing an entrenching tool, water bottle, rations, rifle and a pistol.

There were rumours that the method of attack in France would be changing based on the lessons learned from the losses at Second Ypres. What these changes entailed they did not know, which was unsettling, but it was for their own safety; if captured, they would not be able to reveal any attack plans.

Mike looked up at the many brave faces around him. Tonight, they were all writing letters home. Several officers walked around, picking up the letters one by one, throwing them into a postal bag. Mike wrote quickly and sealed the letter, tossing it into the bag.

"We'll be travelling to France soon, men," the Lieutenant said. "Get some rest! You'll all need it."

CHAPTER 23

Mike and Stan arrived at the Vimy front in staggered marches with the 2nd Canadian Infantry Brigade in late October.

Protecting the coal mines of Lens and the city of Arras, Vimy Ridge ascends to a height of 360 feet from the muddy plain. The uppermost point is Hill 145. The climb looks gradual but rises abruptly at the northern tip.

The Canadian Brigades began setting up on a line that extended approximately 9 miles in length from north of Arras to Lens. The Germans dominated Vimy Ridge and looked down into their opponent's trenches. Mike heard men talking about it being called the Valley of Sorrows because so many lives were lost here; some still lay scattered on the battlefields. Approximately 150,000 French and Germans were killed here, many unburied corpses and fragments remaining. The land was filled with craters of foul, muddy water and decaying remains of the fallen. It was a huge rotting mass of mud.

In the centre of the Canadian lines was the war-ravaged skeleton of a town called Neuville-St. Vaast. It had many underground tunnels and strange labyrinths. To the north was another German-dominated ridge called the Pimple. Stationed at this point, the Germans were gunning down any Canadian or British that came near with artillery and trench mortar fire.

The Canadians were also well-armed, though. Each brigade was equipped with Lee Enfield rifles, Lewis .303 hip held machine guns, stationary Vickers machine guns, trench mortar weapons and much more. They were an intimidating crew. The 2nd division's commander was Henry Burstall, a Canadian gunner, who survived two years of battle and twenty-five years in the army. He was a highly respected man.

To the north of their position was the 3rd Canadian Brigade with the commander Louis Lipsett, who was an educated, respected officer as well. Further to the south was the 1st Canadian Brigade, a battle-ravaged brigade that had fought at Ypres, with the commander Arthur Currie.

There wasn't a specific date set for an attack, but they heard rumours that the Canadians were waiting on one more brigade. So far, there were approximately 75,000 soldiers in total, including the specialized units of the Canadian Machine Gun Companies and the Canadian Trench Mortar Battery, which made up each brigade.

Mike and Stan set up their tents amidst thousands of soldiers, as the wind blew with a chill that sent shivers to their bones. Snow started to swirl as they settled in to call Vimy home for the next little while. It would be a long cold winter.

∾

The 4th Canadian Brigade had arrived by the end of 1916. It was one of the coldest winters on record. Mike was glad that the 4th Brigade had arrived. The frozen ground was hellish, and waiting to attack was even worse. The men had fought boredom stationed in the front lines, then rotated to the rear and back again. Six days at the front, a week in the rear trenches and then a week out. Mike spent most of the winter shivering and shovelling, although sometimes, he would go out at night and use his rifle to sharp shoot several Germans, returning to his bed as if nothing had happened.

The Canadians were 100,000 strong now. The 4th Brigade to the north was newly formed and commanded by a Major-General named David Watson. The Brigades were stationed numerically from the south being 1st, 2nd, 3rd and the northmost being 4th. Every now and then, during the winter, there were skirmishes where Germans and Canadians were killed, but it never escalated out of control. Until February, it seemed.

As March approached, a plan of assault was being formulated slowly between the four Canadian brigade commanders. In the first week of March, the Canadians set up stationary Vickers machine-gun teams to commence a steady barrage. By tilting the guns up to the skies, gunners showered the German lines chaotically with thousands of bullets. Sixty-four guns began firing during the day and during the night, keeping the Germans under a harassing hail of bullets. Machine gun teams switched duty to keep the steady hail of bullets raining down on the German lines. The enemy was forced to restrict their movements to the trenches.

Mike noticed several battery units beginning to focus on eliminating the enemy barbed wire. An impressive new 106 graze trigger fuze was used, the shells exploding on contact with barbed wire. But the effort seemed to be in vain; Mike saw the

Germans laying new wire every night. Mike fidgeted nervously as he peered through his scope.

The next step was crucial; a massive infantry assault. He could feel it in the air.

The intense training began behind the Canadian lines. The infantry assault would follow a creeping barrage, moving methodically at 100 yards every three minutes. The men had to be well-coordinated and stay within 40 to 70 yards of the wall of fire, where the bullets would be steadily showering the German lines. There were several units of the creeping barrage; first, the attacking infantry in front, then the mopper uppers 50 yards behind, then sectioned columns in irregular formations 100 to 300 yards, then finally carriers and support 400 to 500 yards back. Every soldier was assigned based on their skills; a hunter would be placed with the riflemen and snipers; a base-ball player would be with the grenade throwers, and machinists would be with the Lewis Machine gunners. The groups were well matched with abilities.

Mike and Stan were placed with the riflemen as snipers in the irregular formations 100 yards behind. The snipers had their choice of weapons; Mike and Stan had both favoured the Ross rifle for accuracy. Both men were interspersed with the riflemen in the formation, evenly distributed among the ranks. Mike was stationed to the far left, and Stan was his backup slightly behind. During training, they had to be cognisant of the yards travelled. If they arrived too quickly, they could be inadvertently walking into friendly fire.

Mike was dressed in a uniform shirt and trousers with his lower legs wrapped with puttees to keep the mud out. The leather boots were durable but stiff. Around his waist was the webbing containing many pouches, including a small shovel type tool, water bottle, two days of rations, ammunition, a flare, cigarettes and three empty sandbags. On his head was the standard steel helmet, which had reduced many head wounds since being introduced in early 1916.

They trained every day amidst the firing barrage and increased fighting of late March. The commanders were speculating early April as the attack date.

After training, Mike and Stan ate their slop, a stew of some sort.

Mike finished, wiping his mouth. "So, do you think we're ready?" he asked.

Stan chewed with a mouthful of food, then swallowed. "We are ready," Stan said simply.

They were awakened on Easter Monday, April 9, 1917, at a very early hour. The skies were still dark, and a light snow was falling. Mike shuffled into line quickly to grab some warm porridge. Stan was late and not so lucky; he had to dine on cold meat and bread. They ate quickly and nervously, then sat awaiting orders. Some officers started passing around the battle rum. Mike took a quick swig and grinned menacingly. It was strong alcohol, and it seared his throat all the way down, although it did calm his nerves.

Finally, the call was heard.

Mike and Stan hurried along with the men and marched onto the battlefield into formation.

It was 5:28 am, 230 Vickers guns started their barrage. Everyone stood silent as they watched the assault rain onto the German lines.

Two minutes later, the barrage opened up fully, the heaviest ever seen. At 5:30 am, 863 field guns, howitzers, and 120 mortars opened fire. It was still dark, but the skies had ignited with flashes, fire and smoke. It looked like a sheet of flames had been detonated on the German lines. The soldiers stood there in awe, watching the early morning skies light up.

Then the front line advanced.

Mike timed it, glancing at his commanding officers for the call. He reminded himself, every three minutes, another 100 yards. Mike stood still, waiting for the command to advance. He watched as some front-line men fell while some men crept steadily forward. The 2nd Canadian Brigade was farther from their objective of Zwolfer-Stellung, the German Black line. The 4th Canadian Brigade was closer to this line with less distance to travel overall but mostly uphill to Hill 145.

The 2nd Brigade was longer and flat landscape, but also farther.

Finally, the call was out. Mike inched forward through the chaos. He walked and crawled over several dead and injured Canadians, grimacing at the losses so far. The Canadian shells rained over their heads consistently as he moved. An artillery shell landed on the barbed wire ahead 100 yards, exploding the ground into a wet mud lake. He firmly walked forward, then crouched down into a rut, he steadied his rifle and aimed at the German line. The smoke was heavy, obscuring his vision. He fired into the smoke and waited; nothing moved. He crawled out of the rut and frogged through the mud. When he reached the mopper uppers, only a few stood with their Lewis machine guns, bravely standing amidst the bullet chaos. Mike rolled into another crater, sliding onto his stomach. He watched the Lewis gunner in front of him advancing and followed his aim towards the German front line. Suddenly the Lewis gunner fell, shot in the chest. Mike cursed, narrowed his eyes and followed the estimated fire path into the German line. He spotted an enemy helmet; he aimed and waited. A German appeared, bending down to lift the ammunition belt. Mike fired. The enemy soldier flew backwards into the mud. Mike immediately crouched into his hole, expecting return fire. A barrage hailed onto him as he crouched in the hole. He waited patiently for the pause.

When it was silent, he peered over and watched another Lewis gunner walking forward, firing at the hip. He followed the fire path and located the German nest; Mike aimed and fired at the German gunner. The bullet made contact. The enemy's arms flew overhead as his body catapulted into the air, hit squarely in the chest by Mike's bullet. He immediately slumped into his hole again, bracing for the return fire. A barrage of bullets kicked up the mud around him. He waited for the reload. Then he cautiously peered over, shuffled out swiftly, crawling through the muck and came along a team of soldiers trying to take out another German nest. The gunner was hosing down the moppers and front-line soldiers. Emotions bubbled up into Mike's throat. He fought the anger down as he watched some of his comrades fall. Mike breathed and slipped into another hole. He steadied his rifle and aimed, just as a front-line soldier jumped into the German gun nest! Mike switched his aim to the stunned German gunner as he began to respond, tilting his weapon quickly towards the front-line soldier. Mike fired, his bullet whizzing through the air, hitting the enemy directly in the face. The German gunner flew back into the hole as the front-line soldier stood stunned and bewildered but grateful for another chance at life. The Canadian soldier quickly snapped out of it, surging forward and sliding his bayonet into one of the remaining German soldiers. Another enemy in the nest reacted, dropping the ammunition belt and picked up a rifle, swinging it towards the front-line soldier. Mike fired, and the bullet smashed into the German's upper chest. The front-line soldier smiled with a mixture of relief and jubilation. Several seconds later, the courageous soldier waved, and two more Canadians crawled into the nest, securing it. Mike smiled and continued along the line, looking for more gun nests. He crawled over the body of a soldier younger than himself. He was horrified at how many Canadians were being slain.

Mike moved stealthily, finding another gun nest. Several mopper uppers were providing suppressing fire so the front line could get in. Two soldiers fell right in front of Mike. He caught one and laid him down. He was bleeding from an arm wound but still alive. Mike whispered in his ear, "Stay still," he said. "Keep pressure on your arm. You will be alright. Help will come soon."

Mike crawled several feet forward and slipped into a deep wet crater. The hole was filled with watery cold mud. It seeped into his bones; it was so frigid. Mike flinched as something nudged his shoulder; he turned and was appalled. A dead soldier floated beside him in the water face down. He grimaced, goosebumps travelling all over his arms. He looked away, trying to shake the image out of his head. He exhaled and brought his rifle to bear. Mike scanned the area for the nest in the chaos. The German gunner was spraying bullets into a line of Canadians, several fell, although some still miraculously advanced, injured and bleeding. Mike aimed and fired into the enemy nest, his bullet piercing the German gunner's shoulder. The secondary German gunner grabbed the gun hastily, aiming it into the line of moppers. Mike fired again, and the German's face shattered. The hail of bullets never came.

Immediately, a front-line soldier ran and jumped into the nest, poking the bayonet at the two surviving Germans. "Surrender!" he growled angrily. Their hands went immediately up into the air in defeat. Another Canadian soldier jumped into the nest, bayonet ready, supporting the team.

The Germans were surrendering!

Mike surged forward and met the men in the nest. Several other Canadians jumped into the nest as well.

They were celebrating, clapping each other's hands, as two men led the German prisoners back to the Canadian lines, prodding them along with the points of their bayonets.

"You have to keep going," Mike said to the remaining men. "I'm one of the snipers. I have your back." He grinned, relief flooding his heart. "Good job, men!"

"You were the sniper that took out that gunner!" one young man said, slapping Mike on the back.

Mike smiled. "Yes," he said. "Now get going, leave behind two soldiers to secure the nest. I got this. Don't look for me."

"Yes, sir!" they all shouted.

Three men jumped out and advanced onto the muddy plains of Vimy Ridge, leaving two behind. Mike watched as the men advanced, one front line soldier and two Lewis gunners. They stepped over bodies and walked over the plains steadily. Mike waited until they were 25 yards ahead of him, then he scrambled out, frogging through the mud. He was entirely soaked with mud. His body, his shoulders, his legs, even his face! Good camouflage, Mike thought crazily.

He slipped into another hole and observed as they walked forward steadily. The barrage of German bullets was quieter here. They were reaching the first Black Line objective

Zwolfer-Stellung! Mike scanned the terrain carefully. Some movement to the north. A few Germans scurried about. Mike aimed.

Suddenly a burst of shellfire came from the Germans, smoke obscuring his sights. One of the Lewis gunners fell.

"Fuck," Mike swore. He aimed and fired. A German fell, then silence. He must have hit the shooter, but he didn't know. Something was wrong; he could feel it. It wasn't the same kind of shooting as before. He peered up, and two direct bullets greeted him. He ducked down. Those shots were very accurate, he thought. A chill ran along his arms. A German sniper had spotted him.

"Shit!" Mike cursed as he huddled in the hole, unable to move.

"I see him!" A familiar voice shouted through the air, approximately 20 yards to the south. It was Stan! "It's a German sniper! I'm going to try and get him. When you hear my covering fire, run!"

Stan surveyed the small hill the shooter was on. His head bobbed, then disappeared. Stan steadied his rifle and fired; the German head ducked.

Mike ran hard and fast as the German head cautiously bobbed back up, firing at him. Mike dove into the mud, digging as a bullet seared into his leg. Mike breathed in sharply and seethed through the pain. He slipped into the shell hole, ripping a field dressing out of the special pocket in his tunic and wrapped it tightly around his leg. He lay down on his back, breathing heavily. Mike took a deep breath in and out. He took a swig of rum. I can do this, he thought. I'm hit but not down. He tucked the rum back away and rolled onto his stomach, wincing from the pain. He steadied his rifle, fear jumping into his throat.

He told himself that he was in Gimli hunting deer with Afi. They were going to the small clearing where Grandma Anwa had first taught Nathan where the deer herds were hiding. The exact same place that Afi had first taught Mike to shoot. Breathe steadily, become one with your environment, Nath would say. The deer should think you are nothing more than the leaves rustling in the trees. A reassuring calm fell over Mike.

He rubbed his helmet and face with the mud, then very slowly peered over his rifle. Be one with the soil, his instincts told him. He winked one eye and saw the German in his sights; he steadied his rifle. Mike fired and ducked quickly down.

The German sniper died instantly with a bullet in his face.

"You got him!" Stan shouted, as a hail of bullets rained down on his position. Stan retreated, shuffling down into a crater, bleeding from a minor shoulder wound.

Mike watched as another machine gun nest sprayed mercilessly towards Stan's position. Mike steadied and aimed at one of the final German gun nests. Zwolfer-Stellung was just 25 yards away! Mike fired and hit the German gunner, his head spun from the impact of the bullet, but not before another German threw a long evil-looking grenade. It sailed through the air directly at Mike, tilting one end over the other. Mike tried to run, but his left leg wouldn't take the weight; he knelt and half-crawled as quickly as he could to get out of the path of the German stick grenade, not really knowing which way to run.

It landed and exploded, throwing Mike high up into the air, his body landing with a hard thud onto his back. He looked up at the sky briefly, his eyes open. The impact seared up through his body fiercely, but it was different as if the hurt didn't matter. He watched the smoke rising into the lightening skies; the morning was finally arriving, he thought. All the fighting and the bullets flying overhead were steadily decreasing. Relief and hope filled his battle-wearied mind; he would just rest for a moment. He was puzzled. He couldn't feel the pain. He must not be injured that badly, he thought. He had to keep moving. He tried to move, but his legs wouldn't listen. His mind became clouded with images of the sunrises in Gimli in the fishing boat.

Then his eyes closed, and the blackness took him.

"Fuck, fuck, fuck!" Stan shouted. Stan immediately fired and took out the grenade thrower, his face exploding in blood. Several Lewis gunners sprayed the German ammunition loader, his head lobbed back, and his body flew vibrating from the impact of the bullets. Three Canadians took over the nest, as Stan stumbled over to Mike. He pressed two fingers to his friend's throat and felt Mike's strong heartbeat. He was still alive!

"Hey, Mike," Stan yelled. "I don't know if you can hear me, but you're okay! You're alive. You are a hero, boy! I saw all those nests you took out and the sniper! You better fucking live! I mean it, Mike! Do you hear me? I know you do. We're going to take care of you. Fight it with everything you got, man!"

"Hey, Medic!" Stan shouted, waving as a few medics clambered over with a stretcher and two German prisoners. "What the fuck?" Stan exclaimed angrily, his bayonet immediately against the German man's chest, ready to slice the enemy through.

"No, no!" the medic shouted, waving his hands urgently. "The German prisoners are conscripted to transport the wounded Canadians back with us. Don't harm them!"

Stan lowered his weapon calmly and turned to face the medic. "This man is a hero," Stan said, commandingly. "He was the best sniper we had. He saved many lives. He's still alive, dammit, bullet wound left leg and shell shocked by stick grenade. Save him, Medic. I fucking mean it."

Medic nodded. "Yes! I will do everything I can!" he replied.

Stan continued up the slope to Zwolfer-Stellung. The Canadians had done it! They had broken through the German front line and secured the first objective. It was 6:10 am, forty minutes after the start of the infantry attack.

Monday, April 9, 1917, was a long day for Stan and the many other soldiers who survived. At approximately 7:10 am, they had overrun the Red line Zwischen-Stellung position. By the end of the day, most of Hill 145 was in Canadians hands, taken by a daring bayonet charge from the most junior Battalion soldiers. With a blood-curdling cry, the last Battalion from the 4th Brigade was sent in by Watson as a last resort. They charged the hill with their bayonets ready. The Germans were taken by surprise by the suicidal attack but soon responded with Mauser rifle shots and then machine gunfire. Many of the 85th Nova Scotia Battalion soldiers were beaten down by the enemy's machine gunfire, but the survivors refused to go down to ground. The remaining Canadians rushed the hill, running, shouting, shooting, stabbing and clubbing the enemy to their deaths in a vicious courageous attack. They took control of a portion of the hill and continued to fight for the remaining portions overnight.

It was a victory, and the Canadians were now occupying most of Vimy Ridge. However, the victory came with a huge cost. This day would end up becoming the single bloodiest day in Canadian military history. The total casualties for the day were estimated at 7,000 Canadians, including 2,000 dead and the rest injured. The stretcher-bearers were still going through the fields, gathering the wounded and dead. Some stretcher-bearers were loading the injured onto light rail trams, and some medics were treating soldiers in the German dugouts. Screams and moaning filled the air. There were so many injured soldiers that the doctors were overwhelmed. They began accepting only the ones that could be saved. Many of the more severely injured or unconscious soldiers were being moved to the outside of the military hospital tents by triage. These soldiers were left to the elements, blankets laid over top of their prone bodies, the snow slowly falling on them. Mike better not be one of them left outside, Stan thought angrily.

He looked down on the field. It was strewn with bodies, some facedown, some just lying there on their backs motionless with gaping holes of blood. Some were not even recognizable as bodies, just fragments of limbs and portions of human remains everywhere. It was a sight that he would never forget. It would be burned into his memory for eternity.

Stan sat on the ridge, smoking a cigarette and guzzling the wicked rum. A battle-weary soldier from the front line joined him. They shared the rum, taking swigs, passing it back and forth, inhaling on their cigarettes and blowing plumes of tobacco smoke over the ridge. The view up here on the ridge was commanding. The plains below were clear and detailed. Stan now understood the significance of the taking of Vimy Ridge. It was a dominant position.

"What do you think about tomorrow?" the older soldier asked. "What's in store for us now?"

"We follow orders," Stan replied. "We need to stay overnight and defend our position with the Vickers guns they finally brought in. Those guns were heavy beasts, but we got them up here. A little late, though, I had to mow down the counter-attack a few times with several Lewis guns taken from the dead." He dragged slowly on the cigarette, momentarily remembering the grisly details. "Tomorrow, we will go on with the other Brigades to continue taking the rest of Vimy. But tonight, we will try to stay alive defending our position here."

"We have succeeded though, haven't we?" the soldier asked, seeking confirmation.

"Yes," Stan blew out another plume of smoke over the ridge, the little cloud rising over the dead and injured. "We have taken Vimy Ridge."

Chapter 24

There were a lot of voices around, none of which he knew. His eyes felt heavy; he couldn't open them. He tried, and it was just useless. Where was he?

Someone was holding his leg up. Then they stuck a sharp pin into it, pulling a string or something, then another pinprick, then pulling, as if they were sewing, then suddenly a murderous pain seared all over his body.

Fuck, that really hurts, he thought. What are you people doing to my leg?

His body involuntarily jerked. He wanted to sit up and shout at them. He wanted to throw their hands off of his leg physically. But he couldn't even open his eyes. It was so frustrating!

Then a tablet was pushed under his tongue. Soon after, a silky, warm feeling danced throughout his body, and the pain slipped silently away. The voices grew dim, and his mind shut off, leading him back to blackness.

Annabella sipped the hot tea while Nathan spooned honey into his. They were at Nathan's house, looking out over the expansive beach, while Jon and Vlad wrestled in the snow. Her older daughters, Katya and Natalie, were back home preparing several dishes to bring over later on. Easter celebrations had come and gone. They had spent it as a large family, cooking, eating and praying for Mike's safe return.

Then yesterday, they had heard the news about Vimy Ridge. Annabella's face was streaked with tears. They had not heard from Mike since late March. It took so long for the letters to arrive from overseas, sometimes several weeks. They had no idea if he was alive, dead or wounded. It was heart-wrenching. They knew that Mike was a sniper in the 2nd Canadian Brigade and that he was stationed at Vimy Ridge, nothing else.

Annabella broke down emotionally, and the tears started flowing freely. "We don't know anything!" she said. "How long do we have to wait? He could have died, and we don't even know about it!"

Nathan wrapped his arms around her and rocked gently as her tears dropped onto his arms. "It'll be alright," he said. "We will have some kind of word soon."

"What if my boy didn't survive?" Annabella shouted through her tears. "What then?" Her sobs took over her body. Nath grabbed her tight and rocked her just like he did when she was a little girl. After several moments her sobbing reduced to a few tears.

"Are you feeling better?" Nath asked, sympathetically.

"Yes, a little bit," Annabella said. "I'm still so worried that I might have already lost him, and I don't even know."

"Well," Nathan said. "Then, all you need to do is feel deep down in your soul what you think has happened. Do you feel like you've lost him? Does a part of you feel like he's gone? Or, do you feel like he's alive?"

"He's alive," she said immediately.

"I agree. I feel the same," Nathan said quietly, nodding. "I don't have any confirmation, nobody has told me this, but deep down, I can feel that he is still a part of this world," he paused. "A part of our world." Nathan turned his body and lightly lifted her chin. "Look at me, Bella." He turned her face and stared into her blue eyes. "Trust your instincts; trust what your gut is telling you. Remember what I told you that your Momma used to tell me all the time, become one with yourself, trust yourself." Annabella blinked hard. "You will know the answers; you always do, Bella. All you have to do is trust those answers. He's alive. He's still here with us. We will hear word from the army soon."

"Thanks, Pabbi," Annabella said, hugging her dad fiercely. "You are the best dad ever. Do you know that?"

"Yes," Nathan grinned. "I know that." He laughed.

Annabella chuckled and kissed him on the cheek. "Okay, let's get this dinner going," she said. "Ivan and the girls will be here soon. Let's have a big family meal all together for Mike."

"Wonderful!" Nathan said, smiling. "Maria should be back home soon from school. Let's throw some wood in the fireplace and celebrate the family that we have."

Vira was distraught. It had been over a month since anyone had heard anything from Mike. She feared that he was never going to come back. She knew the war was difficult, and he couldn't always write. She knew that it sometimes took weeks just for one letter to arrive from overseas. She understood all of this, but her heart was bursting out of her chest with worry. She was not sure what to do about it. They had just spent a few days together, but the short time that she had spent with Mike were some of the loveliest moments in her life. She wanted them to continue; she wanted to spend more time with Mike, to know him better, to spend the afternoons sailing together and to finally kiss him.

The letters they had sent back and forth throughout the war were often weekly comments of what was currently going on, sometimes nothing vastly important, just normal everyday stuff. He once responded that he loved hearing about the farm, that it warmed his heart and furthered his resolve to help end this war so he could come back to Gimli.

Their letters grew romantic over the past few months. Several times, she had mentioned that she loved the way he thought. He had mentioned the same thing. Mike had told her that he admired her strength and conviction. Not too many women could run a farm as she had and succeed too! He was proud of her. She had overcome many obstacles with the wheat and the cows, some of the animals becoming sick. Vira had turned things around, the cows healed, and the crops were salvaged. But the biggest test was the coming summer. If she could get the wheat growing and harvested, hire additional labourers, maybe she could leave farming and join Mike with operating the fishing business.

He had agreed.

He warmed her heart like a hot fire on a cold night. She wanted him back in Gimli. She needed to hear some kind of word that he was okay. It was terrible to be kept in the dark like this.

Vira poured an ounce of an unsweetened Icelandic schnapps into her glass. It was illegal, of course, because of the prohibition, but the family had bought it previously from locals during the winter. The strong drink was made from fermented potatoes. It was sometimes called the Black Death. It tasted strong, but nothing so extreme as its name should suggest. It was just a small bottle, and they had it hidden well.

Vira sat down on the sofa and put her long legs up, sipping the strong, clear drink. She stared at the ceiling where the roof met the wall and daydreamed.

Maybe one day, she would have little children running around and would rush after them, feeding them and keeping them out of trouble. She smiled; hopefully, one day, she mused.

She was falling in love with Mike Kozak; she could feel it. She hadn't heard anything for several weeks. Was he still at war? Was he alive? Her thoughts went grim. She tried to dispel the bad thoughts with good ones. He had said that he was coming back. Every single time he had written. And he said that he was going to kiss her when he gets back.

She sure hoped so.

CHAPTER 25

He could hear the voices again. His eyelids felt very heavy, and his leg hurt badly. His back felt twisted, pain shooting up his spine. He groaned and tried to move. Every part of his body screamed back at him in an awful type of pain, crippling his mind's ability to deal with it.

"Hey, hey, soldier," a female voice said softly. "Be careful. We need to keep your leg stationary."

He tried to talk, but it felt like a thousand cotton balls were stuck in his mouth. So, he willed his eyes to open instead.

The sunlight and the white tent immediately assaulted his pupils. It was painfully bright; he squinted and looked at the nurse tending him. She smiled sweetly. "Well, good morning Private Mike Kozak," she said. "How do you feel?"

"In a lot of pain," Mike mumbled the words out.

"Mmm," she said. "Well, you need a lot of recovery time. I can give you something for the pain."

"No more drugs," Mike said, coughing, attempting to clear the cotton balls out of his mouth.

"Geraldine!" the nurse shouted. "Bring this soldier some water!"

A small girl, the age of ten, arrived with a jug of water and a glass. She poured it and handed it to Mike. Realizing that he was not grabbing it himself, she tipped it immediately to his lips. He sipped the cool liquid gratefully.

The nurse checked his pulse, felt his forehead and examined his leg. She grimaced and looked up at him over the sheet. "Sleep soldier," she said. "You need more rest."

As if on cue, Mike closed his eyes appreciatively and drifted back off to the blackness.

Annabella and Nath worked at the Willow Point cabin, cleaning it out and fixing the yard up. It was a very windy day. The waves were rough, and the gusts whipped at their faces. It was a cool early May morning. They had finally received a notice from the military informing them that Mike was indeed alive but severely injured. He was currently recovering in a London hospital due to an acute full-body concussion, a broken left femur, shrapnel and severe shell shock. He had briefly awoken several times over the last month, disorientated, but often fell back asleep immediately. Once he was stabilized, they would try to ship him back to Canada. The doctors said that he might not be able to walk again. His spine was damaged heavily in the grenade blast. He was awarded the Victoria Cross for his bravery and saving hundreds of lives on April 9.

Annabella looked at Nath. "So, you were right," she said. "We all knew he was still with us."

"Yes," Nathan nodded. "I knew it in my gut."

"Ok, let's get working so we can get this cabin fixed up before he gets home," Annabella said, grabbing small piles of logs over to the far shed.

"Are you sure?" Nathan asked skeptically. "It's going to be a lot of work."

Annabella slapped his arm. "Stop it!" she said. "I told you we are going to make this our summer cabin. The entire family. We will roast deer, have stew and drink illegal alcohol!" She laughed mischievously.

Nathan laughed. "Bella!" he said, feigning shock. "I'm glad you came up with the idea. I love the thought of fixing the cabin up and making it new again, sharing it with you and the grandkids, maybe even another future sibling of yours."

Annabella laid down the stack of wood and walked back to the cabin. Did she hear something right? "What?" she asked, momentarily confused. "A sibling?"

Nathan smiled. "Maria missed her period for two months, so we are hopeful," he said, slyly.

"Oh, my Lord!" Annabella shouted and hugged her father strongly. Then nudged him in the arm. "Why didn't you tell me earlier?"

"Oh," Nath said, grinning. "Because we weren't quite sure if we could even conceive. We are both a lot older than you were when you first started having babies."

"That's because you waited thirty-nine years, Pabbi!" she shouted playfully at him.

"It was well worth the wait," Nathan said, smiling gently. "She's the best woman I could ever ask for. She's beautiful, intelligent and kind. I love her dearly."

Annabella stood with her hands on her hips, smiling broadly. "I'm so happy for you, Pabbi," she said, the words coming from her heart. "You deserve this kind of happiness. You really do, Pabbi." Tears welled in her eyes.

Nathan grabbed her, hugging her, feeling his eyes growing moist with happy tears. "You are the best daughter any father could ask for," he said, the words muffling into her shoulder.

"I love you, Dad," Annabella said, into his ear.

They hugged for a long while, happy that things were finally looking up. Mike was injured, but he was alive and coming home. Nath and Maria were very happy together. Annabella was so thankful that her father had found love again, and her son was coming home. She was going to have a sibling! She chuckled and rejoiced at the thought. Sometimes life takes interesting turns, and you just never know what's going to happen next, she thought.

Bella and Nath continued working. They laboured tirelessly, cleaning, clearing out the deadwood and fixing the summer cabin. They wanted to get it all ready as a family surprise when Mike came back.

They both sat on a log, taking a break to eat their lunch. Bella laid out several slices of homemade bread and cheese. Nath ate ravenously; Annabella chuckled at her father's strong appetite.

Annabella looked up, a slice of bread poised at her mouth. Several horses whinnied in the distance.

Nath jumped up, obviously forgetting something. "I'll be right back," Nathan shouted, stuffing the remaining bread in his mouth. "I forgot! Please stay here!"

Annabella crinkled her nose, confused at his sudden disappearance. What was he up to now?

Nathan stomped through the bush to the road and waved to several horseback riders. Three of his old cousins, Aron, Kristjan and Viktor, reined the horses in, pulling a trailer full of building supplies. Wood, nails, roofing materials, everything they needed to build a larger cabin at Willow Point. The old cabin would be a guest cottage and a place to rest while they were building the bigger house.

Viktor hugged Nathan roughly. "Nath!" Viktor said, smiling. "You old man! Didn't anybody ever tell you that you should look your age?"

All four men burst into raucous laughter. Aron, the oldest, hugged Nathan warmly. "How have you been, my cousin?"

"We're doing great! I'm the happiest that I think I've ever been," Nath replied, wiping his dirty hands on his pants. "How's Julia and the kids?"

"They are good!" Aron answered. "The kids are too many, to be honest. Five children and ten grandchildren now." He paused thoughtfully, scratching his grey beard. "I think it's ten. I may have lost count."

They all broke into boisterous laughter.

Kristjan shouted. "It's true!" he said chuckling. "My wife and I only had three children, but the grandkids! I can't keep count. I think we have seven."

Viktor laughed. "I only had the two children with my wife," Viktor said. "So, I'm the black sheep of the family. But my daughter made up for it by having five children! What kind of children did we raise? Colonists, I guess. Make as many children as possible!"

All four men burst into laughter again. They continued in the friendly banter, laughing so hard that tears welled in their eyes.

Annabella crashed through the bushes. "What is going on here?" she shouted. Surprised that her second cousins were here, she shrieked and hugged them all. "What are all these supplies for?" Annabella said, pointing at the trailer full of wood.

"I wanted to surprise you," Nathan replied. "But it's kind of hard to keep a construction project secret. We are building a grand summer home for all of us to share! We will keep the old cottage as a guest cabin. We hope to have it finished in the next three months, just in time for summer."

Annabella shrieked and jumped into her dad's arms. "Oh my God!" she yelled. "Momma would love this. Thank you, Pabbi!"

Nathan hugged his daughter fiercely as Viktor and Kristjan started pulling the supplies closer to the site. Aron tied up the horses loosely to the trees, and they all entered the summer property on Willow Point.

"What a wonderful surprise!" Annabella cried, with tears streaming down her face.

"We will all have a beautiful lakeside summer cottage to call our second home," Nath said, smiling with all his heart as the men got to work, surveying the expansive land before them.

CHAPTER 26

They loaded him carefully onto the ship. Mike winced as his battered body was jostled side to side. He could move his arms now, but his left leg was still in an awful state of constant pain. The blast of the stick bomb had thrown his body into the air, and when he had landed, his injured leg had crumpled underneath his body somehow, breaking the large femur bone. His back and head had suffered from a severe concussion, making it very difficult to sit, stand or even move at all for that matter. He had murderous headaches often. He continued to refuse the morphine because it made him so sleepy and out of sorts.

The sniper bullet that hit him had travelled cleanly through his lower leg. They had disinfected the wound and stitched him back up. The broken femur made it impossible to put any weight on it, even moving hurt. He was lucky that gangrene had not been a problem; many other soldiers were not as fortunate.

He was lying on a cloth stretcher among many other injured soldiers, some on stretchers like him, some in wheelchairs, some with legs and arms missing. He felt blessed that he still had all of his limbs intact, albeit very painful ones, but he was altogether in one piece. The doctors told him that it would take six months for his leg to heal, if not longer.

Mike wondered what happened to Stan. He had asked several times and was told that Stan was most likely still at war since they hadn't heard any different. Mike was worried. Stan was competent and brave but was still out there battling the evils of war. Mike felt uneasy and concerned about his best friend, praying that he would see Stan again.

The boat was crowded, and the horn blared, preparing to leave the dock. Slowly, he felt the boat slide into the harbour, and the shipload of injured soldiers began their journey back home to Canada.

Vira was shy and nervous. She was not sure what to think of the Olason's and Kozak's. They had invited her to be with them, even though her place in the family was unsure. No one had said that they were dating as far as she knew, so she felt a bit awkward standing with this extremely large family, awaiting Mike's return to Gimli.

Annabella hugged her warmly and kissed her on the forehead. "We love that you are here with us," Bella said. "Mike always spoke fondly of you."

"He did?" Vira asked, her eyes blinking nervously.

"Yes," Annabella smiled tenderly. "He told me often of how much he admired you. Even before he left."

"Oh?" Vira said, smiling. "I wasn't sure. He always said to me that he wanted to stay friends."

Annabella cocked her head to one side, grinning affectionately. "My dear," she said. "I believe he said that because he didn't want to fall in love. Not right before leaving for war."

"Yes, I suppose," Vira said, her eyebrows wrinkling. "Do you believe he might think differently now?"

"Possibly," Annabella said. "My son is a very good man. He will always do the right thing. Never expect anything less from Michael."

Vira smiled, shading her eyes from the bright sun, as the boat came into view. It floated slowly to the Gimli dock as the crowd surged forward, anxious relatives looking forward to seeing their war-torn loved ones.

Nathan, Ivan, Kristjan, Viktor, Aron and all their wives, children and grandchildren stood together in a large group awaiting Mike's return. The town had several nurses ready to transport the most injured men into their homes. Several apparatuses, including stretchers, wheelchairs, walkers and canes, were arranged on the dock. Several bearers stood ready, most in military uniform. Someone started playing a happy song; the music lilted into the air from an Icelandic Langspil, a long triangular string instrument with a soulful sound.

The Olason's watched as the injured soldiers disembarked one by one, some walking, some limping, some in wheelchairs. They were dismayed to search every face and still not see their beloved Mike.

Then the stretchers were taken off the boat, one by one. A collective gasp sounded as the bodies of the severely injured were handed over to the relatives. Nathan felt his spine tingle as he grasped Annabella's hand.

Then they saw Mike's head bobbing on the stretcher. He was awake and waving. Nathan and Annabella rushed forward.

Bella pushed her way through the crowd until she finally reached Mike's side.

"Mike!" Annabella shouted. "Oh, my Lord. I'm so happy to see your face again. You have no idea." She bent down and kissed his forehead, tears of joy streaming down her face.

Nathan grabbed his hand. "Mike," he said. "I always believed when you said you would be back. And here you are."

Mike smiled, an affectionate homey feeling spreading throughout his body. "Afi, Momma," Mike said. "You have no idea how lovely it is to be back home."

Annabella pointed at the cross emblem on his tunic pocket. "Is this the medal?" she asked. It was a bronze cross with a lion in the middle suspended by a dark red ribbon, with some wording below.

"Yes, I was awarded the Victoria Cross," Mike said solemnly.

Nathan smiled. "Yes, we heard. For bravery," he said proudly.

"Bravery and outright courageous stupidness," Mike said, laughing.

Nathan chuckled. "Somehow I doubt that," he said, grinning. "You are the best marksman around here, and I assume you were just as good during the war."

Mike smiled warmly. "You may be right, Afi," he said, brightly. "They said I was the best sniper in the 2nd Canadian Brigade and saved hundreds of lives. Except I didn't pay attention to my own leg or my spine. The doctors say that I may not walk again."

Annabella inhaled sharply. "They said that?" she asked.

"Yes," Mike responded truthfully.

Annabella looked at her father, searching his eyes briefly. Something he once said a few weeks ago crept into her mind. She grasped Mike's hand and looked him in the eyes. "But do you believe them? Is that what you think in your heart?"

Annabella asked. "That's the most important question of them all."

Mike smiled affectionately and squeezed her hand. "No," he replied chuckling. "Not once did I believe them."

"Good!" she said. "Now, let's get you home so that you can heal."

The evening was a long one with so many people at Nathan's house that it became severely overcrowded. There was food, cousins, children chasing each other in the sand, running in the house and parents chasing after the littlest ones. It was a lovely homecoming, but Mike was tired and needed rest, so each family member was heralded out the door. Ivan spent many hours with his son, recounting their military pasts, stories and techniques. He was relieved that his son was back home and safe. He knew the horrible atrocities of war and the daunting aftermath.

"You are a strong man," Ivan said. "You'll recover. Don't ever think anything otherwise. You have all your family here to help you on your road to recovery."

"Thanks, Dad," Mike replied. "I've been dreaming of coming home for so long."

Ivan patted his son's hand and left with the children, leaving Annabella behind to care for him.

Once the house had cleared, Mike noticed only a few people were left. Nathan, Maria, Annabella and Vira. He had seen her, of course. They had said hello, but with all the relatives around, they barely had time to talk. Now, it seemed they had a private moment. Nathan was in the kitchen with Maria, and Annabella was off preparing a warm medicinal tea.

Mike nodded at Vira. "Come here," he said firmly.

She smiled and walked to his side.

He grabbed her hand and laced his fingers into hers. "Thank you for being here," Mike said. "It means a lot to me." He gestured to the room with his other hand. "I know my family is a bit overwhelming, but they are all good people with good intentions, you know. They all want the best for me."

Tears started forming in her eyes, the emotional turmoil she had endured for the past month bubbling up to the surface. "Your family is lovely," Vira said softly.

"You are crying," Mike said gently. "I'm sorry. It has been too much for you."

"Yes," Vira said, the tears falling down her cheeks, one by one. "I thought I had lost you before I ever really had a chance to be with you."

Mike pulled her close and leaned up. "Kiss me," he said.

She leaned down, and their lips met. She felt her body shiver and release all the stress of the past month. It all poured out of her as their lips met.

Mike pulled back and looked her in the eyes. "Do you still want me? I'm an injured man," he said solemnly.

"Yes," she said, without hesitation. "I accept you for who you are today and tomorrow, no matter what happens."

Mike smiled, his eyes watering. "That's the best thing I've ever heard since I left for the war," he said, smiling. "Will you stay here beside me tonight? Please."

"Of course," Vira smiled, tears dropping onto his arms. "I will be here for you as long as you'll allow me to be."

"Good," Mike said, grinning. "Now come here and kiss me again."

She laughed as their lips met, sweetness and honey, mixing in with the salty tears of relief and joy.

CHAPTER 27

It was July 29, 1917, and they were all gathered at the Willow Point summer cottage. The entire family had shown up, including all the cousins, Aron, Viktor, Kristjan, as well as Joshua, Aron's son, and all the rest of the grandchildren. Annabella hugged Joshua warmly, kissing him on the cheek. They were born only one month apart in 1876. She had grown up as a baby with Joshua, her childhood friend.

"It is so good seeing you again, Josh," Annabella cried, hugging him strongly.

Mike stepped gingerly onto the path. It had been a rough few months for him. Vira and Annabella nursed him as much as they could, but he still had difficulty. He had to elevate his leg 18 hours a day, so his movements were still limited, but he was now walking upright with the crutches for a few hours. His pain had lessened, and his back was slowly healing from the blast. He was determined to go fishing before the season was done for the year.

They had finally heard the news about Stan. He was killed shortly after, during the night of April 9, 1917, defending the hard-earned Vimy Ridge against the German counter-attacks. Mortar fire had hit the ridge where he was stationed. The nurses did not want to tell Mike at the time because they felt it would impede his recovery. Several weeks ago, Mike and Vira had visited Stan's fiancé, Shirley, in Matlock. They had brought flowers and a special wood ornament Mike had carved of a soldier. Stan had been awarded the Victoria Cross posthumously. It had been an emotionally challenging day for Mike. He had survived, but his best friend had not.

Vira had been there for him; throughout everything. She was a lovely fiancé, and Mike was falling deeply in love with her. It had been an arduous road, filled with difficult moments of weakness, headaches and gruesome war flashbacks in his mind. But every time he awoke in a sweat, shaking, she was there, right beside him, hugging him tightly, letting him know everything was alright and that he was back home safely. He appreciated her so much that it made his eyes tear up, just thinking how lucky he was to have her in his life.

When they had arrived at Willow Point, Mike was astounded by the size of the new summer cottage. It was built for the entire extended family. The cottage was an expansive one-story home with a large front and back deck. They had built it in the old-style log design, with large round timbers as walls, cemented with mortar to keep the holes sealed. The roof was an expansive square roof, pointing upwards to the skies. In the middle of the cottage was a large wood stove, the fire already burning, with pots of deer stew and delicious pudding for dessert bubbling on top. The yard was littered with beautiful little blue flowers that had randomly grown everywhere, even growing in the grass. Closer to the sand, there was the sweet smell of wild blueberries. Nathan picked the blueberries with his pregnant wife, Maria, throwing them into a pail for dessert. He looked up into her eyes and smiled. Her belly was round and protruding in front of her, making it hard for her to bend forward. She was only five months pregnant but looked like she was eight months. Her belly rose directly in front of her as if she was holding a large round balloon.

"Maria," Nathan said gently. "Don't strain. I will get the blueberries."

She straightened and flipped her long blonde hair back. "Thank you, my sweet," Maria said. "But I'm fine. It looks bigger than it feels. I don't know why, but it honestly doesn't feel like that much weight. It's all in front of me, it seems." She laughed, picking some more blueberries and depositing them into the bucket.

"Maybe there is more than one," Nathan said, chiding her.

"Don't laugh," Maria said. "My aunt had twins in Iceland. It runs in the family!"

"Interesting," Nathan said, straightening. "I would love to have two children instead of one. If that happened, I would truly think someone was blessing us with good fortune. God knows, we have had to live with enough tragedy."

"That's life, though, isn't it," Maria responded. "Love, death, joy and hard times. It's all part of life. It ebbs and flows around us and through us. All we can do is pick up the pieces when they fall and build our lives over again, keeping a smile on our faces. The future is always brighter when you keep thinking that it is."

Nathan leaned over and kissed her lips gently. "I love that about you," he said. "Your optimism, your spirit; it has helped me grow into a better person." His hand fluttered onto her waist. He pulled her into his side, and they both admired the cottage they had all built. A lovely homey feeling spread through him.

The smaller guest cabin sat in the distance, farther into the wooded area, gleaming with pride and love, the exterior walls washed and stained a dark honey colour. The front door was replaced, a new wooden door with a skeleton key lock installed. A wreath of flowers hung on the door in memory of Anwa. Every time he walked in the guest cabin, he still felt the strong urge to fall to his knees, but now he stood steady, his eyes happy and his heart warm. "I will never forget the memory of Anwa, she will always occupy a special part of my heart, but Maria, you are the one who has helped me to love again. I understand that life is what you make it now. Death is, unfortunately, a part of life, just as anguish is part of love. To live, you need to accept the good and the bad. It all exists together within our spirits. And when someone comes along and loves you so fully and wholly, accepting all those broken pieces, you need to love that person without boundaries and never let them go." Nathan hugged her closer with his right arm still around her waist. "And when life knocks you down, stand up and be proud that you are one of the last men standing."

They watched as Vira hung a wood carved sign beside the front door to the guest cabin. Mike stood a few feet away; his head cocked to the side. He had spent weeks carving the sign. It was approximately three feet long by one and a half feet high. It was carved from the local oak trees. He had polished it, stained it and sculpted the elegant letters into it.

The sign read, simply:

Olason's and Kozak's

Paradise

A symbol of a Victoria Cross was etched on the bottom corner of the sign.

"It's crooked," Mike said, laughing, leaning on his crutches. "Turn it just a bit to the right. Yes, there. It's perfect. Thank you, darling." He hobbled over to Vira and kissed her. Her face glowed like a thousand warm lights.

Nathan and Maria walked towards them. "It looks good," Nathan said. "Simple, I like it."

"Thanks," Mike said, smiling. "It took me a long time. I put a lot of work into it. You know its strange; I feel emotional going into the guest cabin. I don't know why. It's the strangest feeling."

"I know," Nathan said. "So do I, so do I."

Suddenly, Annabella came crashing through the bushes to join the small group by the guest cabin. "What are you guys doing?" she said loudly, laughing. "We have a lot of food to eat, a lot of celebrating and things to be grateful for." She glanced at the guest cabin. "I cleaned that cabin so well. Ivan, Vlad and myself; we all washed the walls and stained the wood. Pabbi fixed the rotting floor and the roof; it looks perfect now. This summer property will always have a piece of my heart; I love it here. It is so calm and serene. I'm so glad we all came together as a family and put our love and effort into this." She dabbed at her moist eyes. "I love you all." She hugged Ivan first, then Nathan and Mike joined, waving Maria and Vira to join. They embraced in a lovely group hug. "We've been through so much, but we're still here together."

Nath kissed her forehead. "Yes," he said. "We're still all here, wearing our battle scars, inside and out. But the most important thing is we all have each other."

"I love you, Pabbi," Annabella said softly, with tears dropping from the corners of her eyes. "I love you all," she added, smiling despite the tears streaming down her cheeks. "Okay, let's start celebrating! There's lots of food! Let's have dinner together as a family!"

THE END

Don't miss the next book in The Olason Chronicles

Available Fall 2021

FINAL NOTE TO READER

In the fall of 1915, the 108th Overseas Battalion in Selkirk began recruiting soldiers to fight in World War One. Approximately ten percent of the Battalion members were Icelanders. The 108th was quartered in former chicken coop barns in Selkirk in the winter of 1915-1916. They were moved and completed their field training at Camp Hughes, Manitoba, from May to September 1916, living in Bell tents on straw mattresses. On September 19, 1916, the 108th Battalion was deployed aboard the SS Olympic, the sister ship of the Titanic. They arrived in England on September 25, 1916. The 108th Overseas Battalion was absorbed into many other Brigades and Machine Gun Corps, some of those soldiers fighting and losing their lives at Vimy Ridge.

The events in my story have been sculpted to fit within my fictitious saga of bravery, hope and love, using the details to propel my story. I have attempted to be as accurate as possible although some differences were unavoidable or intentionally skewed to keep the story moving forward. All my characters are fictitious, with the exception of the following individual:

Lieutenant Colonel George H. Bradbury, Lieutenant Colonel of the 108th Battalion

The Strong Within Us is a fictional saga of overcoming obstacles, growing through the forest of grief and pursuing your passions with your family by your side. It is the dramatic sequel to The Strong Amongst Us, following the path of these courageous Icelanders and their descendants.

I am immensely grateful to Colonel Roy Boehli (Ret'd) from The King's Own Calgary Regiment Museum, for notes about the lives of soldiers during WWI and the assistance with photographing the Ross MKII. This rifle developed into such an essential part of my novel that I needed to obtain an original photograph of the weapon for the cover. What I didn't know was that this specific rifle is almost impossible to find now. The MKII and MKIII's were reused in WWII as well as the helmets, resulting in many of the original rifles ruined beyond repair or sometimes just left in the fields. It proved extremely difficult to obtain a photograph in the position that I needed for the front cover. I searched everywhere, military surplus shops, everybody told me, "Good luck with that." Finally, my search led to The Military Museum, and during the April 2020 COVID-19 lockdown, I was granted supervised access by Roy. I took many photographs of the beautiful rifle at all angles for my cover designer. It was one of the most thrilling days of writing this novel! I was also led to the bowels of the museum and into the vaults to photograph the WWI helmet, another artifact that is hard to find. I am forever grateful to Roy Boehli and The King's Own Calgary Regiment Museum for granting me this special access, and the experience was out of this world!

I would also like to thank Larry Morrison, a Canadian Veteran that was posted to 2 PPCLI in addition to many other regiments throughout his 12-year military career. Larry provided much-needed assistance with the military training and war scenes. Thanks, Larry, for the nights listening to my war chapters, offering suggestions and allowing me to pepper you with questions all night. You were a great source of valuable real-life military information.

Another enormous hug goes to Gord Crossley of The Fort Garry Horse Museum and Archives, LCol Harcus Strachan, VC, MC Armoury in Winnipeg, Manitoba, for his excellent notations of the war scenes. It was like finding gold in my research efforts! Gord helped me immensely in creating a more realistic portrait of life in WWI, the 108th Overseas Battalion and Vimy Ridge. I was thrilled to have access to the expansive knowledge inside his head and am forever grateful to Gord. My book needed this man like the desert needs the rain!

In the end, this book meant so much more to me than people can ever understand. I was raised by Hungarian Revolution refugees in Canada. My father was enlisted in the Hungarian military in the 1950s and fled during the revolution. I was born in Canada but was a product of and lived with the aftermath of the atrocities of war, PTSD and my father's buried pain. Many of my father's war buddies were missing limbs, fingers and had severe PTSD. My father lived with undiagnosed PTSD his entire life until his early death from cancer in 1990. His death devastated and splintered my family but left me with an immense appreciation of soldiers and what they do for us citizens. It is the single most significant sacrifice that any person can make for their country, and I deeply appreciate all military personnel, past and present. All you men and women deserve so much more than you are given.

My acknowledgements page would not be complete without the mention of my closest family and friends. My heartfelt thanks go to my teenage sons, who stood by me throughout many long nights, flights when mom wasn't available and dealing with my emotional tears as I wrote this passionate, heart-wrenching story. My numerous friends, including Matt, Wendy and many others, were always there for me when I needed them too. I am grateful to have this wealth of support.

One other special person in my life deserves my appreciation and gratitude. His name is Mike K. I met him after the majority of the book was complete. It just happened by coincidence that his initials were the same as my supporting character Mike Kozak. I didn't even realize this until I neared the end of the editing process. Mike K. has been my biggest fan throughout Book One and Book Two. Without him, I honestly don't know if I would be where I am now. He was always in my corner, lifting me up when I fell down and encouraging me with his words, his love and his optimism. He believed in me more than I believed in myself. I will forever be in your debt. Thank you, Mike K.

My biggest thanks also go out to all my devoted readers and followers. Without you, I am nothing but just words on a page.

J. A. BOULET was born and raised in Western Canada. Both her parents were landed immigrants from Hungary, a direct result of the mass emigration during the 1956 Hungarian Revolution. J. A. Boulet was born many years later as a Generation Xer and a first-generation Canadian. She started writing poetry at the age of five and subsequently progressed to short stories and novels. Writing has always maintained a strong current of passion throughout her life. She recently left her career in finance to pursue her dreams of being an author. She currently lives in Canada with her two teenaged sons and a pet crested gecko named Mossio.

You can learn more at:

Website: jaboulet.ca

Twitter: @ love_walk_life

CPSIA information can be obtained
at www.ICGtesting.com
Printed in the USA
BVHW030725051120
592542BV00024B/4